C000084799

MAIRE O'CIARAGAIN

The Red Curse

KARIN ELDER

BALBOA.PRESS
A DIVISION OF HAY HOUSE

Copyright © 2020 Karin Elder.

All rights reserved. No part of this book may be used or reproduced by any means, graphic, electronic, or mechanical, including photocopying, recording, taping or by any information storage retrieval system without the written permission of the author except in the case of brief quotations embodied in critical articles and reviews.

Balboa Press books may be ordered through booksellers or by contacting:

Balboa Press
A Division of Hay House
1663 Liberty Drive
Bloomington, IN 47403
www.balboapress.co.uk
UK TFN: 0800 0148647 (Toll Free inside the UK)
UK Local: 02036 956325 (+44 20 3695 6325 from outside the UK)

Because of the dynamic nature of the Internet, any web addresses or links contained in this book may have changed since publication and may no longer be valid. The views expressed in this work are solely those of the author and do not necessarily reflect the views of the publisher, and the publisher hereby disclaims any responsibility for them.

The author of this book does not dispense medical advice or prescribe the use of any technique as a form of treatment for physical, emotional, or medical problems without the advice of a physician, either directly or indirectly. The intent of the author is only to offer information of a general nature to help you in your quest for emotional and spiritual well-being. In the event you use any of the information in this book for yourself, which is your constitutional right, the author and the publisher assume no responsibility for your actions.

Any people depicted in stock imagery provided by Getty Images are models, and such images are being used for illustrative purposes only. Certain stock imagery © Getty Images.

Cover artworks by Tori Peter

Print information available on the last page.

ISBN: 978-1-9822-8171-7 (sc)
ISBN: 978-1-9822-8173-1 (hc)
ISBN: 978-1-9822-8172-4 (e)

Balboa Press rev. date: 07/24/2020

WHO KNOWS WHERE THEY HAVE BEEN?

WHO KNOWS WHICH LAND THEY HAVE TRODDEN?

ON EARTH AS IT IS IN HEAVEN.

One of the joys in life is discovering who you truly are. Trust you. Express yourself. Be Free

Ask and you shall be given.

Eivør – Trollabundin

This lady artist's deep spirit of truth though her own words, helped me to fierce myself up to find the warrior that wrote these words.

"I am no longer hidden in the shadows of darkness."

xx K

MAIRE – THE YEAR 1433

My ample flesh reclines on my rock of distinction. Baring shoulders that surpass the average lass. My calves teeming with thunder laid bare on the cold stone. Waves rippling in from afar, roll towards me wildly as I do in my thoughts. In remembrance of a day gone by, a moment, transgressed into reality. My life sucked to return again into destiny, oblivion.

A tear, moisture, behold thy kingdom is nigh. My cries distance themselves on other shores. For my feet shall thunder, put asunder the very man I loved. The north wind blows. My auburn hair takes up in the gusts. Rises and falls, reminding me of my kinship. My clan. My sept. Self-doubt shall never cross my path again. I am broken, free.

"Johnny." I shout out into the frothing seas. My body now standing, trembles as it did that day three years ago. When my virginity was unleashed. "Armageddon!" I have nothing to be romantic about. Sentiment does not exist. Tera shall bring terror. With my arms outstretched to the old ones, I kiss each broad shoulder of power. Then place my hands in a gesture of prayer. Give myself to the elements. A fresh ambitious wave, slashes at my full length nature green dress. Refreshes my bare feet. Takes with it back into the ocean, forever, my hesitation. For today I have dressed as woman. Next week the warrior will once again preside.

KELLY – THE YEAR 2017

My alarm goes off. I wake with a bang. Turn it off, flop back on my crumpled warm bed. Wow, what a dream, so real. Lifelike. I take a few moments to relish in the dynamism bestowed. Time to ponder its place in my subconscious. I find none. I don't want to get up, I wish to take myself back into the mysterious place. With the youthful strong woman. I sense her power rushing through my every atom. Well, whatever it was, it certainly has bludgeoned me into a new day.

My beautiful cat, Cinders, jumps on the bed, as she does every morning. Her lush white coat shines, her tail twitches with delight. She comes closer. Purrs. Nuzzles into my neck. Licks my cheeks with her thin, rough tongue. I am so grateful for that fateful day, some three years ago. I'd taken myself to the local nick knack shop to find a present for my mother. The owner, a strange bedraggled women, seemed to have no care in the world for her appearance. Commenced her tale, of how she works rehoming cats. Two days previously, a bag of kittens had been found on the river bed. Three in all. Two dead, drowned. One survived. The rest of course is history. My Cinderella. In my mind the lucky one who survived is now my beloved companion.

"Come on princess," I coo to her. Breakfast time. She eagerly follows me down the stairs of my mid-terrace house. Takes herself off through the cat flap to do her ablutions. I do the same. Return. Boil the kettle. Tend to her feed bowl, fill it. Check her water dish. I always see to her first, Cinders would not have it any other way. Definitely the boss of number three now! I take my usual bowl of rice krispies. A habit from childhood, never dropped. Besides, I'll have hands full of grease shortly. "Mummy's leaving now. Back later." My daily words of goodbye. I'm so grateful to have my own business. Small mercy. That way I can bide my time, with my Cinders, meandering around the town and outskirts. It's remarkable how easily she was to train on a lead. I know some of the locals consider me potty, but what's the difference really? If a cat likes to walk out as dogs do, a cat likes to walk out. Simple.

Simple is the name of my breakfast café. Simple as it's not posh. I take my time getting there. It's a cold, sharp morning here in Banbridge. Typical early December. The sun yet to rise. I always take the long route through Church Square. Seapatrick Parish Church, draws me to pass by its large welcoming doors. Its magnificent arched, stained glass windows, nourish my soul. There's one in particular that I often wander in to stare at, after lighting a candle. It tries to tell me something I have yet to grasp. This little custom helps me to connect with Our Lord and Lady. Gives me what I need. Helps me to give the most of myself to my people. This year, two thousand and seventeen, has so far been rather mundane. I arrive. Bob on time, six thirty am. I open at seven. That's when the customers start to arrive. I swear I do the best Irish breakfasts in all the world. Well, that's what I'm told. I like to believe it too.

Having let myself in round the back, I commence my routine. Fire up the oven. Turn on the boiler. I look down whilst I tie my apron. Yep. My belly's still there, sticking out at least six inches from my hips. Oh well. I place my wiry dyed-brown hair in my catering net. Reach for the box of plastic gloves. There's a knock at the door. I guess the light spilling from the kitchen gives it away, that I am, yes, indeed present. Whoever it is, they are early. They know my rules. The knocking persists. I peek through the serving counter. It can't be. It can't be. Yes it is. I excitedly fumble for the front door keys. Fly to unlock it, and let the persistent fella in.

"Arthur. My dear Arthur. How wonderful. Come in." We encase each other in bear hugs. I've not seen or heard from him for near-on two years. My, he's looking good, must be approaching his eighth decade now. "What's brought you back?" I teasingly ask. "I had to come and see you myself. I wanted to catch you before you get busy in here. I have the most wonderful news to share."

"Well, whatever it is you seem to be beaming." I reply.

"May I trouble you for a cuppa?" He winks. "Same as usual?"

"Of course, sit down in your old favourite place, I'll have it out in a jiffy." I hurriedly make us both a cup of tea. Place them on the plastic table cloth, sit myself besides him. He takes both my hands.

"My dear. Do you remember the conversation we had shortly before I left for Florida?"

"Why yes I do." I say, nodding.

4

"I cannot thank you enough. After my wife died, as you know I was somewhat lost. It was you. You who pressed me for my dreams. You who led to me take those gigantic first steps. You who reminded me of my glory days, when I used to dance in all the local competitions. Winning most you know."

"I do. Carry on Arthur, I'm intrigued." I nudge him.

"Well, it's never too late. The loss of one you love can bring you down, wear and age you. Or you can honour all that you shared, honour the gift of falling days. And live them. That's what you said."

I give him a warm smile.

"I'm in love." He exclaims.

"What?" I joyously shout out. "Oh my God. Tell me all."

"I did as you suggested. Rooted out an Irish jig school. Started to attend their over fifty's dance nights. I felt a bit of a fool at first, you know being somewhat over fifty myself. Your voice, your words drove me to walk through that door, on that first fateful evening. That's how I met Miriam."

"Oh, Miriam." I raise my brows in wonder. "Do you have a photo?"

"I do. He opens up his old tweed jacket. Pulls out a crisp white envelope, opens it. Here, here is Miriam." He places the picture before me. "I know you." He pipes in. "You're going to study it, aren't you?"

"Yes, give me a moment."

As I focus on the dainty face. I'm first drawn to the palpable sadness. "Widowed?" I ask.

"Yep."

I look more deeply. "I see the sorrow Arthur. It will always lie there, as shall yours. However there's definitely something endearing in this lady. I see she has danced before, started in her forties with a somewhat stocky man."

"She did, that was Alan. She's much more nimble on her feet than I." He laughs, then continues. "She nearly didn't go that first night either. Hadn't been for many a year. Felt she'd be betraying her husband if she was to dance with another. As I entered the dance hall, I spotted her straight away. Miriam was leaning back against the wooden stage, eyes down. Looking terribly anxious."

"So, how did you get talking?" I enquire.

"It was like this. I'd treated myself to a brand new pair of Corrs hard shoes, also poodle socks. It was as I was putting them on, and tying the laces that she meandered over. Drawn to the shoes, she said, same as her late Alan's. That's how we started. We both sat silently whilst the others in the hall started to form couples and groups, to dance to the music. Two, three melodies passed. Then bravery awoke in me. "One for the road?" I asked her. "Yes, alright. I'm sure that won't hurt. I'm Miriam." The lady spoke. "I'm Arthur, at your service." I replied and did a half bow. "What happened after that is nothing short of a fairy tale for old folks. We very slowly, and very carefully fell in dance, in love." "Arthur, I am delighted for you. You've always been such a giving man. Worked so hard all your life. Provided so well for all your family. It was the right thing to do you know. Take off to a warm climate, warm your old bones."

"That's not all Kelly. We are engaged." I gasp.

"This is the best day of my life Arthur. The most amazing news. Congratulations." "You'll be able to congratulate us yourself." I look to him quizzically. "I've flown back home early, to give me the time to see you firstly. My savour. Also my children. I want to face them as I am you.

"What are you trying to tell me?" I ask. "We, that is Miriam and I are to be married. In a fortnight." His face is radiating bliss. "Oh my goodness. I guess I shouldn't be surprised, patience is not on your side here."

"Indeed. We have chosen the registry office in Armagh. Wouldn't be fitting to marry here in Banbridge, too many memories. It's a new and final chapter in our lives. It needs to be fresh. Her family can afford to come over for the ceremony. So there will be quite a crowd. And you. You my dear. Miriam would love you to be her maid of honour. She firmly believes it is your insight that brought us to this wonderful union."

I gasp, my mouth flies open. I jump up, wrap my arms around his broad shoulders. "Thank you. I'd be honoured."

"December 21st." He pipes up. "Winter Solstice. To honour my time line. And you, of course. Besides, seems fitting, as I'm coming to the end of my days!" He winks.

"Arthur, I am truly delighted. Yet, I have to crack on now, or they'll be grumbling stomachs."

"I know flower. I'll pop back in when Miriam arrives, so you can meet her properly."

I hand him back the photo, which he lovingly tucks away. I get up. He nimbly rises, pushes his and my chair back in place, always the gent. "Isn't it about time you were wooing again young lady? Your baby clock is ticking." He smiles gently.

"Arthur. I've come to realise that this is my second home, this café. And all that enter here are my family. I don't know why, I just know, my place is here, at Simple. Serving freshly prepared meals with utmost care and love, and helping those that pass my threshold." "You always said that my love. Always did. Well you do a good job pet". I guide him to the door. He kisses me gently on the cheek. "Thank you. Thank you." He utters. Raises his collar on his jacket against the cold and leaves.

Another wonderful day, half way through. It's two in the afternoon now. I've been so light on my feet all day, after my earlier encounters. The strange dream. Arthur's ground breaking news. I lock up the café. All things away and in order for the next day. I amble home, stop in at Doreen's newsagents on the way. Pick up a copy of the Banbridge Chronicle. Some fresh skimmed milk for me and kitty. We will go for a short walk up to the golf club and back before it's dark. Those golfers are the ones that give us the weirdest looks of all. Who are they to judge? I'm walking my cat. They, their golf bags with clubs. I know which I'd rather walk with. I'm planning a night by the fire. Lit by me, not always successful first time, but hey ho. A homemade mixed mushroom pie. Mashed potatoes and peas. Umm. With Cinders curled up next to me on my old worn sofa, which is covered with a throw to hide the kind damage Cinders did as a kitten. Whilst waiting for supper to cook through, I pick up the paper.

As the aromas start to waft through, my eye catches an advert. To be held in Dromore, our neighbouring town. Starting this Saturday, late afternoon. A jewellery-making workshop, using little gems and crystals. This is something I've often fancied having a tinkle with. I pick up my phone, call the number. The organiser Jackie swiftly answers. We have a little chat. And then that's that. I'm booked in. I look to Cinders. "Perhaps, I could make you a special collar with pretty little stones." She looks to me with slight disapproval. "Ok, princess. I'll make myself a collar. I know what you want, saw it in your eyes earlier. You want a little cosy coat for your walks, don't you? Just like the small dogs wear. Well, your wish is my command." I go to pick up my laptop. Tap in on Google "cat coats". Sadly there are few choices compared to dogs. "Bugger it." I say. "Here princess, take a look." She eyes the screen as I flip through various sites. She's not impressed I can tell. "Ok, dog ones it is then." I instantly find a site which caters for the particular. She gently curls her claw on my lap, as one picture of a bright red one, lined with black fur comes up. Perfect. I go through the buying process. "There done. It will be your Christmas present. I'm excited to be doing some craft work. No rubber gloves needed there." I scratch the base of her spine, just as she likes it.

KELLY 2

It's Saturday. I had a very busy morning at the café. I do sometimes consider getting a little helper, however, I like the intimacy of how it is. I cook, present, clear up. Listen. There's a young woman who comes most Saturdays with her two children. Sophie, a little stick of a girl. Long brown hair reaches to her lower back. Eyes so blue, so Irish blue. A wasp like face, pointy little chin, high cheekbones. Her brother, two years younger at four, is quite the contrast. Stout, tall for his age. The type that often gets comments of how he'll make a good rugby player, just like his father. Brown eyes, square jaw, scruffy brown hair that's always sticking up somewhere. He makes me laugh. Conor is cute, though he loves to rile his sister. Their mother Teagan, who certainly takes after her name, is stunning. They've been coming less and less. My initial happiness to see them soon waned. There's certainly something amiss here.

Teagan is normally full of beans, today she looked tired. Haggard in fact. Thinner, if that's possible, from last they came in. There was a distinct nervousness about her. I let them eat, cleared their table. I have an innate sense for others' pain. I never leave it be. I took over, on the house for the two bairns, an extra chocolatey hot chocolate. Together with two pages from the drawing book I keep in the back, with old crayons, ranging in colour and length. With them happily distracted, my heart goes in.

"What's the matter?" Teagan looks shyly to me. "If you want me to leave it I will. However, you know how I am." Her eyes water. She uses her left hand to gently release her long blonde locks from behind her ears. This I know is an instinctive manoeuvre to hide her emotion. I notice there's a spare table by the window. "Come with me, let's move over there. Children. Mummy and I are just going to have a little chat in that corner, is that ok?" "Yes." They both hardly reply, engrossed in their colouring. Conor's tongue, stuck out, darts from side to side in absolute concentration.

With us now having some privacy, Teagan starts to open up. "It's Ian. I. I." Her tears roll.

"Take your time dear, I'm here for you." I gently tell her.

"He's. I think. He's having an affair." Her body now quivers.

"Ian, really?" I question.

"Don't mock me. I know." Teagan injects.

"It's just that he has everything. You for a start. Your lovely children. A thriving re-established career." I try to console.

"Evidently not." She breaks for a while, I allow her space. A moment later she starts to talk again. "You know how he got that job, presenting at the rugby matches, being an old boy, he's got all the knowledge. Well, it's been taking him away from home regularly. And now he's away a lot. A lot more than I know he needs to be."

"Are you sure that an affair is the real reason? Perhaps he is just working more." I try to reassure.

"He's not, there's more." She states.

I give in. "Ok, tell me what's been going on."

"He keeps his phone firmly by his side, that's when he is at home." Another pause. "He nips out into the garden. He's started smoking again. That's his excuse for getting away from me, for his private little texts. He's dumb if he thinks I am." Teagan starts to mess with her fingers, twiddle her wedding ring, clearly agitated. I noticed how pale her skin is. "There's more." Teagan looked down, as if embarrassed.

"What is it dear?" I ask.

"He's. He's different in bed. You know, does different things. Little things, yet they are there. Things we never did before. New things." Teagan looks to her children. "Small mercy they are none the wiser." She says. "But I don't know how much longer I can keep up this charade. Don't know how much longer I can keep this in."

"My dear, you've taken the first step opening up to Aunt Kell." I reassured her again, with a look of concern and determination to help her through this awful nightmare. "My dear, you don't seem to me to be strong enough to confront this. If you want my advice, I'll gladly pass it to you."

"Yes. Please." She shoots out in pure desperation.

"Ok." I sigh. "How long have you been together?" "Ten years, since we met, eight since we married."

"Ok, pet." I reply. "My last question to you now." Teagan's eyes lift. "Do you still, after this, wish for your relationship to flourish again?"

"I do." Comes her humble reply.

"Well then, here goes. You won't like all you hear, but hear me out." I take a deep breath, focus myself. "The truth is my dear. That most men will stray. The fact that it is an affair Ian is having, would indicate to me this is the first time he's strayed. Men come in three forms. Those that are wholly loyal, rather few, I might add. Those that look for a take-up one-off opportunity at every turn. Then those that, well, let's say perhaps, are trying to regain a part of their youth. I believe Ian is one of the latter.

"Really?" Teagan's curiosity grows.

"Yes, my dear, really. You see, your husband, is what, around thirty eight now?"

Teagan replied, "Thirty nine."

"Ok, so here it is. He's been happily with you, and at my guess loyal for the best part of his middle youth. Approaching forty, sometimes makes a man feel that he's losing his vigour. A younger maid, can falsely provide him with false beliefs. Make him feel tough, fill up his chest with pride, like a lion, like a, "Yes, I've still got it." Kind of thing. Do you follow?" Teagan seems to be a little relieved by my words, as if they have made her realise she is not alone, nor is she in any way to blame for his otherly activities. I'm pleased. Feeling guilty that perhaps, she has in some way been inadequate, can really debilitate a woman. The way she walked in earlier, easily summed that up. I carry on, happy that my words have resonated. "Furthermore. With his recent appearances on the sports channels, this would without a doubt draw to him those in want of a free ride, a bit of celebrity, status, power over their contemporaries. An expensive handbag to show off. These young ladies will stop at nothing to get what they want. They care not for the wife, she's competition for them. They enjoy their wickedness, feel they have the upper hand. They care less for the children, or proposed family destruction. All they care about is themselves. Full stop. We have to carefully consider therefore, how to use our given female talent of being the sly winner that casts out the sinner. In this case the lady, if I could call her that. Let's just call her It. Takes away her power over you. As that is what she is, an "it" to your husband. A mere prop in his life, and mere podium to his testosterone thrust. You, need to make him realise, that what he has with you is as good as it gets. Otherwise, he will fall into the endless cycle of turning, to what he now sees as youth dew. We can see this every week in the endless articles of aged rock stars, billionaires who, by their own undertaking, seem to believe that by having a body lie next to them that has no wrinkles, no droopy bits, that somehow this eliminates theirs. Fools. Funny, really, we should feel sad for them, in their forlorn mistakings. The foreboding cycle of marriage, children, divorce, broken hearts, homes, and crushed children ensues."

"I suggest you look to his diary, book a surprise family holiday, make it two weeks, not just one. Do you see this will really piss off the it. So instead of you two having it out, she will turn into the nag. This will hopefully push his buttons, as to the welfare of his family. This will really push her buttons too. It will whine and moan. It will create the drama. It will show, it's real face. It will endlessly text, try to draw attention away from his children, this will anger him. Show him just how selfish it can be. Give him the space he needs, yet encourage as much interaction with the kids as you can, push his guilt button a little, Poppet. In other words, don't be needy yourself. Stay strong, aloof in a manner, yet pleasant, as if all is well. This cheesy little tart will fail at her continued manipulations. She will show him how she herself is but a needy child. Get this done sooner, rather than later. The quicker the sexual bond is broken, the better."

The kids come over. I'm not too concerned, I think I've said enough. "Oh, and one other thing." I bend over, whisper in her ear. "Do yourself some research." Teagan looked puzzled. I giggled. "Have a new trendy hair style. Get yourself some hot underwear, and hot new naughty tips. Search the web, it's all out there these days. Remind him that you are his one and only lioness. Oh, and kill him with kindness."

Teagan and her children gathered their small belongings and left, not before Sophie and Conor proudly handed me their drawings, which I promptly stuck to my achievement board, each with a little gold star placed in the top right corner. Pleased children, and an empowered mother walked out into the street. I'm happy there's been no mention, nor sign of violence. In my experience, that type of violation certainly, sharply or slowly, ends everything. I'd been so engrossed I hadn't realised the remaining customers had left. Each as honest as the day is long, having left the correct sum of money on the table cloths, along with a few extra pennies. I tidied up what remained. Shut down the office. Went promptly home to my Cinders. Showered. Washed the oily smell from my hair, and found I was just in time to make my little journey into the unknown world of jewellery-making. Yippee.

Feeling really pleased with myself as I head off to Dromore in my little old red Mini. Had the girl many years now, never lets me down. I glance at the note of instructions on my passenger seat, follow their directions. I arrive at a relatively modern semi-detached house. Park up. Get out. Go through the delicate iron gate, which has been left open, leading to the front door. Lots of little trinkets adorn the front yard. Together with several different types of chimes, hanging from the branches of a now-dormant cherry tree. I knock twice. The door swings open. A very jolly middle-aged woman greets me. I quickly take her in. Similar height and build to myself, deliciously curvy is how I describe myself. Her hair is tied back into a high bun, the beginnings of grey wisps give way to a bright orange mop. "Come through, come through." She utters. "Jackie, pleasure to meet you, Kelly is it?"

"Kelly I am." I answer. Jackie leads me down the narrow hall, through an open kitchen diner, to a conservatory at the back. She indicates for me to take the last seat at the round glass table.

Four other ladies are perched. All chatting away, evidence that they have met before. "Hi, I'm Kelly, call me Kell." I chirp. They all say hello back and proceed to introduce themselves. Jackie starts to talk.

"Kell, you've missed the first lesson but don't worry, we are all here to help each other. We did bracelets last week, and are moving onto necklaces today. Ladies, I have set out on top of the drawers everything you will need. Go to the lay out and choose which stones you wish to use today. Jackie, I will bring you up to speed, once they've chosen their colours."

The ladies rise, chat amongst themselves. Gather each a small basket of small irregular stones, each having different hues, each too a hole through the middle. Jackie goes to the laid out tools, places them at the centre of the glass. It seems to be a collection of small various-headed pliers. A crimping tool. Tape measure. Wire cutters. Wire thread, and a small tube of glue. "Ladies." Starts Jackie. "Today, as it does appear to be fashionable we are going to create ourselves each a double threaded choker. You will need to measure and cut two pieces each of thread, fourteen inches for those of us blessed with narrow necks, up to sixteen inches for us bonnier ones. Allow a few inches extra for knotting etc. We can tidy the ends when we are finished." Jackie then goes back to the dresser. "Arhh." She exclaims. "You, Kell, appear to have been left with the beads of amber. Lovely, they will really suit you. The ladies quickly get to work. I panic for a moment. "Don't worry." States Jackie, who drags a smaller old chair from the corner of the room, kindly asks a lady to shove up a bit, slips it in besides me. Sits herself down.

"Right. Take the wire, measure it as I mentioned before. I'm sure fifteen inches will suffice for you. I'm following her instructions as best I can. Jackie intercedes a bit, when she notices I'm struggling. One of the ladies has nimble fingers and finishes her two lines of turquoise stones first. Uses the appliances laid out.

"There all done. Shall I make us all a drink?"

"Good one," replies Jackie. The lady takes our orders and potters back into the kitchen. I'm done. Complete. The pliers used, the ends cut. The glue and tiny clasps in place. I look down to my work. Umm quite satisfied. The lady with the teas returns with a tray, which she places where the baskets of beads had been.

"Ladies. We shall have our drinks whilst the glue sets." We chat some more, get to know each other's basic life stories.

Thirty minutes later, the drinks cleared away. Jackie claps her hands. "Ladies, the moment you've all been waiting for. Your chokers are ready to adorn your necks. We each lift our endeavours and place them proudly in place. One lady, asked another to help as her fingers are a little stiff with arthritis. Jackie then hands around a hand mirror. We all coo at our creations. "Lovely. Lovely. Beautiful." Flattering words fly around. I look to my watch, stand up.

"I'm afraid I have to leave now. May I say I've truly enjoyed myself! Thank you to all of you for sharing this afternoon with me. I have to get home to walk my cat."

"Your cat." The elderly lady questions.

"Yes my cat." I get those familiar looks from all five faces. "It's just a pussy cat." I laugh. Say my goodbyes. Jackie lets me out. I hand her the agreed amount for the workshop. "I hope to see you again." She says as I walk down the path.

"I'll see what I can do, I have a few busy weeks ahead. Bye now. And, thank you again."

MAIRE 2

"Come hither, daughter." A man. Tall, robust, long grey curly hair with a tidy beard to match. My father approaches. He's adorned in all his finery. Black trousers, knee-high black leather laced boots. Black long sleeved, high collared tunic. With bronze buttons down the front, around the waistband and at its cuffs. Looking every much the substantial character that he is. For he is ruler of the Sept Fermanagh. Chief of clan O'Ciaragain. I, his only child, am Maire. It is autumn. The year, fourteen twenty.

"The feasts, celebrations and fires of Beltane, have worked wonders this year in voluminous ways. I have a tremendous gift for you. Follow me." I jump up from my tapestry work with great enthusiasm. My father is my life. I obediently walk behind him, out of the main room, into the great hall. Passing the stone walls, either side furnished with elaborate wooden chests. Countless animal heads decorate the walls, amongst the largest wall set candle sconces known in Armagh. Perhaps in the whole of Ireland. Two guards, heavily clad in chain-armour. Both wearing a scabbard bearing the toughest of iron swords. They stand at each side of the main entrance, instinctively heave open the heavy wooden doors when my father approaches. He does not greet them.

"Take my hand child." I do as asked. Slightly taken aback.
My father is not known for being tactile. I sense a different
air today. As if something is about to change. We walk
around the back of the manor, where our finest horses are
kept. Enter the wooden barn. Railings separate each horses
stable. I often take myself here to tend to them. Horses are
my very foremost pleasure. Father leads us to the last horse
box. "Cover your eyes Maire, let me guide you in." I obey.
"Now, remove your hands." There, by the side of our best
chestnut brood mare, lying silently in the straw is a new-
born stallion. White as the moon. Legs long, lanky, make an
effort to stand. He does fairly quickly, a good omen. His nose
leads him to her teats, his mother nudges him into place. He
suckles. I am in awe.

"Maire. He is yours. Born just in time for your coming of
age. You'll be twelve next week. He is a gift from me, via the
gods." I cry, sob in fact.

"Really?"

"Yes child. Really. You are to allow his mother to do her job.
Interact when she allows it. Get to know him. You are to be
his main keeper. It is you that shall teach him the ways of
man. Feed him, tend to him. Bond with him like no other
before. For it was prophesised at your birth, that the white
one would come. The druid was indeed correct." Father
laughs. "As if I doubted it." He puts his hand to my shoulder.
"This horse is no battle horse. He is to carry you to your
preordained fate. He will lead you to where you are destined
to travel. That is when you both are old enough." Again
he laughs.

"There is one other thing." He regains his usual serious
pose. Pulls from round his neck under his tunic, a small

round hessian pouch. He tips the contents onto his palm. An exquisite necklace, made of tiny amber resin balls, spills out. "Now bow your head Maire, look to the ground." I feel cool beads being placed and clasped around my pearly white neck. Father lifts my chin. "There, perfect. These, dearest one belonged to your mother. She had me make an oath that I'd pass them to you this year, if she herself was unable to. I truly say I can feel her around us this very moment, blessing this blessing. From the otherworld herself. That is not all. Your mothers' mother, her mother before, your great grandmother and all the ladies of our clan, wore this. Consider it more of an amulet. It brings the power of ultimate wisdom, great protection. Also creates a bridge to the past. You are to treasure it. Guard it with your life. Pass it on when the time shall come. Do you understand?"

"Yes father." I reply, slightly worried to take on the responsibility.

"Oh you'll be fine. No man will dare take it from you. As you know, I have no son. The druid, my seer, does not see one forthcoming. Therefore, from this day you are to be trained in the art of war. For there are many who have come before, and many who will try again to take our lands, eradicate our people, plunder our possessions. There is a third gift for you this day. Ivan. Stand." My father orders.

From the other side of the barn there is a rustling, a heap of hay moves. Falls away. A man rises. Rises and rises. He is three heads taller than any man. My body starts to tilt backwards, away from him. "Don't be foolish Maire. Ivan will guide you. Cherish you to womanhood. He is to teach you the way of the sword, the dagger, the javelin, the axe. Every tool of death. Every way to kill. No more time for needle work my dear." Father laughs so much now his body jolts up and down. "He is to stay close to you until you are fully learned. It is his duty. Trained the venerable Earl of Desmond's fine son before you, he did."

"Father, I don't know what to say." I state.

"A thank you would be nice." Again he's entertained by my naivety. "May I hug you?" I ask.

"I think, on this occasion. That would be appropriate." I step forward. Throw my arms around his waist, up to his bold shoulders.

"I don't intend to release my mortality yet. But just in case, you shall be prepared." The conversation is drawing to an end, I can sense that. "Now back inside. You start tomorrow. First you'll check your horse, then start to grow in the ways of a warlord. What are you to name him?"

"Pardon father."

"Your bloody horse idiot."

"Oh." I think for the slightest of seconds, the answer pops into my head. "Raphael father. I shall call him Raphael." Tears fall again. At the wonder of my special gift. "Raphael it is." Father shouts out as he leaves. I quickly follow, slightly unnerved at the prospect of remaining behind with the gargantuan man.

KELLY 3

There's a knock at the door, which startles me. My first thought is where am I? Fell asleep on the couch again. That thing is just far too comfy. My second is, who on earth? My third, typical, woken up again on a Sunday. "Wait a moment." I holler out. Very quickly check myself in the mirror above the fireplace. Get rid of that toucan thing my hair does. Then go to open the door, taking a peek though the small round glass spy hole. There's a delivery van parked across the street. A man in my doorway, holding a cardboard box. "Hello, parcel for a Miss Kelly Duffy?"

"That's me." I reply.

"Sign here please." I do, he leaves. I turn, close the door, and return to my second bed. The amount of times I've fallen asleep on that, woken up there none the wiser.

My grumbles at being disturbed soon dissipate. "Fab." I say aloud. I'll be able to catch the morning service at church. Missed a few of recent months. It is appropriate for me to attend today, to give thanks for the support the good Lord and Lady, who gave my old friend Arthur his second chance of happiness. Warms me, it does. So now to explore the box. I take it to my recently repainted kitchen. I fancied a change, so paint it was, from blue to grey. Couldn't really find the means to change much else. Reach for the scissors stored in an old pot vase, by the side of the sink. Cut open the tape. And. "Hey. Cinders. It's your new coat." She meows, comes into the kitchen, well she will be hungry now. "Look what's arrived for you." I pick her up, put her on the work surface. Pull the neck bit over her head, fasten the buttons under her tummy. "There, look at that. You do look a treat. Fits fine. We'll take it out with us later. As it's a crisp, dry day, I'll take us up to Drumkeeragh Forest. Would you like that?" I remove the coat, put her down, Cinders walks circles round my ankles, rubs herself against my legs. I feed her. Make myself some scrambled eggs, return to my sofa. Turn on the television.

I'm happy to have made the decision to walk through the forest today. Sometimes we get to see the local riders out on their horses. I've never ridden. One thing I regret, I love their majesty. My neck itches. I scratch. Holy, I'd forgotten to remove the amber necklace. My thoughts race back, to recall my latest dream. What does this imply? I pick up the remote, push pause. What is going on? That young girl. Maire wasn't it? I remove the necklace, place it in my palms. This is uncanny. My mind races. Grasps. Puts two and two together. The girl Maire, she's the younger version of the woman I dreamt about last Wednesday night. There's no doubt of it. I normally dream a load of rubbish. This is odd. Two in a row. Two very clear scenes. No flying pigs in these. I get up. Dump my plate and cutlery in the sink. Best get a move on or I'll miss Mass.

I look to the clock on the spire. I'm just in time, just. Three minutes to ten o'clock. I try to walk calmly down the aisle. Not wanting to disturb contemplation. I take a pew five rows from the front, park my bum. Glad to sit here, it gives me a full view of the archway, behind the altar. The stained window in it depicts the last supper. The morning sun streams though. I cross myself. Cannon Liam Stevenson conducts his service. I relish every second, as he recounts the old tale, of how St Patrick is camped on this very spot in the fifth century. This spot is very sacred indeed. I'm affected by it. Nowhere else makes me feel so at ease. So at peace. During the prayers, I give my little thanks to God for his grace with Arthur. I also plead with Our Lord and Our Lady to help resolve young Teagan's marriage. The service draws to its end. The choir sing as we take our leave. The Cannon shakes everyone's hand as they pass through the doors. Shares a few words, accepts his praise. I walk home solemnly.

"I'm home," I call out to Cinders. Perhaps the neighbours consider me mad, talking the way I do to her. Pooh to them. I go upstairs, change my attire for something more suitable for the forest. Return to the bottom of the stairs, reach for my long quilted coat from the antique coat hook, bequeathed by my late Grandmother. Grab my scarf. Call my cat. Take her coat, put her on her lead. Kick off my day shoes, retrieve my walking boots from the back door. That's it. Ready.

When we arrive at the forest, I put Cinders' coat on first. Oh is she happy. I open the glove compartment, take out my old felt gloves. "Come on." She hops over my seat, onto the ground. We set off in a northerly direction, Cinders' tail held high. The sun has warmed the earth. Any earlier frost gone. Better for Cinders' paws, I am pleased. We've been walking now for a good half hour. The pines stretch up their might to the sky. The odour is wonderful, clear, clean, an alpine smell. Upon the path ahead of us, a pony, small rider and a man leading them appear from a bend. I pay little attention until they are closer. I decide to pick Cinders up. She's a little wary of anything much bigger than a dog.

As they pass, the girl, and the man I presume to be her father, greet us with a hello. People often stop to ponder why I should walk a cat. I answer their question. "Say hello Cinders." I tell her. Then discretely nuzzle her near the pony's head. "Pony, meet Cinders." I teasingly say. "Raphael, say hello." Pipes up the girl.

I stop breathing for a moment. What did I just hear?

"What a lovely name Raphael is." I recant. "Thank you. Enjoy your walk pussy cat." The girl smiles, along with her father. "Enjoy your ride too. Bye now." I reply. "Bye." The girl responds. She pats her pony, they carry on past us. With not knowing what's just triggered a shiver down my spine.

MAIRE 3

My father and I, Mac, to those that are close to him, are
leading our clan's precession. I am on Raphael. He grew into
the strongest, most admired horse ever bred by us. The ladies
and children follow behind. Flanked by our guards. Some
are walking, some, like the bairns and elderly, travel seated
in long four-wheeled chariots. Our men went before us to
set out the tents and provisions. Gather firewood. Set out
the games.

As I turn to look behind, I smile. We are quite a clan. Flags,
decorated with cultural symbols bring a mass of bright
colours to our parade. We are one of many clans, coming
together at the sacred forest to celebrate the festival of
Lughnasadh. In honour of the God Lugh, the bright and
shining one. Although this is a peaceful event, guards are
required, as we Irish are volatile. Conspiracies abound
after the coming of the British (below our lands). People
can easily be bribed. Caution prevails. However, we fiercely
defend our ancient traditions and beliefs. As usual, a third
of our protectors have remained at our fort. These are
treacherous times. Our grounds must be kept safe, just in
case. The faces of the men left behind saddened me. Yet
there is a rota devised so they each get their turn to enjoy
the celebrations. The two in the watch tower above the gated
entrance, lowered the draw bridge across the deep ditch that

proceeds the walls that surround the grounds. We left a jolly, gabbling lot.

'Tis the last day of the month of July. The year fourteen twenty six. We breach the outskirts of the deep forest by midday. Go to our usual camp site, which is always in the same spot, as are those of the other clans. Fires have already been lit. Father and I proceed to our main tent, elaborate as it can be. Dismount, pass our horses on to their keepers, in my case Ivan. The others find their close family quarters. All settle in. I'm excited, as father has told me, that, now at the age of eighteen, strong in muscle and calm enough of mind, that I can participate in the most arduous of the competitions. Swordsmanship. To be held tomorrow afternoon, just before the great feast.

The merriments have commenced. The people drawn to the music at the opening ceremony. Gather at the open field to the west of the woodland. Children and youths are swirling, stamping and hollering around a great fire. One which will not die down for three days and nights, as is custom. Sounds of flutes and drums complement each other. Rhythmically, hauntingly, recalling past tunes of old. Nursing mothers form an outer circle, together with the infirm on mats crafted from straw. These mats will be the final offerings to the fire for Lugh.

The chieftains sit around a highly decorated round ash table. As every year. Here they raise their drinking horns, to cooperation. Each with the clan's emblem carved meticulously around them. A large vat of mead rests in the middle. Each replenish from it when needs be. Which is fairly regular. I will take the place of my father one day. To form alliances, to keep the peace. Or to talk up vengeful war.

Which there is belligerent talk about. As the English of the Pale try to take hold of more of our plentiful Isle.

The music dies, the dancers stop. This first afternoon is now dedicated to the children. Mothers and fathers encourage their male offspring to partake of the first game, which is brutal, given the Irish innate violence. Stick and ball. Toughens our youngsters. Long thin wooden branches carved into the shape of a new moon, with a little catching cup at the end. The ball made from tightly stitched leather. Four teams form, to represent their province. There are few rules. Blood may spill, yet just a little, there is no forfeit for that. The parents and on lookers shout out commandments. Tick their children off, should a simple mistake lead to loss of ball control. In fact this game is one that raises the most of hackles. The aim is to toss the ball cleanly over the fire. The team that gains the majority of clear landings on the other side, become the winners. Once a landing has taken place. The ball is thrust into the air from the place it landed. By the one that scored the point. Of course many a young head, arm, leg gets struck in the ensuing boys efforts to win. A good early lesson. Time is called by the chieftain's wife from the team that won the year before. Of course this can be easily manipulated. Another good life lesson.

Next it's time for the younger children to be entertained. They gather, sat cross-legged, in front of an old man, the story teller. The bard. He stands before them. Clicks his fingers, two younger men appear, carrying a small wooden box. A series of little puppets are laid on the ground before them. The old man starts to tell his stories. The puppeteers use the appropriate props to convey visually to the children what is being told. Myths and legends are clearly and profoundly spoken about. The adults themselves hush to hear. Although they have heard them many a time. The tales of old continue to entrance all present. Chronicles of adventures, folklore. History, battles. Tragedy. Romance. Otherworldly creatures, half man, half beast. Yarns of interaction between druids, gods. The Fae. Small eyes stare in bewilderment. From the very start. Our descendants, are taught the way of the Celts. The old man and his assistant pack up, depart the circle. The children, entranced, excited, put on their own little display, reenact what they have observed, heard. The elders whoop. The elderly women enter to quieten the children. Gather them. Take them away to settle them down. It's time now for the adults.

As is our custom. It is now time for boisterous drinking, copulating. Invoking the essence of sex so to heighten the magic. The blessing to Lugh. The most powerful night is tomorrow. The sexual rite, initially held only at Beltane, has now become a part of most of our rituals, as it pleases. Maidens emerge from the woods. Clad in nothing but a cow-skin loin cloth, tied loosely to reveal a hip. A burning torch in hand. For it is they that are in charge of choosing their mate for the night. An erotic, enticing dance is firstly performed for all to see. The loincloths rise and fall provocatively, revealing more flesh. Once they are ready, they break their trance. Walk towards the expectant young men. They tease, half approach. Pull back. Carry on doing this until they feel drawn to a particular male. One by one they use their flaming torch, point it towards the heart of their chosen. Use their other hand to offer their honour. Take their prize to a premade den, deep in the forest. For here they will spend the night, calling to the gods. Making love continuously until they can no more. I am not allowed to partake in such rites, such is my standing. The older and married retire for the evening. A band of druids will watch over the fire at night. Keep it alight. Perform their secret rituals.

I'm awake the next day at the crack of dawn. Ivan ordered me to go to the large stream that sits beyond the idol rocks. "Go there. I shall follow behind, behind to protect you. Not to see you. Take off your clothes, lie in the cold water. Have your head facing down stream, so the pure waters can wash you from your feet up to your crown. You are to close your eyes. Don't worry. No harm shall befall you. Use your imagination. Believe the water sprites are clearing any negative thoughts or feelings about your abilities. For you shall win the tournament today. Stay there until you feel completely refreshed. Get out. Shake like a dog, then redress."

I do as I am told. Strangely, the water though cool, warms me the longer I'm in there. I do feel as if any weaknesses are being drawn out into the waters, all up my body, finally leaving through the ends of my hair. Shake like a dog though? Seems stupid. I do it. It fills me with prowess. I dress. Set off back to camp. I become aware of Ivan's presence. He follows in the early morning shadows. Back at the camp he asks me to put on my simplest of robes. "Gather your sword." He commands. I do. He has his also. We take off to a small clearing, away from the crowds.

"Look to your sword." He tells me. "Really look to it." I do. The blade is made from the lightest of iron. The sharpness unforgiving. The hilt, dipped in pure gold. Three ravens each facing west are engraved on the front. These form part of our coat of arms. "The ravens." Ivan continues. "These are there for a reason. That will be imparted to you on one of your further journeys. For now. Slip off your sandals." I bend down, untie the lace. Toss them aside. "Hold your blade up, way above your head with both hands. Stretch as far as you can. Close your eyes. Connect with the sky above. Spread your legs a little. That's it. Now let go of any preconceived ideas about today. Ask the sky to open up to the gods' inspiration. Ask them to reach down. To bless the very tip." My arms start to quiver. "Good. Now ask them to deliver their power through the enormous blade, and into the hilt. Then into your hands. Right down your body, through to your feet. See your feet as growing roots. See this bright golden white light going down from those roots right into the centre of the earth itself. Now jump."

"Jump?" I enquire.

"Yes jump."

I do. I land. I sense a new strength. As if the very earth herself has encased me.

"Stay on the spot on which you now stand. I'll go through all the manoeuvres I have taught you. Remain closed-eyed. I will do these at an extremely slow pace. Slower than we have practised before. Pay attention to every tiny sound, every movement of air. Every breath I take. Follow my sword with precise precision. If our swords clash, you have failed. I am to commence." At first I'm aware of nothing. Then, instinctively I move my head from side to side, bit by tiny bit. I become aware of the bird song. The trees' whispers. My heart beats. Ivan's breath. There, it's coming. I'm aware of the slightest sweep, cutting through the air. I take up my weapon. Avoid from the ensuing blows. To the side. To the ground. Sweeping up high, crossing though the middle. Darting, diving, sweeping. All in slow motion. My feet feel Ivan's movements. Every grain of soil he steps on, causes a vibration into my soles. I respond. Listening with every sense a human has. Responding with the skills of a goddess.

"I sensed that." Ivan cuts in. "What?" I question.

"Vanity. Do not let vanity take hold. Ever!"

"I'm sorry." I reply.

"We are done. You may open your eyes. Replace your sandals. We shall return now. Get you a breakfast to fill a true warriors' stomach.

The afternoon games begin. I stay in my tent contemplating. I cannot, will not be distracted. I shall win. I have seen the performances before many a time. There will be archery. Spear throwing. Wrestling. Each contestant dying to prove their skills are unsurpassed. As I envisage success. The acknowledgement of my earned place in this, our society. We are considered barbarians to those of the Pale. We are not. We are of true bloodlines. Keepers. Carers, defenders of our realms.

"My lady it is time." Ivan is by the tent opening. He goes to the chest, set in the middle of the tent. Opens it. Brings out my attire for the show. No armour is to be worn. This is a battle of will, skills. Patience and nimbleness.

I walk to my first initiation. Approach the five druids, who are stood in a line. They are as usual adorned in white, full, hooded robes. Plain tan pixie boots on their feet. A symbol of their connection to the otherworld. My father's personal magus is one of them. The other hopefuls come, stand in line in front of them. We are six in total. Four men. Two women. I do not weigh them up. Again no distractions. They eye me though. The druid in the middle steps forward. He pulls from his pocket fresh blades of grass. All of different length. Closes them lightly in his fist. He approaches us from left to right. Each one of us invited to pull a blade at random. My turn comes. Like the others before me, I take one. Hold it up for all to see. The druid inspects our blades. He numbers us. Six to one. One being the longest blade chosen. I am number three.

Number six and five, pick up their swords, move forwards. They turn to face one another. Bow. Commence. I know deep down I shall not battle against either of these opponents. So yet again, I pay no attention. Ivan warned me of trying to learn anything new at the last minute. Number five, the slighter of the two men, goes through to the next round. The same procedure starts up again. This time the slighter man is up against a large, well-honed man. He wins. I am to be up against this person. Larger in all ways to me. I step forward. Bow. Face him. The crowd remain silent as is required. He looks to me with disdain. A look of how flaccid this woman before him seems. A look of this is going to be easy. He is proved wrong. It is only a matter of less than a minute before I have him in a death hold. He curses to me under his tongue. Moves away. "Beginners luck." He mutters through twisted lips. Number two places himself before me. He is tall, lanky. Tries to disable me through his glare. Fool of a man. My reaction to such looks left me long ago. Again, I win. Again no more than a minute. He retires. The final number approaches.

Standing before me is a woman, around my age. Her left eye lost. Her long blonde hair braided at the front and sides. I notice slash scars about her skin. Tell myself to stop it. This is immaterial. The contest is all that matters. Not the look of ones foe. The druid from the middle takes a step forward. "Let it be known. That the final two opponents to commence their claim to the title of Swordsman of the Year. Are. Maire O'Ciaragain to my left." He indicates towards me. "And Gwyneth O'Hare, to my right.

The druid then blows the final horn. We are to fight. For a moment I hesitate. I've never raised my sword to a woman before. She looks to me. Evidently the same is not true for her. She shows no hesitation. Takes up her sword, lurches towards me. What ensues is a battle of wits, strength, prowess and sheer determination. Unlike men, she tries to lure me, trip me up. Belittle me with jest. I must admit I admire her strategy. Stop thinking. Remember this morning's exercise. I do. My resolve returns. "Yah." I lift my blade, bring it clashing to hers. Our blades meet by our guts. I use my strength to shove hers away. The blades screech. The crowd gasps. The druids are forced to move back as our movements become flowing, cover more ground. Neither of us with a care to our surrounds. A mere will to win. After much, lurching, leaping; spinning, squatting, I have her prone, sealing the final blow. My blade to her open neck. I am pronounced the champion. Gwyneth returns to her feet. Both of us panting, sweating. She, shows her camaraderie. Approaches, offers her hand. We shake. Something tells me our paths will cross again. "Time to feast," the druid states. Giving a theatrical wave of his hand, towards the field to the left. Where everything has been prepared. Music strikes up. The people readily make their way to the source of the night's fun. Eating, drinking, merriment. My father's beaming smile catches my eye. He thumps his fist to his puffed out chest. Juts out his chin. I have made him proud. I don't see Ivan. I understand, he will not congratulate me. Will not feed any need in me to be recognised.

I'm about to join in, when my father's druid pulls me to one side. He has no name. His eyes are ice blue. Large. They see though all men. The darkness, the light. Nothing is hidden to him. "You are to be shown some of the ways of the magi," he informs me. "Not all, as you do not have the twenty years required to do so. However, I shall in time make arrangements for you to learn what you must. Great prowess. You are now on your way to your destined chosen path." Then he slinks away. The day has been long. My first victory gained. I take myself to the field of food, wine, dance, with gratitude for my father's pledge to me.

I wake up on the last day of the festival still wearing my combat clothes. Oh dear. My head feels a little heavy too. That's usual for this time of year. We all have one more game to play. However this one is one the druids closely watch. As it foretells the plenitude, or not, of our coming harvest. Two sets of chosen participants stand to one side of the fire. They are to play War of the Rope. A long rope, is to be held at either ends, by each team. Each member takes a place along the rope. They prepare their grasps. Using various grips. The middle druid calls the start. Lifts the rope, at perfectly equal lengths to each side over the head of the fire. "Begin," he calls. The two teams start to pull away from each other with all their might. One side represents the Sun, the male. The other the Moon, female. Although all players are male it matters not. The line moves more to the left. Then the right. To and froing in each direction, back and forth. Just as it seems the Sun team are to win, a mighty force from the Moon side gathers ground. It is firmly longer to their side now. Grunts, moans, fill the air. A final challenge. And it is done. The players fall back and to the ground. The rope is burnt through, broken. The Moon side has won. The druids nod to each other with satisfaction. The Moon, the female. The fertility side has the longest part of the rope. A major omen of a good yield of crops this coming autumn.

MAIRE 4

Samhain is approaching. This is the close of our year. The
new year starting on first of November. This is normally
a time when I would join in the closing of the sacred fire.
The lighting of the new one. When in turn, each labourer,
carpenter, forger, everyone in fact, takes a light from the new
fire, to bring to their hearth. As a sign of new beginnings.
A time when we don animal skins. Some even wear animal
heads. The great new fire is given sacrifices of crops. Stocks.
However I shall miss this this year.

Father's druid has planned for me, himself and Ivan to take
a sacred journey. To the uplands of Fermanagh. Nothing else
has been divulged to me yet. It's cold. So I am in Raphael's
stable, preparing him for the trip. He whinnies to me, letting
me know that he appreciates my care. I place over his back
a hand knitted, thick woollen blanket, of the finest Tyrian
purple. It was given as a token of appreciation to my father
from the late Earl of Desmond. Father said it was likely stolen
from British travellers. But we don't care. They are the greater
thieves. The Black Death some eighty years ago, all but nearly
wiped them out. I wish it would return to eradicate them. So
now this prestigious blanket, well, here it lies on my horse's
back. Where it belongs. I tie the straps to the front. Then
place my saddle to secure it in place. Attach the travel bags
to either side, along with my sword and dagger. Put on his

bridal. The druid is to take my father's black mare. Ivan is to walk. All are packed up and ready. I have on my amber necklace. Many under layers, topped with a green felt cloak. It is cold. Yet there's no sign of rain. A good thing, as the uplands are known to be harsh in winter months. It is a three day ride until Samhain. We are to arrive by late morning on October thirty first. The druid has arranged cover for us at night fall.

The last leg of our journey takes us by a stunning lake. Little fishing boats bob. Their occupants toying with nets. With the honouring mountains rising to one side of it. We begin our ascent. The wind kicks up. I love it when it does. It shows Raphael's true majesty. His mane, it whips up. Normally plaited to keep him from eating it. His mane, white like his coat, it falls to the top of his legs. Now it's dancing with the wind. My red hair takes lift too. He starts to jog. A sign to me that he realises his grandeur. The druid has remained mostly silent the whole way. Ivan's been quiet too. So I follow suit. It's as if talking would detract from the reason for this trip. Having climbed for some time now, we take a turn to the right. The terrain now is mostly rocks, mosses cover most of the stones. Eeriness abounds. I am entering into a vault of a different time. The air dampens. My stomach turns. All around, seemingly strategically placed, are the skulls of rams. We stop.

Further down the slope a black hooded figure stands motionless. Facing a black large upright stone, which appears to be an entrance place. We draw closer, the figure does not flinch. The druid dismounts. Ivan helps me down. Takes hold of my reins, goes to the druid, takes hold of the mare. "With me now." The druid exclaims. We walk to the hooded figure. Still it does not move. The druid directs me to stand in front of it. I do as obliged. I'm startled. It's a woman. An old hag.

I try to hide my alarm, having never seen such an aged face before. She cares not. She brings her eyes to mine. They are as dark and as deep as a sacred well. She stares at me. I stare back. She transforms right in front of my eyes. Back through the years of her life. She shows me all her faces and facets. Until she stops as a young woman. Beauty exudes. Beauty. Charm. Wisdom. Charisma, enigma, which I cannot fathom.

"I am Meghan of the Morrigan." Her voice sweet, alluring. She raises a finger, indicates for the druid to draw near. "Bless her." She tells him. He removes a tiny flask from his belt. Opens it. Tips a drop of holy water to the tip of his finger. Uses it to draw a Celtic cross on my forehead. It tingles. From a black leather bag, Meghan then draws two black ebony wands. They possess an energy of their own. They glow. She passes one to the druid. They move to the black stone. Both mumble unknown words to me in synchronicity. Holding the wands between their hands in prayer position. Then together, from the prayer position, both reach out to brandish the wands to the stone. It starts to vibrate. Slowly, its denseness crumbles. In seconds it's gone. What lies behind is an opening to a cave. The druid tucks his wand inside his cloak. Meghan returns hers to her bag. It starts to rain. I worry about my horse. Look over. Happy to see that Ivan has found shelter. "Quickly now." She says. "We need to pass the portal before it closes again." She takes my hand. Energy surges from her palm to mine. "Now come." She commands me, we walk through the opening together. A mist rises from the ground and the stone returns. We are left in the utmost darkness.

Panic takes hold. I hear a cackle. "Trust child. Trust." She claps her hands. Immediately the walls illuminate. Lighted torches line the cave walls. Revealing the true extent of this underground world. I've heard whispers of these places. Never before have I seen such a sight. I feel in awe, bewildered. "Follow me." She mutters. "Take care it's slippery." We move deeper into the belly of the cave. Further down, a small lake appears. As we near it, a silver canoe comes into sight. We go to it. It is lined with sheepskins. Tied to the side by a metal pole, with a rope attached. Meghan draws it towards us. "Get in now," she tells me. Meghan helps me aboard. I notice there are no oars. "Now wrap yourself up with those covers. You need to keep warm." I sit there in wonder. "As you know it is the day of the open veil. The day the dead come alive. The day of visions of the future." I shiver. "You need to lie down now. I will set you adrift. The rope will remain attached here. You are not to stop the process. The canoe will take you to where you need to be. Trust me. And do not, whatever you do interfere with this right of mystery. Whatever comes to you, whatever situation you find yourself in, you are to lie still. Any movement will destroy the magic. When the time is right, I shall draw you back to me." With that she gives the canoe a little push.

I'm quite calm until I realise I am meandering from the light. Slowly, slowly into blackness. The canoe gathers momentum. I detect small sounds of running water. It dawns on me that I'm on an underground river. It dawns on me also, that I am utterly alone. I'm doing as I was told. Sometimes with my eyes peering into nothing. Other times with my eyelids closed. I'm trying not to think. Trying to take in this experience in wholeness. Suddenly the canoe collides with a solid object. It jolts, then settles. I am moving no longer. I look around me. Nothing. No sounds. Nothing.

Then something starts stirring. The cavern in which I lie, takes on its own existence. Faces start to appear to me. Faces I can't identify. They come out through the walls. Down from the roof. Various faces of every age and colour. They start to sing my name. "Maire. Maire." Softly at first, then rising to a crescendo. The voices start to overlap, so there becomes a constant calling of my name. No beginning. No end. Has my imagination possessed me? Next I hear gushes of water. I realise the water level is rising, my canoe moving upwards, towards the roof of the cavern. What is happening? Am I to drown here? I try not to panic. Remember not to stir. This is a trial of faith indeed. The water continues to raise my tiny vessel. I close my eyes. Surrender myself. Give in. A whole world opens up to me. Oh my. Oh my. I know where I am. I don't know what to expect. I've heard the ancient legends of good and mischief makers too. The lands the sorcerers speak of. I observe the lands, they look rich. All things shimmer. The ground. The trees. The river. I glimpse small balls of light coming out from the woods. As they get closer they materialise into tiny folk. They have transparent wings. Little pointed ears. They all excitedly chatter between themselves. Come to face me. Look over their shoulders back to the woods. Larger balls of light now appear. They too change. This time one is a miniature horse. White like Raphael. The others, rams, goats, foxes, badgers and stags. The fairies jump onto their backs. Wildly run around. Cheering. They ride the animals bareback. Animal and rider move as one. These mysterious people are all female. Suddenly they change their clothes. From delicate pretty frocks, to fearsome warfare garb.

The fay on the white horse (the leader), calls to the rest. They form assembly as a battalion. The leader of the fay, has dark skin. Long black hair reaches down her back. She speaks to me through my mind. "I am Faye. The leader. The time will come when you will need us. We will be there to outwit your enemies. To play tricks on them. You will succeed. The druids summon us when the time arrives." With that, her miniature horse, which I intrinsically know is a tinker, bared his teeth, reared, bucked, took off and farted. Instantly they disappear. Gone on a gush of wind. A human form approaches me now. She looks on me with great kindness, love. Within a second, I recognise her from the portrait hanging in our home. It is my mother. She holds out her hands, I take them. She pulls me into her. I weep.

"Weep not Maire. I've been watching you all this time. It shall soon be your duty to protect our Sept, alongside those of others. Your father will pass, naturally, in a few short years. Meantime you must prepare. People will see his death as a weakness to our people. You, my dearest, shall prove them wrong. Take no prisoners. Be as bold, brave and merciless as the best of our ancestors. You have the Celtic blood. Let it boil. I shall unveil a vision now, a part of your future. To help you make the right decisions. Place you valiant for what's to come."

I'm aware I am galloping at full speed. My horse's neck is protruding. Flecks of foam from his mouth join sweat, streaming down his withers. It is not Raphael. It is of a slighter build, chestnut. I am wearing armour. I hold my falchion sword high. I am charging towards a garrison, bellowing in frenzy. They carry the English flag. On my left side another horse runs. A bay. And its rider. Its rider is Gwyneth O'Hare. She is straining forward, determined, eyes ablaze with anger. We are in unison. There is another riding to my right. I cannot see a face. A whole army thundering in my wake. Now the vision is gone. I am sinking. Down, down. My little canoe spinning. My mind racing. All is black again. The canoe judders. I'm being drawn backwards. Rapidly. Awkwardly. I heed the dim lights coming closer, brighter. I am back at the edge, whence Meghan pushed me off. "Here," she says, offering her hand to steady my exit from the canoe. I feel refreshed, almost reborn. Meghan silently starts to walk back up to the doorway to this magic world. She removes her wand. Places it against the stone. The lights dim, then extinguish. Total darkness returns. Thankfully the doorway opens. There is the druid wielding his wand as before. We walk through. As I turn to thank Meghan, she smiles. Turns back into the old hag. Retrieves her wand from the druid. She stands, places a wand in each hand. Lifts up her arms, changes right there in front of us into three huge ravens. They fly up for a second. They disappear.

What to do now? What to say? Indeed, whether opine or hold my voice. I just go to my horse. Fling my arms around his neck. This horse, I realise, is my otherworldly companion. He will never ride with me into battle, nor should he. He's too precious. He's my angel. We journey home. Again in distracted silence. There is one thing I do reveal. "Ivan, do you know where it is, that the woman I fought with at the festival of Lugh, resides?"

"I don't. But what I do know, is that she will be at the jousting tournament to be held next spring at the D'arcy's family castle Dunmoe, by the river Boyne. Which sits to the western edge of The Pale's boundary." "How do you know that?" I sweetly enquire.

"Because, Miss O'Ciaragain. Her family are renowned for their horsemanship skills, particularly in the re-enactment of old battles."

"Then Ivan, you shall take me," I finally add.

KELLY 4

Wednesday morning I waken. It is eight days until Arthur's wedding. I'm expecting to meet Miriam any day now. Cinders has nestled under my chin. Her long white fur tickles my nose. She starts to twitch with delight as I tickle her tummy. Unlike most cats, Cinders likes a tummy rub. In fact she likes a rub anywhere, and as many as she can get. I'm sure she'd have me pet her all day if she could. She raises her eyes to face mine. Her right eye is yellow. Her left eye pale blue. I'm sure she has the breed of Ragdoll in her. All her mannerisms, her pink little ears. The bendy, floppy body. I bloody love her. How anyone could have thrown those kitties away is beyond me. With the usual morning home routine attended to, I leave for the café. "Bye my beauty." I coo to Cinders as I shut the front door.

The early morning diners, as I call them, have all left. It is ten o'clock now. Everything is set for round two. I go back to the kitchen, to make myself a warm, sweet, milky brew. The little bell above the customer door gives a little tinkle. That's my ten minutes' peace gone then. I put down my mug, breeze through to the dining room. Yay, its Teagan. Instantly I see a different air about her. "Teagan, darling. How wonderful to see you again, and with that spring back in your step. Come in the back. I'll make you a cup of tea. We can have a chat."

"Thank you, Kelly." She seems pleased that the café is empty of customers. We go to the kitchen.

Teagan is beaming. "I've been rather sly," she states.

"Good girl. Tell me." I respond.

"I decided in order to avoid my Mr trying to dip out of a proposed trip, that I'd make it more about the children. I've booked to go to Disney Land in Florida next Thursday." "Why, that's cool thinking. But what's sly about that?" I ask.

"Well. I went to the local travel agent. Paid for it all on our joint credit card. Had them print off all the documents there and then. Then that night. When Daddy came home. I sat both the kids next to him in the lounge. I passed him the envelope containing the travel arrangements. He opened it immediately. I could see his hesitation. However, with the print outs of the Disney Park in full view of the kids, he had no choice, but swallow the bait. I did it! We did it," she pronounces. "Kelly, I can't show you how much I appreciate your input in all this. Had I not broken my silence to you last week, I know, I would have flown off the handle at Ian. I was seriously about to lose it. That, I'm sure would have driven him further away."

"You did the right thing darling. You did the right thing." I let her know.

"Here." She fumbles in her handbag, brings out a small pink box with a cream ribbon on top, tied into a petite bow. "This is for you. A small token. A big hug from me, Sophie and Conor."

"Why you didn't need to." I'm surprised.

"Open it then," Teagan instructs. I do. Inside is an exquisite charm.

"My charm bracelet, you remembered." I gasp.

"Yes, turn it over, it's the wrong way round."

I do. On the other side of the silver circle is a neat, embossed, unmistakable raven. I'm aghast, transported back to the three ravens. I feel my cheeks blush. As they do when I'm either embarrassed or taken off guard. This time. It is the later. I try to hide my shock. "Teagan." I stammer. "Many, many thanks, this will make a charming addition to my Pandora bracelet. You are thoughtful. How kind." I give her a special Aunt Kell hug.

"I'd best crack on now Kelly. You've been a tremendous help to me. I'm off to get my hair restyled now, like you suggested. I've looked up those, er things on the internet. I have indeed come across some, let's say interesting alternative activities for the boudoir." She grins. "My mother has offered to look after the children again tomorrow. So that I can go to Belfast, peruse the lingerie shops. I am so glad I came in last week. So glad. You are a true treasure. Bye for now. I'll of course pop back in after our trip." She gives me a kiss on the cheek, then hurriedly walks out. "Bye. Safe and successful journey." I call after her.

Those dreams. They just keep returning in profusion, stronger each time. I swear they intrude every night, though incredibly I wake up more refreshed than ever. Every time I forget about them, something pops up out of the blue. Draws my attention back to them, just like this charm. I look to it. "Holy Mary, Mother of God. What is happening here?" I ask aloud. Perform the cross. The door bursts open. The bell goes like crazy. I go out front. A group of youngsters, all male, tumble in. I know one of them. "Hey Aunt Kell." Ricky balls out, rather too loudly. "I've brought my mates here. We are on our annual Christmas pub crawl. Thought it best I bring them here. Take in some of your nourishment before we take in too many beers." They clumsily sit themselves down at the largest table. Ricky gets up again promptly throws himself at me, almost trips. I hold onto his arms, stabilize him. "You don't mind do you? Us coming here? Only last year I was as sick as a dog. Don't want that again. Need to fill our bellies with your finest brunch."

"Not at all. I can't believe you're old enough to drink now. That's why I've not been seeing you, hey. Taken to the local pubs now?" I wink at him. "Right lads, what can I get you?" Already a bit too gone to concentrate on my small menu. So I say. "Leave it to me lads, I'll line those stomachs of yours, well and good. Plenty of spuds for you me thinks." I leave them to their frivolities, go to rustle up a good, beer soaking meal for them. They eat quickly, pay quickly. Leave quickly. Not wanting to waste their drinking time I guess. "Take it easy guys. And, Ricky, say hi to your Ma."

"I will." With that they spill into the street.

I'm so busy cleaning up the plates the lads left. I hadn't noticed someone else had entered. When I return to the dining room to reset the table, I am quite taken aback. Tucked in the right hand corner of the room sits a rather elegant looking lady. Advanced in years, yes. However she looks fabulous. She has a wedding magazine out open on the table. She licks her finger, turns the page, glimpses the various images. I get it. I approach. "Hello, I'm Kelly." I reach out my hand.

"I'm not merely taking a hand dear." She pushes back her chair. Stands. "Well look at you. You're all Arthur said you were. Now give me a big old squeeze." We hug, tighter than I'm used to. Boy this woman has some strength for her size. She almost has me off my feet, and that is saying something.

"May I get you a drink?" I enquire.

"Why yes please." She responds. "I'll take a small pot of peppermint tea."

"Good idea. I'll have one with you." I'm soon back with the best tea set I can muster up. "There now. Miriam. What a pleasure." I raise my tea cup. She follows suit. We say "Cheers."

"I know I'm a bit silly, looking at these pictures," she pipes up. "They just make me feel so grateful, that my golden years are to be a pure bliss. I've been alone quite some time you know. How lovely it is to have Arthur by my side to share life's little pleasures."

"He's a good catch." I laugh. "No really. He's a true gent. Always has been with me. I've missed his old-fashioned mannerisms. Not to mention his humour.

"Arh, yes. His humour, he tickles me pink most days. A real ray of the brightest sunshine. I am blessed to have found him. I'm sincerely thankful to you for encouraging him to make his move to America. Without you pushing him to do so, we may never have met." "Well, met you have. I'm delighted for you both. Now, tell me the wedding plans. I'm enamoured to be your maid of honour. Truly I am. But what am I to wear? Do you have any thoughts?" I ask.

"My dear. My dear. You come as you like. It's you I wish to stand by me on our special day. Your attire does not matter one jot." Replies Miriam.

"I have had a little look in my wardrobe. I do still have a pale pink designer suit, which I purchased many years ago, it still fits. Just. Would that be appropriate? I do not wish to upstage the bride," I say.

"My dear. Well. That would be perfect. I have chosen for myself a lovely pink dress. Made from fine silk. It is minimally beaded. Don't need to much fuss at my age."

"Give over," is my response. "You look terrific."

"Arthur thought it best I come to meet you alone today. So we can really get to know each other as well as we can. Before we do that. I just need to let you know a few details." Miriam starts to fill me in. "The service is to be held at the Armagh Registry, as Arthur told you. However, they now hold the civil services at the Palace Stables. At the Palace Demesne. Do you know it?" "Yes. I do." I assure her.

"Excellent. I chose that particular office, as it sits in the grounds of Primate's Palace, where many archbishops of the Church of Ireland resided. I still want it to feel a little religious. The service is to be held at twelve, midday. If you could arrive by eleven thirty, I would be grateful."

"I'll be there, wouldn't miss it for the world. Only eight days now. You must be excited." I reply.

"Excited? I'm bursting. My children arrive next Monday. They want to take a little tour of your lovely country before the wedding. After the service, we are to go to Arthur's friend's house. He has a wonderful old manor. It will be more cosy there than in a hotel. His old friend Brian. Do you know which house it is?" she asks me.

"Yes, Yes I do. Further down the river isn't it, the one with the long tree-lined drive? Perfect setting for a perfect couple." I exclaim.

"It is, we checked it out yesterday. They have a lovely large hallway for us to greet our guests. Along with a huge lounge. These old Georgian properties were built to entertain well. That's the formalities over with. Let's really get to know each other now," Miriam commands. We while away the next few hours. Miriam pouring over her magazine at the times where I'm needed to serve. What a lady, what a sweet lady, are my finishing thoughts. This wedding will be a cracker.

KELLY 5

It's Monday eighteenth. Ricky's mother, Heather popped in earlier. She wants me to have a chat with him. Seems she's worried he's going off the rails. Losing direction. Her concerns that a once promising student is now failing at sixth form. Having completed his A2 levels last summer, coming out with less than his usual straight A's has made him lose faith in himself. Many a young lad finds this predicament. He, as most sons, will not take a mother's advice. Nor his father's, who is constantly remonstrating. She wishes me to meet him after I close up today. Having the wedding just three days off, this has thrown me. However I agree. "Ok Heather, I'll see your bairn, tell him to arrive after three pm. To bring a coat. I'll take him for a stroll. See if I can have any input. I can't promise. I'll do my best mind. He always had a soft spot for me." Heather left grateful. It's best I do this today, as my excitement for the wedding is mounting, distracting.

Three pm prompt, the little doorbell jingles. A sheepish Ricky enters devoid of the cheer whence I last saw him. "Take a seat poppet. I'm almost done." I go to the back, ensure all's shut down. Grab my coat. "Right come on young man, off we go." Ricky hangs his head, gives a wry smile. We set off across the road, over the bridge, down to the river Bann. I consider it best to have these conversations out in nature. Where a fierce wind can blow away our troubles. A soft breeze waft away the doubts and fears of a mind askew with anxiety. The sun light up and lift droll faces. We stop at a spot away from other walkers. Sit down on an old bench. We while away a few minutes, settle. The river is running full flood. Broken chunks of ice from the morning frost race along, allowing the river to take them. I turn to face him.

"Ricky. Look to the surging water. Let your misgivings swirl off you. Imagine them being shifted by the torrent. Let nature's mood clear your mind." He sits, forearms on thighs, hunched shoulders. He lifts his head, straightens his spine. Stares out. Now he's receptive, I say to myself. "Take deep breaths. With each exhalation, let go of your troubles." He relaxes. "Tell the big bad wolves to flee. Banish them for ever. Your mother told me her concerns. These are nothing new. Feel the power of your mind. Be kind. Bring kindness to yourself and all you are. Believe in yourself. Follow your own heart, not the words of others. Exams contribute to your life, help you succeed in in any way that you are already bound to. Care for yourself, nurture yourself. Give to yourself. Honour and enrich yourself. Exams do not define you, they are merely a ladder to an adult world. See them as this and nothing more. You are "somebody," life will enfold and enrich you in the way that is right for you. Follow your heart's dreams, for they shall bring you happiness, fulfilment. Sleep well so you can think well. Get into the well of knowledge deep inside you. Your brain is a computer, boot it up and see it all. The screen's view is in the imagination. So, you may lose a part of yourself, but gain a part of something others don't want. You."

"Wow Kelly." Ricky quietly says.

"What are your hopes, aspirations? What makes you happy? What does Ricky enjoy, wish to achieve? Evaluate your assets."

"I like maths." He pipes back. "I'm good at quick thinking, problem solving. I'd like to travel. Be excited. Put my quick mind to the test. I want to see the world. Be part of a team. Be of help somehow. There's an innate protector in me too."

"Why that's lovely Ricky, so positive. I put my arm round his shoulder. "You know what Ricky? I have always felt that in you. That solid, intelligent, steadfast young man. A man of the world with intent. Your mother is proud of you. She just wishes you to be happy, focussed." I add.

"The problem is Aunt Kell, my mother will be devastated if I reveal my thoughts. That's why I've been drinking. I really don't want to upset her. Everyday life is not for me. I want to join the Royal Army." He shyly states, expecting it to surprise me the way it would Heather.

"Ricky, tell her. If this is what's been affecting your life, get it out. She will understand. Maybe even prouder than you think." I supportively give my opinion. "So there's a bit of a traveller in you then?" I tease. He looks to me.

"Yes, Kelly, Yes. I've dreamed of this since a young boy. I could never speak of it. My father had so many desk jobs planned for me. I'm just not cut out for that. I want to travel the seas, explore other cultures. I want to be a medical technician. To administer immediate first aid on the front line."

"Now it's my turn to say the "wow." I laugh. "Have your researched this?" I ask.

"Why yes," he replies. "They look for logical minds like mine. Those that can master multiple tasks, without worry or loss of concentration. Have hardened stomachs. I'd have to go to Pirbright, for fourteen weeks on a basic infantry course. Onto combat medical training which takes fifty weeks. I'd love it Kell. I'd serve an infantry regiment. Then I can help. Deploy my brain."

"Then you must go for it. Gather your courage, inform your mother. Let her tell your father, she knows him better. Mothers are good a softening blows with a light touch."

I carry on. "See, all those years of fearing their reactions. And you've just exploded with it in these twenty minutes." I raise my eyebrows, mockingly.

"Kelly, you're a star. How come you understand so much about people, their thoughts?"

"It just seems to come naturally," I reply. "Right, come on now. Get off with you, you've a conversation to be had." He gets up, says an earnest thank you. Leaves. I shout after him. "Hoist your sails. Soar." I remain in contemplation, pondering his question. "Where indeed does all this insight of the human spirit come from?"

KELLY 6

"It's the day. It's the day." I sing, full of jolly as I prepare myself. My sweet neighbour popped in early this morning, as planned. She has certainly done an excellent job of placing my hair tidily in a French plait. Bless her. Although we seldom meet, when we do it's warming. Tilly is an endearing old lady. I guess she's well into her nineties. She will not divulge her age. Considers it a nonsense. "If you're alive, you're alive." Is her moto. I passed her a key, to tend to my cat whilst I'm gone. Now time to wriggle into my old suit. Put on some heels. Not like me. That's it. Ready. Off.

I turn into the entrance of the Palace Heritage Centre. An old ruin catches my eye. I'm a little early, ever curious. I take a walk over. There is a placard explaining the history of this Friary Church. I'm taken over by the strange eeriness of the place. Peaked large archways loom. Crumbled stones dotted in the surrounding grass. A feeling of a connection to this site emerges. I shrug it off. Must get to the stables. An old blue Cadillac is parked by the gateway. Miriam is in the back with Arthur. Strange. They leap out as they see me. We greet. "Darling." Miriam exclaims. "Don't you look the part!" "Me, I, it's you that looks amazing." Miriam's dress is perfect on her, just as she described. Arthur, dressed in a dark grey suit, with pink tie, taps on the driver's window. "Open the boot would you old chap?" He obliges. Arthur returns to us with two exquisite bouquets of pure white roses. Both shaped like hearts. He hands Miriam the smaller. She in turns hands it to me. "For you my dear." She says, handing it to me. I take it, smell it. Proclaim my thanks. Arthur then kisses the larger bouquet, places it tenderly in his loved one's hands.

"It's cold. Let's make our way to the café. We pass through an archway under the clock tower, bordered with mullioned stone. As are the windows in the quant courtyard. We enter the visitors' café. Order our coffees, take a seat.

Arthur starts to talk. "My wife to be and I have decided to defy tradition this time round. We will enter the registrar's office hand in hand. You are to follow. Our children and grandchildren will walk behind. It is the way we want it. To be a fully integrated family moment."

"That's lovely," I chirp.

"They will be here soon." Arthur continues. "We wish you to meet with them before the ceremony." The door bursts open, three little girls, dressed in white frilly dresses, with dainty shoes and little poppet bags to match run in. Followed by two teenage boys. American twangs fill the room. The parents follow. Rush over, gesture to shake hands, I follow suit.

"So you're the secret matchmaker are you?" A tall handsome suited man stands before me.

"I, well, yes, but I wouldn't say that." I reply.

"Well you should, you made this match in heaven possible. We are all so grateful for you encouraging Arthur to change his life. He has certainly changed our mother's. It is damn fantastic to see her so happy again. I'm George. Pleasure to meet you. This is my wife Helen. Here kids." He cuts in. "Say a big hello to Grandma's hero. Two of the boys present themselves. "This is Tom, and this is Brendan." We exchange smiles, nod and all say a few words between us. The smallest of the girls bounds into our circle. "Hi. I'm Miranda." She gives a sweet half courtesy. The two other girls not to be left out, barge through. "I'm Sherry, this is my big sister Lizzie.

"Make way for us." A short, plump woman approaches. "What are they like, so excited I'm afraid. I am their mother Kim, these are my twin daughters, don't they look swell. And Paul. Where are you, come forward. Kelly this is my husband Paul, George's older brother." We all laugh, greet, compliment, kiss cheeks and chatter away.

The next sounds are unmistakable. Arthur's entourage has arrived. We rush to each other. "Long time no see." I call out. His eldest Mark grabs me by the waist, lifts me up. "Put me down you plonker." I squeal. "You'll be bursting the buttons on my blouse." He does, not before planting a sloppy kiss to my cheek. His sister Angela is next.

"Too bloody long Aunt Kell. Too bloody long."

"Where's your kids?" I ask.

"Oh, Sam and Ellie, they are greeting the guests, while their mother Sue is guarding the top few rows of seats." Typical of Sue I think to myself. Always had a penchant for taking over. Mark just concedes. I doubt this little café has ever seen such a display of kinship and animation. "Sue comes in, flustering, waving her arms about. "Right we are ready. Come on. Everyone is waiting. We leave the café, bossy Sue sorts us out into lines she sees fit. Arthur just rolls his eyes in humour. We proceed across the tiled courtyard to the office.

As we enter, music plays. At first I am surprised. Then I gasp and sob. Only Arthur would have thought of this. Bruno Mars' track, "I think I want to marry you." So Arthur, our fun-loving, joking Arthur. Perfect. The theme for the day is set. Celebration of life. The two walk before me, arm in arm, turning, giggling like young children. Grinning nonstop, waving at the awaiting faces. The guests are charmed by the atmosphere. I have never before been so honoured to be part of a procession. The love, pure joy, in the room is tangible to all. Arthur and Miriam repeat their vows in a slightly more serious manner. When logistics are finished, certificate signed, witnessed by Angela and George, Sue again takes command. We follow an orderly exit. All hands clap profusely, the room is dynamic. People make their way to their transport. The newlyweds hop back into the Cadillac. Some joker has had old tins attached to the back bumper. I wonder who that could be.

We arrive at Brian's house. Alas he is newly single. His wife tragically taken away in a motor accident last year. I hope he is not upset by the day. He greets me at the large wooden door. "Come in Kelly." He motions me.

"Brian, this is very kind of you, considering."

"Arhh hogwash," he states. "Everything is as it should be, perfect. It is my pleasure to host this occasion. Beats banging around old empty rooms. House needs a good party to lift its sad bricks. Get yourself a glass of champagne." He indicates to waitresses holding up ready-filled flutes. I smile, leave him to welcome the rest, oblige. The other guests start to arrive, some familiar to me. Miriam and Arthur enter last. A massive cheer greets them.

After an hour or so, Sue ushers us into the drawing room. Wonderfully laid out with tables of various sizes in an oval shape, fencing a slightly raised dance floor. Pink tablecloths host tall thin glass vases, each with white lilies protruding. From the ceiling hangs a network of criss-crossed green shrubbery. The scene is magical. Someone has put themselves about a bit. What a good, generous friend Brian is. Beyond to the conservatory. Long tables have been adorned with food that tempts. We are invited to help ourselves.

After much gourmet's delight is consumed, Brian takes the place of toast master. "Everyone. Thank you so much for attending this special day. May we all raise our glasses to the newlyweds, Arthur and his Lady. May we wish them a long and hearty marriage."

"Here, Here." All respond. Arthur stands.

"We, my wife and I have taken great pleasure to share this day with you. There is no need for speeches. We have planned another way to embrace our togetherness. If you would allow me a few minutes. I will soon return." With this, he gently kisses Miriam on the forehead, then leaves the room. The guests chatter curiously.

What happens next takes us by total surprise. Sue stands, asks for silence. We obey. A group of accomplished Irish musicians enter the lounge. Three men dressed in doublet and hose, move in first, each playing Uilleann pipes. The sound fills the room. A further five men enter, fiddlers, fiddle away. We are all thoroughly enjoying the entertainment. They play their hearts out, jiggle a bit, stamp their feet in turn. Raise the bar. Then they stop, line up at the sides of the room. From the back in walks Arthur, fully adorned as the others in our custom dress. He carries a bodhran drum with tipper beater. He starts with a one beat rhythm, walks to the side of the dance floor. Increases his beats. Behind him, springs a young dancing troupe of girls who line up and start to move to his drum. Little feet point then start to move forward. They twirl, tap; jig. Their legs carry them as leaping leprechauns. My heart leaps with delight as the little deer's kick and twist. I am so amazed by their talent, I well up with pure joy. All are enthralled. The other musicians join in stanza by stanza. They reach their crescendo. Arthur goes to Miriam. He bows before her, takes her hand. Together they rush to the dancefloor. Embrace, face each other; lock hands for a two hand reel. They join the children's folk movements with such accuracy we are flawed. We are stunned by this show of our greatest tradition. The music dies for a moment. Arthur picks up his bride, swirls her round, proclaiming "I love you." Over and over. We all stand up. They stop. Miriam steadies herself.

"Come on, what are you waiting for?" She calls. "Join in." The instruments spring back into action. We do gladly. We dance with such passion. This is the best wedding by far I've ever attended.

Sadly the day ends. Miriam and Arthur lead the way out of the hall to the front door. "It's not over yet." Miriam proclaims. She then turns, throws her flowers behind her without a care in the world. Shit, they are heading for me. I can't catch them. There are plenty of young women here who would love to be blessed. Especially Angela, who was jilted at the altar a decade ago. They are coming, falling through the air. I catch them, I have to. It would be a sacrilege to allow them to bruise on hard ground. "Ah. Woman." Arthur chips in. "Perhaps the Lord does have a plan for you." I blush. We all cheer off the old Cadillac. I look up to the sky, following a familiar call. A beautiful buzzard is hanging in the wind. Circling. The haunting call has always resonated in me as a call to the wild. I smile.

MAIRE 5

Ivan and I arrive via the orchard to Dunmoe castle,
otherwise known as the Hillfort of Cattle. It's bustling.
Women are laying out their wares, garments, cloaks,
blankets, handmade at the mill. In readiness for the crowds
that will ensue. Children, some half dressed with bare feet
are playing in the square. Many of them are that scrawny I
suspect worms. Elderly men fish in the river's weir. On the
banks, the setup of the jousting lanes is almost complete.
The castle itself sits proudly atop the rocks. Vaulted high
windows peer from the two lower floors.

I hear my bird's call. A cross between a cat's yawl, a crow's
call. His calls get nearer. He lands on my left shoulder. I
named him Aodh. Raphael does not flinch as he settles
down, he has formed a friendship with him. Two years ago, I
found a cream egg, dotted with brown speckles, lying under
an ash tree. A tiny beak poked out. I watched as he struggled
to free himself. I considered helping to free it. I decided
against. If a creature couldn't himself emerge into this world,
he would hardly survive in it. To my pleasure, he used his
beak to create a bigger opening, pushed out one of his tiny
bright yellow legs. Used his talons to secure himself to the
ground. The other to break his way out. My buzzard revealed
himself. White upright half formed feathers encased his tiny
body. His eyes showed the fire of purpose.

From hatching I made him a nest in the horses' barn, fed him fresh worms. Used small dried reeds to suck up water to release in his open yellow-lined beak. We bonded. From there our journey began. Today he comes with me, we are now inseparable. His first outing. Fully prepared for the battle of the birds of prey. I was pleased to learn that this game had been introduced at the tournament, it will give him a chance to prove his hunting skills. I have trained him in many ways. He is also my eyes. The slight variation in his calls alert me to views from above. To strangers approaching. To plentiful pickings of food. He answers only to my voice.

We draw to rest in a shaded area, where lies a refreshments table, laid out with various cured meats. There are morsels of fresh fish, dried fruits and jugs of cooled water. We barter with the hunchbacked old woman for our needs. Lead the horse to a water trough. Tie him there to rest. I set about locating Gwyneth, with Ivan faithfully following. To no avail. The trumpet sounds to draw the crowds to the river bank. We reluctantly answer. I take Raphael, we make our way down. Aodh takes off. A tent has been erected to house horses. Those competing and those like mine. The combat men are being helped into their suits of armour. There is much braying. Teasing. Threatening. Weapons are lined up against a wooden frame. We go outside to take a seat and watch. Although this is a friendly game this time, little generosity is shown by the jousters. We observe the various men race at speed to oppose each other, lances at the tilt. Shields close to chest. Wildly kicking their horses' flanks. Each time a winner is declared, the crowd cheers or boos the loser unhorsed in disgrace. Each has their favoured hero.

Whilst the ground is being cleared for the enactment later, Ivan and I head further down the river, where a field has been prepared for the birds. Children are keenly stood by their creations. The competitors are invited to examine the obstacles. Wicker traps holding baby rabbits, with a small opening on top. Mounds containing moles. A hole that holds lizards. Poles with pedestals, from which hang down small flapping song birds, tied by their feet. A pit squirming with rats. A small manmade pond brimming with frogs. The children have been given the responsibility to assemble their own devices. The competitors are weighing up their strategies. They have all attached their raptors to perches in a corner. They obviously do not have the same relationship that I do with mine. No trust. That is in my favour. Hah. We are asked to clear the area. A man comes forward. "Gather round." He calls. "The object of this game, is that each of you in turn, will take your place over there marked with a white cross. You will see there is a basket by the side. You will each be given three minutes to perform. Your bird is to catch and deliver as many of the creatures that they can. To bring them forth to you, to drop them in the basket, which will be sealed upon completion. At the end, a point will be awarded for each creature captured. Two points for each one killed. I requested the raptors not to be fed this day to keep them sharp. Focused. I trust you heeded my words." We all indicate that's the case. "Good. Let's commence. Go gather your villains. You may choose which order you take part." The other competitors go to their perches. Take their protective glove from under the perch. Put it on, Untie their birds, place them to their left held out hand. I call to Aodh. He calls back. Swoops down from a nearby tree. Softly graces my hand. He never harms me. The others scoff at my different approach. The children stand by their posts. They too have baskets. Each containing stock to replenish the sites between shows.

A young bearded dark haired man steps forward with his sparrow hawk. The creature weighs up his task. The

organiser raises a red flag, slaps it down. "Begin." He shouts.
The hawk takes off. Goes straight to the songbirds, collects
three in one go. Retrieves them. Drops them in the basket.
The other birds are each in turn flown. Each seem to prefer
different prey. The men stand in a row with their baskets.
Their birds returned to their perches. It's my turn. I wanted
to go as close to last as possible, so my Aodh could heed
his opponents' tricks. People do not realise how intelligent
creatures are. I do. I take my place to the cross. Stare into
my empty basket. The flag again drops. "Go. Go. Go." I yell.
Aodh leaves my hand at great speed, leaving scratch marks,
with tiny bubbles of blood. His ferocity does not hurt me. I
am pleased. He's a fighter as am I. He knows what it takes
to win.

He goes straight to the frogs, one of his delicacies as a
juvenile. He splashes into the shallow water. His legs,
now darkened stamp into the water. Trust after thrust. In
moments his beak disappears, searches. Rears up. He carries
four frogs to my collection place. He does not pause. Heads
straight back to the pit of lizards, repeats the same tactics.
Returns. Goes again. Swoops straight into the baby rabbits,
pins one down, tears its throat. Brings it to me. Takes himself
to the mound of moles. Ferociously kicks aside the earth. His
head bobs under. He flies back with two. He makes haste
to the song birds, swoops in sideways. Circles the pedestal,
collecting four as he does in one movement. He returns them
to me. Perches on the basket. Uses his beak to slash their tiny
throats one by one. They fall into my basket. "Time." Shouts
the controller. A helper places the lid firmly on, sealing my
trophies. Aodh returns to his tree. The contents of the baskets
are counted by the children. Points awarded accordingly. The
man in charge goes to inspect. "It's a draw." He exclaims.
"The buzzard and the kestrel are even."

"May the two with the most points retrieve your birds. Come stand before me." We do. "Us Irish don't like to lose in any way. So shall we call it a draw, or shall we fight to the death?"

"Fight. Fight. Fight." Bray the crowds. The children jump up and down with glee.

"Make the decision." Commands the man in charge.

"No problem," the owner of the kestrel replies. He is tall, lean. Dark boyish hair crowns his head. He is handsome, clean cut. I stir. I look to my bird. Thoughts fly around my head. Birds tire after much flight without sustenance, and yes he is larger by comparison. However the kestrel is more nimble. I decide to commune with Aodh. "Are you up for this?" I utter, searching deep into his amber eyes. He dips his head in response. "Let's get this done." I proclaim. One of the boys scurries to his basket. A rat is removed. He quickly breaks its neck. The dead rat is placed on the ground. I place my bird to one side, the man who intrigues me does the same. We hold onto them. Then the flag goes up and down again. Both hungry birds race to the prey. Both place a claw to it. They gaze at each other, squawking. Then it begins. The kestrel uses a claw to grab one of Aodh's. He falls back, knocked off balance. Uses his broad wings to reposition himself. A frenzied mass of feathers, and talons turn into one rolling ball. The crowd excites. "Come on, come on," I will my boy. Sending him all my strength. There is a shift, a stillness. Aodh has the kestrel pinned to the ground, belly up. Wings outstretched. He goes for the kill. Opens his beak, pins the other down with it round his neck. Raises his talons to the vulnerable belly. Strikes, over and over. Blood splatters. His empty stomach falls out of the torn chest cavity, below a visible gullet. The kestrel drops its head to the ground in defeat. Aodh takes his reward, flies off out of distance. He has earned his freedom. I let out a sigh of relief. The boy loser slinks off. Leaving his dead, uncared-for bird.

Ivan and I trundle with the others back to the now cleared area further up. I check on Raphael. All is well. Other horses have arrived whilst we've been gone. Further people, dressed in old attacking attire abound. There is an air of joviality. I resume my futile search for Gwyneth, so many people rushing around. I touch Ivan's arm, turn down my lips. "Let us go outside. Watch the battle." We take a place at the back, standing on raised platforms. Others are seated on benches before us. The same man that conducted the battle of the birds takes centre stage. "All those gathered here today. You are now to witness an enactment of the Battle of Cruchain. Whereupon the mighty king of Ui Failghe defeats an expedition of Normans. Pillagers, who came here to gain control of our merchant oligarchy." He raises and outstretches his arms. "Begin," he shouts as he takes his leave. The crowd roar.

A number of our people come dressed in Norman battle garbs. Wearing coats of chain mail. Silver helmets, which cover their noses. Wielding yellow and red shields. Carrying spears and wooden swords. They approach across the ground, acting as idiots. The crowd delights. In comes a man, astride a black horse. Long blonde hair braided back, tucked in a helmet of our own design, a horse's tail attached to the top, at the back. Chest armour. A short square shield in his left hand. An axe in his right. Four other horsemen decked likewise follow him. From the backs of their horses, they gesture to the people. Raising their cries. Then they rush head long into the on-foot Normans. They tease and taunt. Knock them off their feet. Those acting as the Normans let out cries of disbelief. Fall over. Pick themselves up again in a comical manner. The crowd laugh. I laugh. Ivan laughs so much his whole barrel of a stomach rises and falls. Some of the people have tears rolling down their cheeks. This is entertainment indeed. "Kill them. Kill them," chants the crowd. The horsemen roar. With swift accuracy, and without harm they defeat the Normans within a minute. The actors throw themselves around, over-exaggerating their plight. Then they lie down, their bodies at different angles. Pretend to be dead. The crowd leaps to its feet. "Yes. Yes. Bastards deserved to die."

The horsemen start to ride in a circle together, accepting the congratulations. They then line up facing the castle, remove their helmets. The first rider in, takes off his helmet first, throws it to the ground. He flicks his long braid. They then turn their horses. Gallop towards us. Stop their horses in an instance up against the crowd. Take a bow. The first rider, deemed the king, lifts his head. My hand flies to my mouth. It's Gwyneth...!

MAIRE 6

Nineteenth of March, in the year fourteen hundred and twenty seven. We have risen, washed, saddled up Raphael, and set off. Our destination is Kells. Ivan only just informed me of this visit. My father did not want me distracted from winning yesterday. We are now to go directly to King John's castle. Whereupon Gwyneth has hesitatingly invited us to join in the festival of seeing in the spring equinox. She had to leave directly after the enactment with duties to fulfil so we were unable to converse. We are to follow the flow of the river Boyne north side until it joins with Blackwater. Thence to head north. Once we have visited Kells, we are to head north again, then swing back round to Carlingford. This way we will not encounter the Pale.

The odour of the fresh running water cleanses our nostrils. Aodh is following at his own pace. Ahead or behind us, catching morsels on his way. He promptly brought me a mouse. "Why thank you. You can enjoy this little one." I teasingly laugh at him, throwing it high into the sky. He raises his mighty wings, takes off. Catches it, flies off. The sun is now warming us. It's an unusually clear day for this time of year. The riverbanks support all forms of life. We have spotted otters. Swans. Egrets. Ducks. We've eyed salmon jumping. Ivan suggests we stop in a while to catch, prepare and eat one. Aodh will enjoy the scraps.

We approach Kells. A distinctly peaceful feel encasing us. Ivan has told me of the monk we are to meet there. Oissine belongs to the monastic community of the Iona isle. The monks came from Scotland in the ninth century, established their place, away from the troubles of Vikings. "Here," Ivan tells me, "lies the book of Kells'. Safeguarded. Treasured. It is a book of the four gospels of the New Testament." Although not Christian ourselves, we do welcome the monks to our lands. He continues. "Kells is a special place. It had for many years been an imperial centre for spirituality and learning. The scholars took documents and moved to Mellifont Abbey some three hundred years ago. Those with the ancient knowledge know that was a mistake, they remained. The monks that fled abandoned the special energy of Kells. Which enhances learning. Those that studied here gained great prospective on life in Monasterboice."

We arrive by the two churches' graveyard. Celtic crosses rise to the sky. We make our way to a tall bell tower, which we had seen some distance away. Besides the tower, to the west stands a tall cross. I dismount. Ivan ties my horse to a nearby post. He asks me to wait here. Then goes to the tower. Climbs the steps. Knocks at the door. Shortly the door opens, revealing a monk. His brown robes are tied with a rope. Sandals on his feet. His face is round, very white. His bald head is covered by his hood. Then behind him, my father's druid emerges. I am quite shocked. "What does this mean?" I mutter to myself. They approach. I turn back to observe the cross, I am again taken aback. Perched on the top is my Aodh, two tawny owls on either side, quite a sight! What does it mean? The three men encircle me.

The men start to chant in Gaulish, led by the monk. Round and round me. The druid then instructs me to kneel on the ground before the cross. Place my forehead to the earth. I do as I am told. Immediately an energy sears into my forehead. Right between my eyebrows. "Let it come. Let it come." The druid reverently says. The energy is cool, yet warm at the same time. It travels throughout my whole being. Gives me goose bumps. I begin to feel bigger, stronger. The men regain their chant. I feel the earth's power encapsulating me. Taking me. Raising me. My hair gently blows about in the breeze. I do not move. The men stop chanting. Stand still. "You may rise." The druid tells me. I do. For a few moments a dizziness takes me. I regain control. The monk Oissine steps before me. "Bow your head dear." I do. He speaks in a tongue unknown to me. He crosses me. I am blessed. The druid then talks. "Child. A great power has been bestowed upon you. Wisdom too. Use these gifts wisely. If you allow yourself to rise in pompousness, these gifts shall be taken away. You have been chosen to raise our people. To benefit them, to lead you to conquer." I slowly lower my eyes in humility. Place my hands in prayer. Give my thanks.

Ivan steps forwards. Pats me on the back. "Maire, the druid has demanded that you sleep alone tonight at the top of the tower. He wishes for your soul to be closer to the gods. The three of us will stay in the base. You will be protected.

KELLY 7

What's wrong? What's happening? Am I dreaming or awake?
I feel like I'm under a spell. I cannot move. Fear takes over.
I struggle to break free. I can't. I am terrified. Something is
holding me down. Refusing to let me move. I try to call out.
Don't make a sound. God help me. I scream in my head. My
awareness grows. I am locked in a stone circular tower, high
off the ground. In utter darkness. No, it's not darkness. It's
something else. I am surrounded in dark shrouds. They are
holding me down with great force. A menacing voice looms.
"Come with me. Come with me. I shall show you the world.
Give yourself to me." This is not happening to me. I try to
jar myself from this dreadful nightmare. Nothing works.
That voice again. "Maire. Maire. Be mine. Together we will
conquer all. Your fate in my hands will be a towering one.
You shall be feared by all. None will disobey you. You will
have all the treasures of your land at your command." I feel
as if my soul is being sucked from my body. I am sweating,
trembling. "Go away." I shout in my mind with all my might.
Nothing changes. I am drawn to a buzzard. Erratically
flapping at the only small window besides me. It's going
crazy, trying to break its way in. Clawing, butting its head
against the bars. Trying to squeeze through.

Thoughts racing. What to do? I know. I've got it. Pray! Pray
girl, pray. With all my might I recount the Lord's Prayer. I

pretend I am at the church. The Canon giving me the blood and flesh of Christ. I feel the shrouds' power weakening. I call with my heart upon the Holy Ghost to enter me. Can God's will defeat this nightmare? As soon as I do, I see an enormous black face, looming over me. Eyes burning red. It lets out a tremendous roar. The sound pierces my ears. Its breath smells of a thousand diseased corpses. Shuddering, I believe I am doomed. Then it disappears in an instance. An eerie silence abounds. I sign with relief. Was this the Devil, Satan, Beelzebub?

I realise I am still interred in the tower. The buzzard sits on the window ledge. Calm. A good omen I trust. I notice miniscule specks of dust falling from the conical cap above me. They start to increase in volume. More and more fall. They light up. Come alive. Twirl. Hovering in space around me. Even more, this time larger little balls of light cascade from the roof. As if rain itself is pouring through. I look closely. They have little tails which make them spin. They move towards me. Into me. Under the thin matt on which I lie. Suddenly I start to hear and experience vibrations. I feel as if I am being sucked down. I panic. The buzzard at the window nods its head. Thinking this couldn't get any weirder, I relax a tad. Take deep breaths. Surrender. My body begins to vibrate at the same pitch as the noise. The resonance gathers. I feel myself being lifted. Getting lighter. Suddenly I am in a tunnel of bright colours. Speeding upwards, faster, faster. The colours fade to a bright white light. I come to settle. I notice I am wearing clothes of another era. Medieval. Opulent.

As I look up, I discover that I am not alone. I am in the middle of a great hall, whose walls shimmer with a golden white hue. Five tall illuminous human-like beings stand before me. Others, smaller, stand in a circle around us. Their eyes are beaming to me an intensifying resonance of pure love. In pulses. I am lifted, bewildered. Excited. The tall ones talk to me in my consciousness. "We are proud of you. You alone fought off the dark one. You have passed your initiation, the test of old. Your strength has been revealed. We perceive the kindness in your heart. We are pleased. We chose well. We have been watching over you. Guiding you. We know your courage, also your weaknesses. We are the guardians of all the living. The illumined ones. We will ensure you are supported. Maire O'Ciaragain, your soul is old. Older than you could possibly perceive. This is the first time for you to have a position of true trust. You've have reaped it over many incarnations. Congratulate yourself. For you are to keep the lambs of your lands protected." I fall to my knees. "Thank you. I will serve with great purpose, and honourably." Down I am going, down, dropping at the speed of light. Until I feel my essence re-enter my body. I lie in stunned silence. Gradually I regain my faculties. My mind churns over this incredible experience. I am frightened, yet inspired. It is Tuesday, twenty sixth of December. The day after Jesus was born. I sit up on the edge of my bed. My head spins, I feel dizzy. Thankful that today is a day of rest. A day I can mull over what's happened. What it means. Indeed whether it was a surreal dream, or an altered reality. "Oh I don't know," I say aloud. "Come on Cinders. Breakfast."

MAIRE 7

Ivan and I arrive in Carlingford mid-afternoon, having taken route along the Cooley Mountains, via wooded passes. The druid took his leave at first light, having exchanged knowing looks. We soon find a place to stay for the night at a burgage plot, which thankfully has a small stable yard behind. A young boy takes charge of my horse. We leave our belongings in the lodge house. Ivan refuses to leave me to shop alone. So the two of us take to the local busy market. There is a defensive wall built around the town. Urban tower houses stand tall in narrow streets. I had not packed a dress suitable for the night. Yarns of delicate fabrics hung from the stalls we first came upon. They were not of my liking, and not having the liberty to wait for a frock to be made, we carry on searching. I soon spy a stall that promises more highly. A buxom woman and her daughter soon provide me with a dress to my taste. A black velvet dress, down to the ankles. Cream delicate lace to the collar and cuffs. A pair of heeled shoes to match. That will do fine. We barter. Fix a price. Pay. "I need a ladies hairdresser." I state.

"So do I!" laughed Ivan. The stall keeper directs us to where we best could be properly attended to.

"You'll have to wait a while," the young maiden at the door informs us. "It's busy today. They are entertaining at the castle tonight you know."

"We do. My lady is a guest of James White, Deputy Constable of the castle." Came Ivan's stern reply. His demeanour shook the maiden.

"Wait I'll go inside. I'll be back presently."

With that she rushes in, to return within a minute.

"The dresser will see to you at once. Enter."

The room looks more like a boudoir. A heavily carved flat table and chair sit at the back. A clouded mirror hangs on the wall, dressed with burgundy flimsy material. Heavy perfume pervades the air. A thin, tall, sunken-cheeked woman appears through a beaded curtain from the side. Her hair is a mess. I wonder how she will improve mine. "You, fetch the implements." She scowls to the maiden. Who scurries off. "Now, let's see. Hmmm." She ponders whilst tousling my locks. "I am Oonagh. Best dresser in town. You'll see." She smiles broadly into the mirror, revealing a toothless mouth.

The maiden returns, carrying trays containing an array of pretty ribbons. Baubles. Grips. Combs, brushes. This looks more promising. The maiden then returns to her spot at the door. Ivan sits on a small stool, head down, looking bored, twiddling his thumbs. Oonagh makes a start. Pulling at the tugs. Brushing, then fine combing. Her bony fingers as nimble as any, work quickly. She clamps the top half of my hair above my head. Completes four long plaits down to my waist. Returns to the crown, releases more, manipulates these locks into an ornate, raised headdress. Then with the hair by my forehead starts to plait again. She intermingles the plaits with the headdress in spectacular fashion. "Hand me the trimmings tray," she shouts at the maiden. "Quick." The maiden runs over, obligingly holds the tray up. "What colour is your gown my lady." She asks. "Why black and cream." I reply. She fumbles around the tray. Takes out minute black and gold bows. Attaches them with speed at various places around the side plaits. For each of the four long pieces hanging down my back, she takes a black velvet ribbon. Begins half way down, wraps it around the plaits over and over to the bottom, where she secures them with small grips. Her hands return to the held up tray. She picks up a dozen small gold baubles and threads them into the crown. "There, I told you." She steps back to look at her work, smiles, revealing her gums again. I have to say, I am enamoured with her skills. I look as much a lady as ever I will.

Having eaten with Ivan at a tavern, we head back to our lodgings. I go in alone. Wash with a bucket of cold water and cloth. Put on my gown and heels. I meander into the yard, where Ivan is waiting to escort me to the castle entrance.

"Maire."

"Yes," I respond.

"You do know that your father would be angered at you attending this event."

"I do." Showing my appreciation of his agreement to take me.

"Maire, you must be careful. You may look like a lady, yet one wrong word or answer could put you in danger. Stay away from the garrison inside the courtyard there. And more's to the point stay away from young men. They will most likely be British. I understand why Gwyneth has made this arrangement, she will have taken umbrage at her defeat by you. She is testing you. Taunting you to disobey your father's command. For she will know your presence here would perturb him."

"I know Ivan, we already discussed this." "Yes indeed, however I cannot iterate enough to you, as I am not on the guest list, I can only stand guard until the celebration is over."

"I understand." I reply. Don't worry."

We approach the steps that lead up to the castle, it sits on a rocky outcrop looking out to the Loch. Ivan is surprised to see two men guarding them. Each stands steadfast either side. Each wearing pantaloons, half armour, chain mail over their arms and hips, brandishing a battle axe. They cross their axes as we approach. "You may go no further." One of guards points his weapon towards Ivan. He protests. The guard pushes the sharp point to Ivan's stomach. "Invitees only. Now clear off."

"I'll wait for you here." He tells me.

"No you won't," the man says. "Clear off."

Ivan looks to me worriedly. "Go. I will be fine." I assure him. He points to an area across from the road. "I'll be there. Be sure to find you on your departure."

"Yes father." I mock him. Wave, turn. Ascend.

MAIRE 8

Walking up the castle steps, I begin to hear laughter and merriment. With slight butterflies in my stomach, not helped by Ivan's warnings, I proceed to the entrance, in the middle of two large turrets. I take one deep breath, steady myself to enter. Feeling awkward, I square my shoulders, walk through. Flaming torches line the stone floors, against walls draped with fine tapestries. A gathering of well-dressed men and woman of all ages, who are mingling around. There is a mixture of bright, elaborate clothes. Ladies wearing high waisted gowns with slashed sleeves. Sideless surcoats over cotenhardles. The younger wear wimples atop their heads, the older hennins. The men are donning tight breaches, fur lined tapperts over cotehardles. Long houppelands with dagged dalmatian sleeves. Finished off with wide brimmed hats. I consider my attire may be a bit too plain. Too late. Servants are walking round offering refreshments. I try to blend in. Two court jesters doing their best to entertain, receive little attention.

I approach two young servant girls. One is holding a tray of various cups. The other is passing them out. I speak to her. "What beverages are you offering?" I ask politely. "Why, mead, apple wine and ale." "Pass me the mead please." She bows her head, takes a small silver goblet, passes it to me. "Thank you girl." I reply. Then slowly I start to make my way through the gathered groups of gentry and normal folk chatting away. I am trying to find Gwyneth, when I stop in my tracks. There's a group of fine young men engrossed in conversation in a corner. There is no mistaking that boyish mop of hair. One of them is the fellow whose kestrel Aodh killed. I duck my head, change course. Alas he has spotted me. He makes his way over. Something is going on in my belly. I try to ignore it. Blush. The closer he comes the more the fire burns. I've never considered myself in a womanly way before. If this is how it feels. I like it. I clear my throat.

"I'm sorry about your bird."

"Oh that old thing. Don't you worry, I have plenty more." He replies. As I suspected he cares not for the creature, just for the show.

"Let me introduce myself. I am John White, son of James White, deputy constable of Carlingford castle. Those men over there are my brothers." I gaze to the three men. They all nod courteously. "I like a woman with fire in her belly," he states. Embarrassment takes hold. How does he know that? I worry. He continues, as if he hasn't noticed. "I mean, one who likes to win. Will take risks. Is daring, bold."

"Oh. I suppose you could be correct." I tease him back. I sip my mead ever so slowly, raising my eyes to maintain contact with his. I am liking this game. No man has told me of this. I now understand the meaning of the term "aroused." Gwyneth comes upon us, looking less pleased.

"Maire, may we talk."

"Yes of course, will you excuse me John. "Of course." He replies, performs a half bow. Making sure his hand ever so slightly brushes against mine. "I hope to converse with you again later."

I smile daintily, whilst inside me the heat is rising. A damp patch forms in my smallclothes between my legs. My body yearns for satisfaction. I vaguely notice his does too. I will conquer him later.

Gwyneth leads me up a set of internal stairs. She takes me to a deep embrasure with narrow arrow slits. Peers through. Turns back to me. I was so caught up in the thought of being ravished, I hadn't noticed how cleverly she was not exposing her scars, even how she has pinned her hair, thus covering her lost eye. "We are alone. Now speak of that you wish."

"I had a vision of us riding together." I begin.

"Is that it? Is that what you've put your neck out for, to tell me of a vision." She interrupts.

"Yes, well, no." I slightly stammer. I must get a grip of myself. "Call it what you will. I was shown a scene in the future, where we will be heading up an armed force against those that occupy our lands." Her eyebrows raise mockingly. "No. Hear me out. I know this. I feel it. It is to be. With you by my side we shall triumph." She raises her chest. I continue. "I consider you to be of the finest swordsmen. You are renowned also for your weaponry ability whilst seated on a horse. I need to perfect my strikes. I know you can teach me."

"What do I get out of it?" She questions, eye narrowed.

"My father has promised you fine horses. A good sleeping place at our manor. All your wants and needs will be tended to."

"Oh. Like you, you mean." Comes her sarcastic reply.

"I didn't mean to patronise. Apologies." I pause. "My father is not long for this world. That I know. As his successor it is my position to defend my sept, our clans. The British will strike again. It is in their blood to thirst for more power, wealth. They are nonaligned with the fate of those left homeless. Dead, raped, orphaned, starving. They care not for those of our blood. I wish for you to give me wings. Together we can raise an army so powerful, ferocious, that all shall dread. Together we shall make history."

"I shall consider. Give you my answer by the end of the night." Gwyneth informs me.

"Very well. Shall we join the frivolities once more?" I ask her.

"Very well." We leave our place of secrecy, return downstairs to the hall.

My eyes flit round the room, searching for my intended conquest. Eyes are boring into the back of my head. Slowly I move around to face them. We lock gaze. His large brown eyes pronounce his same determination. We spend the next hour socialising separately. Never letting the other out of sight. Purposefully positioning ourselves to carry on our lovers' dance. By the time the night truly darkens, I've felt undressed a dozen times. Every pore of my skin is reacting, as if covered in beautiful flapping butterflies, enticing. I observe him adjusting his collar, to relieve his mounting heat. He cocks his head towards a back entrance. Takes leave. I follow. We rush down a narrow stairwell, him leading, pulling at my hand. Behind the north of the castle, there are ladders to a small jetty, where a little boat is moored. Silently we climb down. Climb in. We sit facing on planks of wood.

He rolls up his sleeves, takes the oars. Stealthily we pass the front of the castle, he keeps to the shore line to avoid detection from the rocks high above. Up ahead of, barely detectable in the new moon light, lies a circular flat rock. We approach. He assists me out. Secures the boat. Joins me.

"It is now my turn to prove my skills, with you my lady eagle." He declares. Then swiftly takes off his upper garments. "Come to me my sweetness." I am in no state to refuse. This is new to me. I shall carry out his wishes. "Undo my trousers, slowly, button by button." I begin. "Do not touch me until I allow it." With each button I release of his breaches, they start to slip over his hips. Tantalisingly revealing the ties of his pants, which start to pleasingly fill up. "Stop." He says. I do. He steps out of his trousers. "Now. Bend to your knees. Kneel before me. Undo my pants with your teeth." Again I do as I am told. "Remove them." I oblige, I have to lift them up first, as the top as his phallus now fully swollen is holding them in place. I cannot resist. I take one of my long plaits. Tickle his piece with the ends of my golden hair. Use it in a circular motion, left to right, around his balls, up to his foreskin, back over his scrotum. I see this pleases him. He arches back. He takes my hand. Stops me going any further.

"Stand before me my love." I arise. He takes his hand to my cheek, his fingers stroke me under my jaw line. I delight.

"May I?" He enquires. Indicating his wish to see my nakedness.

"You may." I reply through deepening breath. Both hands go to the back of my neck, release my neckerchief. Then he moves down my back, still facing me. I can feel the moistness of his breath against my neck. He proceeds to unlace my dress. Which each crisscross he undoes he gives my neck a sharp nibble. I close my eyes. Tilt my neck to my shoulder, allow him greater access. Oh the pleasure. He comes to my shoulders, releases my sleeves. Draws down my garment. It drops to the stone. Only my chemise remains. I am starting to shiver. John gathers my dress from my ankles. Lays it down on the stone, under his own discarded clothing. He unhooks my last garment. Makes it into a makeshift pillow.

He returns. With a look of lust, bends down to his knees. His attention goes straight to my vanity. He uses his tongue. Fervently he flicks around my erection. I gasp. The sensation ripples through me. He starts to suck at it, harder and harder. It's pulling. Again I gasp. He refrains. Begins to gently bite my clitoris. A power builds inside me. I breathe shallowly. My ribs lift in tiny motion, to match the sensations pouring through my sex organ. He inserts a digit. My body rushes, gushes. I can control myself no longer. My reaction begins. Takes over. I fall forward, place my hand to his shoulder for support. Use the other one to systematically tug at his glorious dark hair, then force his face into me. Away and in, away and in. I climax. John removes his finger, lowers his head. His mouth goes to me, his tongue swirls inside me. He laps as a dog. I want more.

He stands, comes to kiss my opened mouth. Our tongues dance, recklessly, hungrily. I taste my dew. Erotica gains. His penis slaps haphazardly against bare flesh. I'm in heaven. We lie down on our bed of wild abandonment. He kisses my lips. Lowers himself to my pert, pink nipples. He sucks as a hungry bairn. I delight. He rises to kiss my mouth once more. Takes a hand to my vaginal lips. Parts them, I squeal. Pant. He takes hold of his phallus, gently, ever so slowly but surely inserts it into my core. A few soft pushes send waves of pure joy through my being. John lifts himself a fraction higher, inserts himself further. Presses his loins tight up to mine. His motion quickens, feverishly he grinds against my pubic bone. Thrusts, grinds. Bites at my mouth, my tongue. Waves gently lap at the rock, adding a further sensation to our pleasure. He begins to grunt. Animalistic grunts of extreme gratification. He quickens further. Rises up like a snake. Grabs at my breasts. A final motion, ejaculation, I join, climax with him. Our bodies contract in unison. He falls to my chest. Rolls to the side. Together we hold hands, looking up at the night sky. Observing this moment in time, under our stars of contentment.

"Alas my love, we need to return." John woefully exclaims.

"Yes, yes. I need to see Gwyneth." I reply.

"What?" He questions.

"Oh. Nothing," I say. We help each other replace our garments. He kisses my feet as he slips on my shoes. "There's a mark on your gown," John states. "Here let me." He retrieves a handkerchief, wets it with sea water. Removes the creamy substance. The rest resides inside me and around my wetness. We return whence we came. I go first into the hall. He waits a few moments to do so. I go to a window, look out to sea. Relive in my mind our ecstasy.

Gwyneth finds me, places her hand in the small of my back. "Maire. I will join you."

"Gwyneth. I thank you for your generosity."

"Anyone who can do what you've just done, certainly has balls," she states. We look to each other as naughty children.

She winks her eye. "You've certainly achieved more than you set out for tonight madam."

"Who me?" I innocently say, placing my hand to my heart. We both giggle.

"I will come to your stead at the end of April. Be sure to have every kind of armament to hand. We shall become invincible."

We place our bodies closer. Stare out to the ocean. Squeeze our hands together, to seal our collaboration.

KELLY 8

I think back to this morning. What a way to wake on New Years' day! Perhaps this is a sign that I am after all yearning for a mate. That was the best wet dream ever. A man made love to me salaciously. I loved it. Couldn't see his face clearly. But that didn't stop me. I feel like a young woman again. Wow. Thank you God.

As I drive up Brian's tree lined driveway. I consider how lucky I am to have such wondrous people in my life. Brian has invited me to join his luncheon, with Arthur and Miriam who have returned from their honeymoon, together with other guests I don't know. I've spruced myself up. Put on my mid-length cream woollen dress, with a scooped chest. My favourite cream and beige scarf. Knee-length black patent boots, bag to match. Long black overcoat to keep off the winters chill. This will be a delight. I park my car neatly along with the rest on the gravel driveway. Head to the front door. Before I have time to knock it is flung open. Miriam greets me.

"Why, I've been eager for you to turn up. We have so much to share with you." "Did you have a lovely time?" I quiz her. "Why, we did. I will fill you in over lunch. Don't want to bore you with repeating the same conversation." She laughs. "Come on through to the lounge. Hand me your coat. There are a few other guests yet to arrive. As you, dear, I do not know them. These get-togethers can be fabulous or a disaster. I trust Brian has asked appropriately like-minded people. We don't need old boring farts."

"Miriam!" I exclaim, rolling my eyes, smirking. We enter.

The room is back to being the way it was. The large fireplace has its mantle prettily decorated with ivy and mistletoe. A fire is burning, warming. We sit in two old armchairs sitting to each side of the hearth. Arthur and Brian are seated on the sofas in deep conversation, which sit in the middle of the room facing a large wooden coffee table. A Persian rug separates the two. A silver tray, champagne glasses, and a bottle of Bollinger laid out on top of the table. Perfect. Arthur gets up. Pours two glasses, brings them over to us.

"Ladies, so lovely to see you two chatting away. And what a great idea Brian had, hosting this day for us. Miriam and I have been invited to stay until we fly back to Florida." "Arthur, you look ten years younger. What have you been doing, rigorous exercise or mere walking?" I joke.

"Now, now." He retaliates.

"I'm going to miss you guys so much, yet I'm happy for you to return to America to start your new life."

"We can skype," Arthur tells me. "A kind hotelier in Bournemouth taught us how, so we could hitch up with Miriam's family at Christmas. Unreal what can be done today."

A black cat appears from behind a lavish curtain, makes its way over. Jumps on my lap. "Sid get down." Brian shouts from his seat.

"It's alright Brian, I don't mind really." I reply. There's a knock at the door.

"I'll get it." Brian states, gets himself up, leaves the room. He returns a minute later. Two women and two men follow him in.

"Now we are all together, I will do the introductions," announces Brian. All approach the fire. I get up. Place the cat on the chair. "This is Dan, Sarah, Jim, and Bree". He now turns to us. "Guys, this is Miriam, Arthur who I told you just got married."

"Congratulations," they all say.

"And this is their dear friend Kelly." Brian hands them each a champagne flute.

"Cheers."

He starts. We follow clinking our upraised glasses. We exchange pleasantries. Miriam winks to me. I can tell she is thankful that our guests are more my age than hers. She is so young at heart. A waitress appears at the doorway. "Excuse me. Lunch is ready."

"Thank you." Brian smiles. "Shall we?" He leads the way to the dining room. An antique table is traditionally set. Eight arm chairs to match are waiting. "Sit where you fancy," inputs Brian. With a little hesitation all of us find a comfortable place. Miriam is next to me. The person called Jim sits to the other side. Brian finds himself at the head; Arthur the tail, next to his wife. The waitress asks me: "Are you the vegetarian?"

"Yes. I am thanks." I reply. Grateful that Arthur has passed this information on. Many a sticky moment has arisen for me in the past. Left to eat just vegetables. She whizzes off, comes back with another lady, wearing an apron. Between them, they lay before us a charming dish of baked goat's cheese, relishes and baby lettuce leaves. After our starters, Arthur and Miriam recant their travels. Well, mostly Miriam who is quite giddy from the bubbles. She delights in telling of her first English red bus ride, around the city of London. Taking in all the sights. Of Bournemouth's Victorian palisades. Eating ice cream on the promenade. Driving through the Cotswolds. How she loved Bristol and Chester, in particularly the Roman ruins. We listen with the same enthusiasm with which she speaks.

The main meal arrives. Everyone has rib of beef, perfectly cooked and pink. Roast and mashed potatoes. Stemmed broccoli, peas, cauliflower cheese. With plenty of gravy. My plate is put before me. The cook speaks to me. "For you, a fine nut roast. With a special gravy." She places a petite gravy boat to the side. "Enjoy." She bows her head, leaves us to our food. The man, Jim, who has mostly been talking to Sarah and Brian, turns his attention to me. "So Kelly, what is it you like to do." I explain about my small café. Some of its customers. How I like to walk out, enjoying the simpler things in life.

I take my turn, ask him questions. "So how do you know Brian?"

"He and my father were the best of friends, "he replies, then starts to recall stories of their times together. He informs me that his father passed away aged just fifty four of a heart attack. How he is pleased they have been invited today.

"What's your line of work?" I ask.

"Ah, well." I notice his accent is decidedly more British than Irish. "I am a barrister. I was called to the bar seventeen years ago. At the honourable society of The Middle Temple."

"That sounds posh." I tease him. "And why is it called "called to the bar?"

"Ah, the bar refers to the wooden benches which separated the judge, barristers and lawyers from the crowds. It was created hundreds of years ago."

"I see. Which part of the law do you serve?" I follow on.

"My advocacy is Children's law. I deal with many cases, not all happy endings. However, it is where I feel I can serve best."

"And why a barrister." I continue.

"That's easy, I love mooting." He states. Placing his hand to his hips. He beams at me. He's been glancing and smiling rather a lot to Sarah, who I notice is wearing a wedding ring. Shame, I'm quite liking this one. With his rounded face, smile lines indicating a fun character. Brown, short cut hair, slightly receding. Oh well.

Dessert arrives, a light chocolate mousse, with raspberry coulis. A ripe, plump raspberry on the top. "Umm, delicious Brian. I'm so grateful for your grand hospitality, yet again," inputs Arthur.

We all agree.

"Here, here," shouts up Jim.

We all raise our glasses. "Good health," we all add. Idle chatter commences with raised voices, as more wine is consumed. Except myself, who daftly decided to drive! An hour passes.

Jim stands up. "Well, I say. What a lovely party we've all enjoyed. To the host."

"To the host." We all pipe up.

"I'm afraid we have to go now Brian, our taxi will be here. If I consumed much more I fear I would miss my flight tomorrow."

"We can't have you doing that," Sarah follows on.

"Work to do, my dear, great work to do." Sarah and Bree both kiss Brian on the cheek. Dan and Jim vigorously shake hands, pat backs. Brian sees them out.

He re-enters the room, reclaims his seat. "I think that went well. You all seemed to get along nicely." We agree. Miriam and Arthur hold hands. "Hey Kelly, what did you think of Jim? You two seemed to hit it off." Arthur points to me. Miriam squeezes his hand, giggles. I'm confused. "Well, I, yes we did. He seemed a genuine chap, works for a good cause." "I didn't mean that." Arthur lowers his head towards me. Grins. "Did you like him? You know. Like him, like him?" I blush. "Arthur, don't be stupid, he's married. Sarah and Jim seem to be very close." Brian roars laughing. "Sarah is his sister! Yes they are close. Very close. As brother and sister. He was quite taken by you." Brian informs me.

"Really, I don't know what to say." Nor where to look. "Where is he flying to?" I blurt out, changing the topic.

"He's off back to Manchester where he is based. Came to see the New Year in with his sister, her best friend Bree, and her partner Dan. This is hilarious, I should have explained properly." Brian can hardly contain himself.

"Is that what you two were so engrossed in early when I arrived?"

"Yes." Proclaims Arthur, howling. "Why was Sarah's husband not here then?" I enquire. Both Arthur and Brian are incapable of answering, so I turn to Miriam. "My dearest Kelly." She addresses me. "That was a prop. Arthur knows how funny you are about meeting single men. We didn't want you to get your "leave me alone," hackles up. To give him a chance."

"I get it, I've been played."

"You have my dear, you have."

MAIRE 9

Ivan and I have been travelling all day. "Ivan. Why have we taken this route?" I am curious as we seem to be swinging out west more than we need.

"We have this slight detour Maire. The druid has requested that we spend some time north of Dartria, at a place known as Edergole." He informs me. "We shall arrive soon, I know you are weary." He does not realise why I am, that I spent half the night awake, listening to the sea, which had stirred up. Letting my imaginations of lust take over. I'd had to wash my under gown as it had streaks of blood and John's excretion on it. But not before I inhaled his odour deep into my nostrils, my memory, once more.

We are approaching hillier countryside. Evidence of an old fortress is visible. Its broken, emaciated ruins sit eerily on the horizon. As we proceed, more hilltop enclosures are visible. Newer, active. "Do not concern yourself my lady. These are the lands of the O'Neill of the Fews. They shall not bother us, unless we bother them. I send Aodh on a tour, as a precaution. He is happy to take flight. "Our destination is ahead of us. Come now." Ivan says, beckoning me to follow.

An elevated ridge lies before us. I dismount, lead Raphael up. Towards the top are two large, separated standing stones. A large flat capstone rests above, creating a portal. It is laden with moss and smaller stones. As we stand before, I see that around this site and over the land close by are barrows of burial grounds. Ivan starts to unveil the reason for our visit.

"Maire. The Druid has asked us to be here this day. He wishes you to go down there." He points to an opening in the ground underneath.

"What on earth for." I ask. "You are to go down into the Giant's tomb. Strewn on the bed are broken bones and mythical artefacts of our old ones. You are to lay amongst them."

"I shall do no such thing." I retort.

"Maire, please, do not concern yourself. Others have been before you."

"I care not of others Ivan. I refuse."

Ivan recounts the words of the Druid. "Take up your bravery. The dead cannot harm you." I soften my gait. "I shall remain out here. You are to make yourself as comfortable as is possible. Lay yourself upon your back. Envisage your own death having passed. You are to imagine your own burial, being placed in your tomb. The voices of your people lamenting outside. The earth eagerly waiting to eat away at your skin. Skin shrinking into black rot. Underground creatures furrowing into your every orifice. Your flesh decomposing, putrefying. Fungi growing from the openings of your wasting organs. Maggots hatching from lain eggs."

"That is disgusting, why would I ever do that?" One last attempt to evade.

"You must face your own death Maire, for in doing so you will become hardened to your vulnerability. This will make you indomitable, fearless savage."

I'm not happy at this. However, I trust the druid's wisdom. "How long am I expected to remain down in that pit of despair?" I ask.

"Until you know the process is complete," he answers me.

I shrug my shoulders. "Right." I say aloud. I get down on my bottom and dangle my legs through the opening. Slide down the muddy gawping mouth of doom. I step on something hard, which breaks beneath my shoe. I retch and shudder. A mouldy, musky smell pervades. Thoughts of bad omens engulf me. I cannot believe I am to endure this. It had better have good reason, if not, my anger shall rise. As my eyes adjust to the dim light, I gulp. The floor is littered with bones, legs, arms, open mouthed skulls. The remnants of children too. Old frayed filthy garments peak out in between. Broken-down amulets. Rotten wooden carvings are lifelessly scattered. I consider making a clearing to lay on, however I daren't disturb a thing. There are rules. I go onto my knees. Consider for a second aborting this absurdity. Putting my head to my hands, I take a deep inhalation, slowly exhale. Courage finds me. I place myself horizontally over the remains. Follow Ivan's instructions. As I do so, a primeval scream rises inside me. Things are poking at me. I innately want to clamber out. Resist. Continue. I allow my imagination to see this through. My life flashes before me. I remember as a child cutting up worms, wondering how the two halves would each wriggle off. In here, it is they that shall feast upon my flesh as my dead body perishes. I cannot stand this. My body starts to jerk. I thrash around. Trying to free myself. I am dead, I am dead. I am dead. The earth swallows me. I scream out for what seems as forever. Then something changes. I feel a great lightness. I quieten. Regain normal breath. My heart settles. I succumb to my fate. A stillness takes over. I bask in my new found serenity. I remain, reposed for a few minutes. Then gather myself. Stand up. Say prayers to those lying beneath me of thanks. Scramble out.

The skies have darkened. The stars are out. The moon peeks from a dark grey cloud. I brush down my clothes, tidy my hair. I hear a loud clap above. I look up. The druid is sat cross legged atop the table. Adoh is settled besides him. The druid smiles. He performs two more, long, slow, meaningful claps. Aodh copies him. He raises on his legs, lets out three caws. I smile back at him. Ivan comes to me, and most unusually hugs me tight. Raises me to his height. "You, my lady, never fail." He says, in a congratulatory manner. He puts me back down. "Come on, let us head home. You've had a busy few days." Little does he know just how busy. "You can sleep in luxury tonight, better than a bed of bones." He laughs at his own words. The druid slides down the stone. Ivan helps me mount my horse. I bend down to his neck, wrap my arms around him. Lay my head in his mane. Inwardly thank him for journeying with me.

KELLY 9

The month of January has been dull. I am glad to be past it. January is always dead in the café. People have spent up over Christmas. The weather, inclement. February has now come. I hope for more customers. I don't like to stand idle. I miss the chats and bustle. The little bells zing their ring. Someone has arrived. "Yes." I cry out loud. "Let the day begin." I steady myself, hear a chair being pulled back. The chair lightly scratches the floor as it is pulled back up to a table. Just one person, I think to myself. Better than no one. I take myself into the front. To my delight there sits Teagan. Looking tanned and youthful once more. She jumps up to greet me.

"Kelly, you star." She proclaims. Excitement uncontained.

"I take it your trip served its purpose," I reply, with a wink.

"Oh it did. Really did. Do you have time to sit a while, I'm dying to bring you up to date. I've been busy."

"Wish I could say the same." I say, whilst pulling a child's grumpy face. We laugh in synchrony.

"What I'm about to tell you will raise an eyebrow or two." Teagan teases.

"Pray do tell." I ask.

"Well, the holiday went well, a slow start passion wise. But the kids soon had Ian back to his former self. I believe the Disney characters helped him too. To bond with his children and his child within. I never once mentioned the affair. I didn't have to, he blurted it all out one night after a few too many beers."

"Teagan, must have been hard to listen to." I guess.

"Yes, but I couldn't believe it. Really, when I persuaded him to pass his phone, reveal the password. He just crumpled, as a man before a priest in confession. He seemed to forget that I was his wife entirely. I remained stoic. Not wanting to stop his revelations. He held his head down as a naughty school boy. Eye contact intermittent. I swear I was shaking inside, how I didn't show my fury, I'll never know. The thought of losing my family kept me strong."

"Share with me the minutest details. I'm all ears," I hopefully tell her. Although I never repeat what I learn. I enjoy being considered trustful, and who does not like a good story? "Ian suggested I scroll down his messages, to view the ones from Josh." "Josh, I…" I interrupt.

"No. No." Teagan giggles. "Not that. He used the name Josh as a smokescreen should I see a text coming through. Her real name is Jess."

"Oh Teagan, I get it. Devious one." I remark.

"When I saw what she'd sent. Her messages of "Woe is me." "You can be my knight." "I hate my job."" Teagan informs me.

"What job? What does she do for a living?" I ask.

"Her living if you can call it that, is to tantalise weak, drunken mindless men." Teagan tells me.

"How the, what the?" I enquire. "She's a stripper, a god damn stripper, and far from a beauty at that. I was devastated to see what had transpired. I mean, I'm not that bad looking am I?"

"Of course not." I assure her.

"Wait a minute, look, I sent myself one of his photos of her. Tell me what you think." Teagan's eyes fly to her phone, she flicks back through her album. "Here," she says. "Check this out." Her piercing blue eyes start to water, her lower lip quivers.

"Teagan, we can leave it here, if it's too much," I say, as I place my hand tenderly onto her shoulder.

"No, no. It's ok. I want your opinion, really I do. I know you are a great judge of character."

I take the phone from her, look to the image before me. I'm as startled as she obviously was. What lies before me is a photo of a young woman. The body of a child. Long straight, boring hair. Pock marked face. Her smile reveals green tinged teeth. "Oh wow." I exclaim. "I think I know what you mean. Hardly Cinderella is she?" Teagan's mood lifts.

"I don't get it." Teagan blurts out.

"My dear one, what goes on in a man's big head when his little weapon is ruling the waves, is any woman's guess." I can see why Teagan would be appalled that her husband would risk everything for this. Instead of revealing my thoughts, my heart speaks. "Teagan my dear. She would have played the wounded maiden. Puffed up his hidden hero archetype. Made him feel needed again."

"Needed again. We need him. Me, Sophie, Connor. We need him." Anger rises in her.

"Teagan. Please hear me out. Look at you, just look at you. Not only are you blessed, fair in face, perfect in dimension. A work of art. Until the last few months, you have been the most together person I know. Perhaps Ian felt unnecessary to you. Perhaps he felt deflated. Incomplete. This Jess, must have appealed to him. Made him feel big, worthwhile. Wanted." You are strong, wise. A lot of men feel demeaned once the children take the mother's attention." She looks to me quizzically. "Don't get me wrong, you are the most wonderful mother. He may have felt on the back burner so to speak. These circumstances are age old. Nothing new. What's the situation now?"

Teagan regains herself. "She's gone. Dumped. He told her the next day. Blocked her number too."

"So that's it then?" I enquire.

"Well, not quite." Teagan grins. "Let me tell you how I got my retribution." She rubs her hands in glee.

"I'm all ears. Go ahead." I plead.

"My old school friend, Isobel, had a shocking idea. One which I relished. I told Ian I was going to London to visit her for a few days. Which I did. Only we did something out of the ordinary."

"Carry on." I nudge her.

"We went out one night, to the ladies of the night. To Stringfellows. You know, the lap dancing club." Teagan leans in. As do I.

"I've certainly heard of the place. Who hasn't? Can't say I'd like to venture there."

"We did. Took some guts, but we were determined to put Jess in her place. We entered after midnight. Wishing to catch her at her greatest time of compromise. Surely enough there she was on the stage, writhing over a pole, as if it were alive, a sex object. Isobel and I, amused took ourselves to the bar opposite. Behaved like lesbians, ogled the mirage of bodies, barely clad. Ordered the most expensive champagne to get the required attention. It worked. As soon as Jess finished her dance, she redressed. God knows how many fannies work that pole. Totally unhygienic if you ask me. Anyway. Jess went to a blonde in the corner. They exchanged words, then slithered over in their high, cheap heels."

"I'm liking this so far Teagan. That must have taken courage."

"It did. With Isobel by my side though, I soon began to see the humour in our mission." Teagan continues.

"True to form, Jess came over, introduced herself as Angel, her friend as Mia. Another lie. I tell you, without that photo, we'd have had to abort. Both girls offered us a private dance in the cubicles beyond the main room. They each wanted two hundred pounds. Isobel and I pretended to confer. Then agreed. Angel and Mia, guided us to a vacant booth. Isobel and I held hands. Showed expressions of expectation. Mia drew the curtains shut. They began. At one point we had to stop ourselves falling into a fit of giggles, as both girls proceeded to show us their lesbian act. They started to neck each other. Run fingers through their home-done hair. Hands started to lower. Each removing the others bra. They played with each other's breasts, sucking, stroking. Pinching. All the time eyeing us up. Lurching towards us. Tantalising. Drawing us into their sexual act."

"Oh Teagan, I can't believe what you are divulging. I hope it has a happy ending." I enquire.

"Just you wait." Replies Teagan.

"Angel feigned to her knees. Played with her protruded fingers around and under Mia's flimsy knickers. Insinuated cunnilingus. Isobel and I feigned arousal. We briefly kissed, to keep them fooled. They swopped places, carried on with their erotica. All the time flicking their tongues towards us, enticingly as lizards, trying to catch their prey. Money. They each removed their colleagues' knickers. Turned away from us, showed us their arses. Parted their cheeks. Urgh! We didn't need that visual memory."

Teagan is obviously enjoying recanting her tale. So am I. "There's more. They then turned round, asked us which of us wished for them to do us a lap dance. "I'll take you, luscious Angel." I told her. She started to straddle me. Lithed her body up and down. I must admit, when she lent backwards over my knees and rolled her stomach, thrusting her bare bits towards my face, I thought that was an excellent tantalising move. May copy it. Blowing her heated breath into my ears. Flicking her hair around my face. She then moved down, licking the air between my thighs over my opened skirted legs. I pretended to be enthralled, as did Isobel with Mia. We exchanged glances when they were unaware. This was so going to plan. Unbelievably so. Do you want to know what happened next Kelly?"

"I most certainly do." I added.

"Once the girls had finished their routine, they became very business-like. Sought our approval, we granted it. "Would you like another dance?" Angel purposefully, innocently asked. I said, I think we've had enough. Thank you. Time for us to get home to our family. I can't tell you how much joy you have just imparted. You're a miracle. I told her. Angel beamed. Mia left and came back within minutes with a card machine to pay for their services. This was it, the moment of retribution."

"What did you do?" I asked Teagan. I had to know.

"The grand finale went thus. After I had paid the price for the naked girls before us, Angel said: "Thank you. Will you come again? I've really enjoyed entertaining you. Far better than middle aged drooling men."

"I'm sorry lass." I replied. I have to get back to Ireland in the morning. To my dear reliable husband, you may know him. Mr Ian Walsh, you may have seen him on Sky Sports?" Well, she flipped, started to scream, shout. A bouncer came and drew back the curtain, just in time to catch her throwing a glass of champagne in my face. Small mercy. He dragged her away. Gave her her marching orders. Mia, red faced receded into the darkness beyond."

"Golly Teagan, I am impressed. Very well done. I'm in shock. See, I told you you're a stout one. That you are."

"That I am," replied Teagan, triumphantly grinning away. "I'd never have guessed you had this in you. That Jess, Angel, shall not be bothering you again, I can guarantee it. Or rather you did. A massive pat on the back to you Teagan."

"I don't know where Isobel got her inspiration from, yet, we sure did rock it." Teagan stands up, puts on her coat. "Bye now Kell. And a huge cheers to us. Thank you." She leaves in a flurry, lifted by her conquest. I sure am pleased.

KELLY 10

Friday second of February. I went to bed last night thinking. Although Teagan has had a torrid few months: she does have a man. Whereas my nightly routine involves myself, a toothbrush and some toothpaste. Nothing else touches my lips. I do sometimes wish I had a cock down there, instead of a load of cobwebs. My choice I know. Not sure I want the entanglements that come with a relationship. I haven't heard from Jim. Shame. There was an attraction there. I shut up early for a change. Having made contact with Jackie. I fancied a little creativity to elevate my pensiveness over the prolific dreams. She informed me that her classes are over now until the spring; however suggested I may like a reflexology session. I have read about this in magazines. So I agreed to go over. A little me time may relax me. Straighten me out. There's a knock at my door. Damn. I was enjoying some peace. I furtively peak though my spy hole.

Well, well, well. This certainly is a week of the Walsh's. It's Ian. Though what he wants with me, nor whether or not I wish to speak to him is another matter. I tentatively let him in. He surges through. His large frame almost knocks me off my feet. "Ian, what is it?" I decide to play dumb.

"I'm a halfwit, a bloody halfwit." He exclaims loudly.

"Come through Ian. Make yourself comfortable, and calm down." I state. Ian paces my small sitting room. "Please Ian, sit down, you are making me dizzy." I tell him. He plonks himself in the armchair by the fireplace. Landing heavily. Then nudges his arse to the edge of the seat.

"Kelly, I am sorry to barge in on you like this. Please forgive me. I just, I just need your council."

"Very well Ian, make it quick, I have plans myself." I reply, trying to hide my disdain.

"A few months ago, having finished a live programme, I let the lads persuade me to join them at a dancing bar," he begins. I think a part of me is going to enjoy watching him squirm, I might draw this out after all.

"Alright Ian. So what's wrong with that?" I goad him. His face flushes. Eyes drop to the floor, a sure sign of guilt.

"This wasn't just a bar with dancers Kell. It was one of them, you know. Err strip joints."

"Oh I see." I reply, feigning surprise.

"I do wish I had stuck to my principles. That I said no. I didn't. Allowed myself to be led astray." He relinquishes.

"Ian, it's not unusual for certain men to drop into such places. There really is no true harm done there. So long as Teagan was none the wiser, it shouldn't be a problem." I console, a hint of sarcasm escapes. "Don't give the game away." I say to myself.

"The trouble is Kell, it went further than that." He blurts out.

"Further, how so?" I question. His neck flushes pink, the colour rises, adorns his cheeks, darkens.

"I know what I've done was stupid, ridiculous, beyond reason," he continues. "There were two girls there that night that hit on me. That's how it works in these situation. You buy them a drink, they sit by you. Listen to your woes. The first girl was wonderful. Bright. Very attractive. She had long thick dark hair, eyes so green, they captivated."

I interrupt. "Ian, I am unsure we should take this any further. I have immense respect for Teagan. I think you should leave." I get up from the sofa. Indicate to the front door. Worried as I know nothing of this other dancer.

"No. Please Kell, I need to speak to someone, need to offload. Need to be honest with myself. There's no one else quite like you."

"Ok. Ok." I reluctantly give in. Reseat myself. "Continue Ian." I retort.

"As I was saying. This girl was together, witty, full of energy. She, Chantelle, she kind of reminded me of my wife. Had her whole life planned. Despite a challenged childhood. She was brought up in a council estate. Mother an alcoholic. Father absent. Her mother's seedy boyfriend did things to her. As she grew up, Chantelle had dreams. Big dreams. She also knew the power of her charm. Used it. Used men to unwittingly draw their cash from them. Chantelle had been dancing for over three years, she told me. That she had saved enough cash to purchase a flat. Almost had enough to gain a second. Her aim to build a mini empire using her wit, or tit wit. I had such respect for her. I paid for a dance, yet wouldn't let her sully herself. She was grateful. Thanked me and left." He informed me. "That was kind. Just like the gentleman I know." I applauded him. Ian lowers his head to his hands, chewed on his lips.

"What is it Ian?" I ask.

"That's not all Kell. Not the half of it." He sheepishly states. I look to my watch. I'm in this now.

"Fill me in." I steer him.

"Once Chantelle had gone home. Another girl came over. Quite different in her demeanour. She was mousy, weak. Yet pushy. I played right into her hands." Ian starts to fidget.

"I don't know if I can listen to this Ian, perhaps you should discuss it with a counsellor, or someone indifferent." I inject.

"No. Kell. You're the best. You are the secret keeper." Flattered, I resolve myself. Ian starts to talk again.

"This girl, Jess. She blindsided me good. Right from the start she poked into my affairs. Drew out my insecurities. Had me believing my life was incomplete. Played a dummy on me. I'm so stupid. I fell into her trap. She listened to every word I spoke. Made me feel cheated. Then turned tactics, informing me of her longing to have designer clothes. Security. How her life was a struggle. She made me feel like it was my job to protect her. To tackle down her troubles. And, I'm ashamed to say, I did just that. She discretely got my phone number before I left. Told me she would be fired if anyone noticed. Insanely I kept it. Wish I'd flushed it down the bog. But. No I didn't."

"At first I took her shopping, spoilt her rotten. Made me feel almighty. She sure knew what she was doing, caught me by stealth. Then things progressed. Before I knew it, I was well in her grasp. I can't believe I was such a cretin. Kell, I cheated on my wife." Ian bursts into tears. His bulky body, spewing as an erupting volcano, bursts out his shame. I give him time to redress. Pass him a box of tissues. He starts to bang his forehead with the palm of his hand. Berates himself over and over. I almost cry myself in response to his utter self-loathing. I wait until he regains himself. It's time for the Aunt Kell's touch down.

I opt out of the, "what the fuck do you think you were doing" route. Only amplifies guilt. Keeps the past present. I begin asking him questions.

"Ian, is it over?"

"Yes."

"Are you still in touch?"

"No." "Does Teagan know?" Ian shakes his head.

"Yes. I told her."

"Good. One feather in your bonnet at least. Has she forgiven you?"

"Yes." "Have you rekindled your bed?"

"Yes."

"Have you learnt the lesson?"

"Yes!"

"That's it then. I am pleased you came to me. Rest assured this matter will remain in these four walls. Now go home. Ensure Teagan feels your appreciation, daily."

"Yes Ma'am." Ian gets up. Composes himself.

"Get on with your future. Don't look back. I doubt Teagan will." I tell him as he leaves.

Phew. That was hard work. Job's done. Now back to my evening. I hurriedly get ready to head out to Jackie. Driving there, I consider: "Why me? How is it I have a knack to cool virulent flames?"

I rock up at Jackie's just on time. She greets me warmly as before. Invites me in. Gestures for me to remove my coat, I do, place it on a hook by the doorway. To my delight she has set up her conservatory in relaxing fashion. Tea light candles lined up against the floor by the walls, glow and flicker mysteriously against the otherwise unlit room. A bouquet of pale pink roses sits atop the sideboard, together with incense which lets off a plume of smoke with a calming aroma of sandalwood. A therapy bed. Made up with pillows and fluffy pink blankets awaits. Perfect. I am in for a treat.

"Hello again Kelly, I am delighted I talked you into this treatment, it will mellow you. If you could just take a seat in the corner," I notice a small armchair, with a stool placed in front, "if you could sit there, remove your socks and shoes. I will be back in a jiffy."

Jackie swans back in with a bowl of water. Sits on the stool. Places a towel over her knees. Asks me to place my feet in the bowl. The water is just hot enough. Delicate white rose petals gently glide along the surface. Bliss. A few minutes pass.

Then Jackie asks me to remove my feet one by one, so she can dry them.

"Is this your way of making sure you have an odourless experience?" I joke with her.

"Well, yes. That and it has a way of enhancing deeper relaxation."

Once dried, Jackie asks me to settle myself on the table. The back is slightly tilted, enabling me to see Jackie when she comes back into the room having disposed of the water bowl. "Have you had this before?" Jackie enquires.

"No. Can't say I have." I respond.

"I will be applying light oil to your feet. With my hands and fingers, I will in a way be massaging them. However, pressure will be applied to specific points, which relate to areas in your body. In the east it is thought that the feet fully mirror the body. So I can detect areas of stress, massage out the tension in your feet, which in turn should alleviate the corresponding area."

Jackie starts very gently on my left foot. My head rests in her left hand. Her right one goes to work. As she travels around the outer edge of my heel, I wince.

"Are you menstruating dear?" she enquires.

"Why yes, how can you tell?"

"Arhh. This is the area that relates solely to women's issues." She informs me.

"That's interesting." I give a chirpy reply.

"Now you relax as much as you can." I do. As I drift off into a semi sleep. I feel her fingers moving in an upwards direction along the main bone in my foot. There are areas that feel like small rocks. She works her fingers over each one, until they disappear. Jackie then takes her attention to my toes. As soon as she starts on my big toe. I feel a crunch. Jerk back into reality. "Ouch." I let out.

"Kelly, is there something on your mind?"

"I don't know what you mean." Comes my sly reply.

"You have a large nodule here. Feel that."

"I do." I answer.

"This would indicate to me that something is troubling you."

"Well, I am having crazy dreams Jackie. Although they have stopped these last few weeks."

"Explain more." She implores.

"I don't know if I can, it all seems weird. It's as if I'm in a period in history, Northern Ireland. Some bits are hazy, however, I do remember the person's name is Maire."

"Fascinating Kelly, would you like to explore it further?"

"Further, how?" I question.

"I've recently qualified as a hypnotherapist. It might help to delve into your subconscious mind to see where these dreams are coming from." She informs me.

"Thank you, but no way. I don't need any crap stirring up. I've heard it can bring up old garbage. No. Thanks again Jackie. That is certainly not for me." I beseech.

"Let me know if you change your mind. I'm always here. It can be quite disturbing stuff though. Give it some thought." Jackie appeals again.

"Jackie, it's a no. Not for me. I don't believe in all that stuff." Our session comes to a timely end. The reflexology has certainly done the trick. I am so ready for my bed. I get myself up. Go to the corner chair. Put my socks and shoes back on. "How much do I owe you for this?" I ask. "Thirty pounds please." Comes her reply. She shows me to the door, I replace my coat. Hand her the money from my pocket. "Thank you Jackie, you were right, I needed this."

"Come again." She calls out as I walk out into the cold, damp night.

MAIRE 10

Tis the month of November, fourteen thirty. A year since the English child king's coronation. He is governed by Richard du Beauchamp. His mind controlled by the regency council. What fools these British are to honour a young boy. In Ireland, yes we have heritage. Yet it is to be proven. Not gifted. The last six months, Gwyneth and I have formed quite a formidable force. News spread of our small training ground. People came from neighbouring lands. Begging for a chance to seal their fate, gather skills. Fight for our kingdoms when the time arrives. An entire village of trainee warriors has grown outside the walls of our manor. Ivan keeps the peace, breaks up the inevitable brawls that the blood thirsty fall into.

I lie in my soft feather bed, under fine linen sheets, nestled in an ornamented canopy. Embroidery hangs either side, depicting our coat of arms. Mainly made of red and white. Shafts of light slice it into my room, through the wooden slats. One shaft falls on the three ravens, recalling my attention back to the Morrigan at the caves. There was no indication of this. Perhaps for good reason. I rub my stomach. It's been lively of late. By my workings I am due to give birth in two months. It is getting harder to hide my predicament now. Although I swear the bairn knows to keep small, I'm hardly swollen for my time. I had the farrier make adjustable fine iron plates, strung together with hard ropes. In order for me to continue with my combat skills. So far, so good. My secret intact. My unborn kept safe.

I raise myself. Take from the bed with me the thick cream woollen blanket. Wrap it around my shoulders, draw it close around me. It is cold. Very cold. Make my way to the window. Pull up the slats. The sky is a flat colourless grey. Fog hangs. Winter's naked branches of trees suspended in the silence, stare eerily back. I shudder, sense an air of foreboding. Two ravens are perched in the tree which grows closest to my chambers, in the same position as my tapestry. Only one is ominously missing to complete the arms. I question. Is this random? Or does this have meaning? My stomach grumbles. I hastily dress to go down to breakfast.

My father is always there before me. This day there is no sign of him. I take myself to the kitchen, where our cook is preparing our food. Oat porridge with thick milk. I notice she is preparing a tray too. "Where's my father?" I ask.

"He's sent word for his food to be taken to his room. My dear, apparently he has woken tired, short of breath."

"Warm his milk," I tell her, then hurriedly go to him. The damp fog weakens his lungs. I'm sure a morning of rest will suffice. I knock at the chief's door. There is no call. I knock again. Silence. I take the liberty of letting myself in. I can see my father is sleeping. I go to him. Pull over a small chair, sit by his bed. Touch his arm. He feels a little clammy. I notice too that his pallor matches the fog outside. Slight concern rises. I shake him gently to waken him.

"Father, tis me. Maire. Father, wake up." He slowly half opens his right eye. Catches sight of me, gives a wry smile. Coughs.

"Father, is it the damp again?" I enquire quietly. I can see he is struggling to catch breath. He calls me closer. "My dear one, it's worse this time." Every word an effort. Panic sets in. Though I don't show it. "Father, how?" I question.

"I'm finding it hard to breathe. It's as if my chest is crushed by Ivan's arse. I tried to get up earlier to piss. I had not the strength to move. You'd better make arrangements, call for the herbalist to come, see if they can mix me up a poultice. Draw the phlegm out."

"Of course father. Cook will be up soon with warmed thick milk. Try to take some. I shall go to send word."

I return to my father, having provided instructions at the gatehouse. Cook has obviously ruffled his pillows. Sat him up. I notice a residue of milk on the sides of his cup. He has consumed a little at least. He has fallen asleep again. I sit and wait. Aware that his breathing is shallow, slow. After a while he splutters and comes around.

"I'm back father." I state, hoping my presence consoles him. I hold his hand, he gently squeezes mine.

"Maire, I fear doom."

"Father, quiet now. Do not speak thus. You are the strongest of them all." I assure him. Which is true, in mind and body. No man has dared to cross him. Which has brought serenity to our community.

"Maire. The baby." I am taken aback. He takes a few broken breaths, continues. "I am not stupid. You're carrying." He proclaims. My mouth flies open. I swiftly close it.

"Father I." He interrupts. Feebly squeezes my hand again.

"Do you not think I would recognise your bodily changes, having walked with your mother through her whole pregnancy? Thought you could get away with proclaiming trapped wind did you? Well I was hoping to deal with this nearer the time. However, you must not divulge your condition. Do you understand?" I nod. Shaken.

"If I am to be taken, trust no one but Ivan. Inform him that he is to spirit you away soon, under my authority, he will think of reason for your absence. It cannot do for the people to know of this. It would undermine their belief in you." I close my eyes in shame. "Yes shameful you may be. However what's done, tis done."

"I'm sorry father." I appeal to his better nature. His reply surprises me.

"I do not want to know who the father is, you understand. I'd kill him myself had I the brawn I once had."

I inhale deeply, exhale slowly. Gut wrenched that I have let my father down. This will be the first and last time, I vow to myself. There is a timid knock at the door. I yell out. "Enter." A buxom woman, appears. Her scraggy greying hair falls to her bosom. She is round in face and body. She carries a material bag with her.

"Let me," she says. "I need to sit in your chair. Fetch me a large bowl, some water, a clean mug and a small spoon." I take my leave, head to the kitchen. When I return she has laid out various herbs on the bottom of the bed.

She gets to work. Takes the bowl, tips peppermint, sage and coltsfoot into it. Pours in a little water, works the mixture into a paste. She retrieves from her bag some cheesecloth. Applies the paste onto it. Folds it. "Lift up his shirt," she tells me. I do. She then gently applies the remedy to his chest. I can't help but notice it is somewhat sunken. Once done, she places his shirt over the top. Pulls up his blanket to cover him. "Make sure the poultice stays warm." She says. "It works better when it heats." The woman then takes a handful of ground thyme. Mixes it with a little water in the cup. Swirls it around. "Here, help me. He must drink from this." I tenderly approach my father. Lift his chin. He opens his mouth. The herbalist assists him in taking it. He splutters again. Half the mixture is dispersed onto the blanket. The woman remixes another bout, this time he manages to consume a considerable amount. The woman seems pleased. "He needs to rest now. You stay by his side. If this does not alleviate his condition, you need to be concerned. I shall take to the kitchen, wait. Grab me some sustenance of my own." With that she gathers her belongings and leaves. Father swiftly drifts off.

Unaware of how I can help. I sit feeling utterly useless. Two hours pass, during which the herbalist has popped her head round a few times. "That's good." She says each time, muttering that sleep is the best thing for him. She has not long left this time, when father awakes. His voice is barely audible this time he speaks.

"Call the men Maire. Now!"

I obey. Rush downstairs, raise the alarm. Shout out to Ivan. Anyone who can hear me.

"The Chief wants the men. Immediately."

Within ten minutes, father's most trusted men congregate in the hallway. I lead them upstairs. The woman is with father. "I'm afraid my potions have had no effect. This is no chest disease. I am sorry to say, I expect the worse. Prepare yourself. The men gather around his bed. I take back my chair. Hold his hand once more.

"He wishes to speak to you," I inform them. They fall silent in respect. Listen to his every word.

"My friends. I am not long now for this life. I wish you to witness the passing on of my title to my daughter. Hear me. Maire O'Cairagain. Only child of Mac O'Cairagain. Is upon my departure. Having earned her place. To become chief of the clan. The ruler of clan O'Cairagain. You are to support her as you have I. You are to protect her. You are to honour her." All the men say "Aye". Father appears pleased. There is a moment of calm.

Suddenly father starts to convulse. I jump up. Bend over him. Speak directly to his ear. "Father, remain. Do not leave, you have work yet to do." I plead, to no avail. His body jerks, contorts, his mouth froths. He cannot breathe at all, he is drowning. "Do something, witch," I shout to the woman. She merely drops her head. Father's lolls to one side. It is over. I suck in my lips with sadness. Not wishing to display my true emotions in front of these, my people. I need to serve. Not wail. The men remain standing. I close my father's eyes. Place a kiss on his bearded cheek. The eyes around the bed, close in mutual respect. After some while. I give my first command. "Leave us." I demand. They do as asked. "You too herbal woman." She bows in respect. Leaves too. I am left alone with my dead father. Only yesterday we enjoyed much frivolity. Though looking back he showed a shortness of breath even then. Sadness prevails. I turn my attention to the child within, talk to it. Tell stories of what a great man he truly was. Hoping the baby could hear. Wishing this day never dawned. Trusting I can justify the honour bestowed upon me.

KELLY 11

I wake up totally disorientated in floods of tears. My hands dart to my belly. "My baby, where's my baby?" I howl. Where am I, who am I? I am sweating, still in the grip of my night terror.

"Collect yourself," I say out loud. I hastily take myself to the bathroom. Splash cold water over my face. Pat it dry. Stare into my mirror. What on earth is going on? I look appalling, rugged. I give thanks to the Lord it is a Sunday. No café to wear a smile in. Church. No church today. I'd frighten off the congregation. I decide to take a cold shower, despite the time of year. Somehow a blast of cold water seems to do the trick when I am perplexed. It had better work this time, I can't carry the day through with this sorrow inside me.

I get undressed. Step into the shower, turn the dial to cold. The cascade begins. The below-zero water hits me hard. Makes me gasp for air. "Stick with it. Stick with it." I orate. It takes a good few seconds, before I feel the benefit. I spin around, making sure every part of my body is blasted, not an inch untouched. The familiar sensation occurs. The water washes away my anguish. My goal accomplished, I turn the shower off. Reach for my towel. My body immediately flushes hot. I am relieved, refreshed. I should do this more often.

I slip into my dressing gown and slippers. Go downstairs. Cinders has slept curled up on my chair. My footsteps alert her. She follows me into the kitchen meowing. "Ok petal. Just a moment." I always have to feed her first otherwise she mithers. Once done, I turn to my needs. Make myself scrambled eggs, veggie bacon, fried tomatoes, mushrooms, and toast with heaps of butter. I'm halfway through demolishing it when I notice a noise at the front. Oh good, my morning paper has arrived. I treat myself to the Sunday paper being delivered, and why not? One little weekly treat. When I get to the door, the paper is lying on the floor below the letter box. There's a timid knock. What? Who? On a Sunday, and with the way I appear. Grudgingly I answer. A young man, no more than twenty, takes one look at me and apologetically hands me a bouquet of flowers. "Oh I think you have the wrong number." I express. He looks to the gift card.

"Kelly Duffy. Number three, is what's on here," he responds. Shocked, I thank him and take them. Pick up my paper. Nothing is going to stop me finishing my breakfast. Nothing.

I don't know why. But I am putting off opening the envelope held on a spike in the flowers. They are gorgeous, a mix of white flowers, roses, lilies, carnations. Green foliage expertly placed amongst them. Who sent them? No. I will not find out yet. I retrieve a vase from my kitchen shelves, place them in with water. Not touching the spike. Pretending it isn't there. So long it's been since I had flowers delivered. I think back to the last time. One last ditch attempt by Adam to win back my affection. I couldn't bring myself to throw them in the bin, so took them next door to my elderly neighbour. She was thrilled. That was five years ago. Five years, blimey, I have been single a long time. Body clock ticking. Am I really bothered? I remember my bizarre dream and shudder.

Arriving back at my house, having enjoyed a lengthy walk with Cinders and still wrapped up, I go to my back yard. Fill my coal bucket from the bunker. Add some logs from the small store. Time for a proper February evening. With no mither. As I walk back through the kitchen the flowers wink at me. I ignore them.

Having spent the last three hours basking by the blaring fire. Watching a chick flick. Drinking a gin and tonic. Pandering to Cinders' scratch requests. I finally succumb. The gin seems to have mellowed me. I go to the kitchen, snatch at the card. Return to my comfy chair. "Here goes." I announce to no-one. Read it, read it again.

"Hey Kelly, I'm back up your way next weekend. Fancy getting together? Call me. Jim." Smiley face, no kisses, phone number. Unsure of how to react, I just gawp at it. I start to query his intentions. It's been over a month since we met. Does this mean he is one of those unreliable ones? Is he simply bored? Searching for a quickie? Or is it me. Am I frightened? Sceptical? Do I, don't I? Another gin and tonic is the answer. Dutch courage. I tinker with my fresh drink, bob the lemon around. Pondering my dilemma. Right I'll do it. No wait, its gone eight o'clock. Is it too late to call? Am I rude if not? Oh blow it. Here goes. I get my phone. Double check the number, press call.

A voice answers. It's a female. I'm thrown, physically flinch. "Er, er, I think I have the wrong number, sorry. The voice speaks. "Who is it? This is Jim's phone. Have you rang for him?"

"Yes."

"I'll put him on." She puts her hand to the phone, it's muffled. Then Jim comes on. "Hello, who is it?" He requests.

"Oh, hello. It's me Kelly. I just wanted to thank you for the lovely flowers."

"Hey, Kell, I'd almost given up on you. How are you doing?"

"Fine, fine." I canter, nervously.

"So, how about it, are you free Friday or Saturday this coming week, It would make my day."

My thoughts race. Am I really going to do this? Grow up. Take control. I answer. "Friday would be great." Trying to keep it cool.

"What do you fancy?" Jim responds. "How about we go to that Little Amsterdam place. They do a mean pancake.

"Good idea." I chip in.

"Great, I'll pick you up at seven if that's ok. Don't want you walking around in the dark alone!"

Is he patronising me, or being a gentleman? God, I have got to stop doubting. "Seven will be fine. See you then." Again, cool.

"I'll look forward to it all week. Bye for now." Jim closes the conversation.

"Goodbye. Thank you again." I disconnect the call. Well, I've gone and done it now. No going back. Brian must have passed on my address. Am I happy about that, or annoyed? Am I excited or bricking it? Who was that woman? And what a coincidence that my Dutch courage, led to dining at the Dutch restaurant.

KELLY 12

I've been trying not to think of my date all week. Not to think about it every five minutes, when it's popped into my head. The house is immaculate on the off chance Jim wishes to come in after dinner. Talk about a build up! I've barely eaten a thing. Walked twice as long as usual. Result. I can fit into my jeans. Whoop. It's been a while. Lots of things have been a while. Never mind full sex, my lips also have served no adult purpose since I split with Adam. Why has Jim shown an interest? He's a highly intelligent, successful man. I'm an ordinary girl, with a simple life. I look to my image in the long mirror, which is tucked on the inside of my wardrobe. Best that way, as I don't get to see my full image unless I choose to. Sleek suede high ankle boots, which zip at the back. The jeans, yep, up to date. A baggy black linen blouse, crosses over my décolletage, revealing just enough of my ample breasts. "Best bit," I pronounce, giving them a quick grope. Who knows what the night may bring. "Whore." I goad myself.

There's a resounding knock at the door. Someone is eager. I fancy. I go downstairs, grab my handbag. Stop myself from grinning too much. Open my door to him. "Good evening Jim."

"Why hello Kelly, your chariot awaits." Jim puts forth. Mocking a bow, I shut the door behind me. Allow him to lead me to his vehicle. It's an old green land rover defender. "I love this old boy," he informs. "Had it many years. My sister Sarah keeps it now." He goes to the passenger door. Opens it for me. I climb in as elegantly as I can.

We are on our way back to my house. I go over in my head the core of our conversation. Jim very quickly told me the voice on the phone was his mother. Phew. He must have guessed I'd query that one. He told me of his childhood. He and Sarah had grown up in a semi-rural area. The house at the end of the road was used as a children's home. All the kids used to play outside. He and Sarah with a few of the local kids who bothered to get to know them. The obvious stress that these children were under had a profound effect on his choice of career. His determination to help others have the childhood he did, led him to his vocation. In his daily life he comes across those afflicted. Orphaned, abandoned. Victims of violence and abuse. He does all he can to bring them comfort, justice. Strongly advocates placing children in foster care, and up for adoption. Some of the cases he works break his heart. However, justice mainly prevails. Even occasionally securely placing the child or children back with their natural parents, when they have wrongfully been taken. We both laughed at the fact that I was an old maid. He never married. Choosing instead to dedicate himself to his cause. He considers all the children he helps as his wider family. When questioned as to my lack of children, I was pleased to inform him, I have the same thought process on the matter. I like him. Will this go any further? Do I want to invite this man in? You bet I do. This might be awkward mind. Rusty Kelly. I'm working myself into a lather. He walks me to my door.

"Do you wish to come in?" I enquire. For a moment his face looks perplexed. What for?

"Yes Kelly. That would be lovely," thankfully comes his reply. I show him into my lounge. Invite him to take a seat on the freshly hoovered sofa. No cat hairs to embed in his clothing. I take more attention now to the way he is dressed. Quite casually, jeans, loafers. Pale blue shirt, dark blue cardigan. Yet still an air of money emanates. Cinders wanders in from the kitchen, inquisitive of our new guest. She eyes Jim up. Decides she likes him. Rubs herself against his legs. I excuse her. "Don't worry Kelly, I'm quite fond of cats." "Here girl." Jim calls. Cinders immediately jumps onto his lap for attention. Umm wouldn't mind a bit of that myself!

"Would you like a drink? I ask.

"Yep, tea please, one sugar, a little milk." "Coming up." I reply, then swiftly take myself away. I return shortly, place the cups either side of the sofa on the small coffee tables. Sit myself down, consider cosying up. All through the meal the chemistry between us was magic. Now I have him in my den, anxiety sets in.

"Relax Kell, I'm not going to eat you."

"Oh that's a shame." I taunt.

"Come here." Jim states. Takes my hand, pulls me closer. I'm that close-up, I begin to inhale him. My, he smells good. Sweet, fresh, with slight odour of a real man. Bingo.

I place my hand to his cheek, he turns with it, drops his head. Takes his hand under my chin. Goes in for a kiss. He begins slowly, gently, running his tongue gracefully around my lips. It tickles. Not for long. Soon rampancy washes over. We begin to hungrily fumble at each other's clothes. Cinders scarpers. Bless her.

"I wish to take my maiden upstairs." He rises, takes my hand, "Show me the way Kell." He grins. He sweeps me in his arms, picks me up. I cling to his shoulders as he climbs the stairs. I notice just how much muscle that cardigan had been hiding. Lucky me. We enter my room. He turns on the light. I immediately turn it off.

"Let's just let the clear night sky light our way." I suggest. Not wanting to undress in the full glaze of a bulb.

"Romantic are you?" he allures.

"I can be." I reply in a mischievous tone. The mood set, we both fall on the bed. Our garments are swiftly removed.

We gyrate, kiss, he pulls back my hair. I like it. Pleased that he's not going to be too soft a bed partner. I feel his penis rising against my belly. I move away a bit, slide my hand down to play with it. Perfect in length, girth. A little banana shaped. Great for my g spot. Bee Jeez, the thing only goes flaccid on me.

"Let me play with you for a while". See if that inspires my little man. Confused, wondering what's wrong? I agree. Jim proves to be an expert in yet another field. He sucks and bites his way ominously down towards my pussy. My body quivers, relinquishing all shyness. Impatience grows. Having been starved of touch, penetration for years, I am desperate for him to speed things up. He's there, at my goal. He inserts a finger into my tight vagina. Uses his thumb in circular movements around my hood. My sex area starts to jerk in response. My breathing escalates. Warmth builds in my abdomen. Oh heavens, I've never been so wet. This is divine. I relax and let go to the pressure building between my legs. I cry out in sweet ecstasy. Mission accomplished. He removes his finger. Takes a well-earned feed. Still gasping, I place my hands to either side of his head. He moves up my body. Kisses me with reverence. I await his penetration.

He flops to one side. His face flushes red. "I'm sorry." He says, looking down. I follow his glance. There also flopped to one side is his soft penis. Disappointment kicks in. Followed by my feelings on unworthiness. "It's not you Kell, it's me. Ever since I met you on New Year's Day, I've been unable to hold an erection. It's all gone, even my bountiful morning glory days.

"Why, what happened?" I whisper to him, not wanting to add to his obvious embarrassment.

"I don't know. This intangible sense of tremendous responsibility kicked in. I've no idea where it came from. No idea what it's about! I almost didn't come in tonight. Dreading it wouldn't perform. Willing it to work. Not wanting to let you down. In fact that's why I left contacting you until now. I awaited its recovery." Jim tells me in a low voice.

I snuggle up to him. "Jim, it's alright. You were amazing. I'm grateful. I hope I don't scare you." I smile up to him.

"No Kell, there's something very special about you. May be next time." He resorts.

"Bugger that." I reply. "Viagra here we come. Thank god for modern intervention." We cling to each other. Jim pulls up the duvet. We fall asleep simultaneously. Each wearing a sanguine smile.

MAIRE 11

The day following my father's funeral rites, Ivan whisked me away. He took me on a journey I found arduous to ride. Five days took us down south west, to the seat of the seventh Earl of Desmond. James and his wife Mary, tended to my every need, whilst allowing me my privacy. Desmond Castle entranced me. Set on the north shore of the cascading river Deel, in the county of Limerick. Although cold, it is by the river's edge, accessed by stone steps, that I sat almost daily. Contemplating my future. My loss. The child inside me soon grew heavy. Now having permission to thrive, away from prying eyes, I was glad of the walled ward. The moat. I felt guarded. Mary checked on me regularly, mostly in silence. Fully aware of my sorrow. My anticipation. She cordially arranged for two women, schooled in the craft of midwifery to attend my birth. Alas the child came early, on the first day of a new year. Having two sons of her own, Mary found herself assigned the duty. With grace, the child was born with ease.

I named her Fianna, after our legendary warriors of old. As I looked lovingly to her, suckling gently at my breast for the first time, she tentatively opened her eyes. A mirror into my soul. Striking blue like her mothers. Her short thick dark hair, the hue of her father's, stuck up to the sky. There will be no mention of his name. No man shall be aware of her origin.

Fianna banged her tiny clenched fists against my chest. My daughter shall be resilient, rugged. Of this I am sure. It took five days for my bleeding to subside. After which I was able to present her to Raphael. He whinnied so gallantly when he saw my face. I unwrapped my bundle before him. He in turn connected with her, nuzzled into her tiny belly. Pawed the ground in elation.

With a heavy heart, my time here was soon to be gone. The Earl's wife, having arranged for a woman from the local village to come to stay at the castle, is to take charge of Fianna, until my calling is done. The woman lost her son two days ago. She has milk, a kind heart. I am assured that James and Mary shall pay attention to her care. Once the woman is known to the baby, happy to feed from her breasts, I shall prepare to leave. The woman return to her abode. Last night, at midnight. The bairn, three weeks old, safely sleeping in her cot by the fire. I went down to the river bed. Sourced dried reeds, caringly made a Brighid cross. Held it to my heart, wept. Blessed it. For the goddess Brighid shall protect my little one now. Imbolc is approaching. The time is nearing for me to return to my seat. My first duty. For we need to prepare. For I know not when our persuit will come. But come it shall.

MAIRE 12

Tis half way between mid-winter and mid-summer. My band are before me. All standing in and amongst the stones at Ballynoe, within the stronghold of Patrick. Wearing cloaks, brandishing our various coats of arms. The sundown is nearing. The sky to the west is aglory with reds and oranges. Perfect battle colours. Gwyneth and Ivan stand as human pillars to either side of me, our backs against the cold north stone. Facing our enemies, the wind blowing in their direction, aiding our intention. We stand in revere, each silently praying to the gods. Asking this sacred site to empower us. Lighted torches follow the stone circle. I look to the warriors. Some have trained with us, others joined us of free will. The Duke of Desmond has sent his men to favour our battle. I am grateful, they are as fearless as my clan. Two years have passed since my intern with the Duke. We plan to attack north of Carlingford. To press the British further from our lands. Unrest has brought us to this point. Warnings whispered in dark houses. The British planning to expand their territory. We are to gather in three days to commence our attack. It is time for me to speak. To bring together these people before me as an almighty one.

"We are here placed on the precipice of our future. Pioneers for our land. Our citizens. Our country. United in hatred. The cantankerous British before us, insult us, fuelled by avarice.

Their minds out of kilter, ruled by dark forces. I call upon the skies. We shall extinguish their fires with our piss." The men roar. "May our fat fingers of death scurry forth, as a demon child taking its first feast on the unsuspecting. We march for justice, peace on our soils. To appease the people who loved and died for us. Reclaim our fathers' house. We shall no longer succumb. They shall beg for mercy, we shall take no prisoners." The crowd shout yes in response. Raise their fists. "We honour those that honour us. The rest can flail, be impaled. We are prepared to spill our blood, to have theirs stick to our mud. To be our fertilizer. We have sharpened our nails. They shall cut like diamonds. Their vanity shall perish. We shall stuff their hair in our pillows, spit on those that have spat on us." Another roar.

I shout into the wind. "We will cull you. Make a beautiful mess. Not warning you of your fate, it will implode in your faces. Your lust for our demise rises in your loins. Your balls shall be annihilated" I look back to my men. "Follow the language you know. Taste it. Feel it. Be it. Get inside your competitors' guts, smell where they are. Drink dandelion and nettle tea the night before battle, to empty your bowels. So they cannot smell your shit. For a warrior eking fear is vulnerable. Have the eyes of a hundred owls. Do not copulate after midnight, I need you burning with desire. Bring out the ale, the drums. Our innards need music to lift up our intentions. Light the central fire in thanks. For this night will mark our impending victory. The bloodiest will win." The men holler in joy, raise up their arms to our triumph. The celebration commences. I am pleased to witness the druid slip from behind the south stone, I had wondered as to his whereabouts, his input vital.

Ivan, Gwyneth, the druid and I leave the circle, walk a little down the cairn. It is time for us to finalise our tactics.

We sit together. A man approaches. He is dressed entirely differently to us. His long black hair curls to his chest. His beard well kept. He is short in stature too. Stocky. "What is it?" Ivan commands. "Allow me to introduce myself, I am Angus of the MacDonald clan of the glens. I've been in Antrim some time now. The Duke of Desmond sent word for me to meet with you. To offer my services." Ivan laughs.

"Aye, do not be fooled by my appearance." Angus states.

"You're wearing a skirt." Ivan jests him.

"Aye, tis my choice of attire. Allows the wind in, not a skirt, a freedom." His garment, pleated falls to his knees. It is made from goat skin. He wears mottled socks, with a dagger tucked in, a belted plaid thrown around his shoulders. He has black leather shoes. A feather in his bonnet. The druid's eyes bore into him. Evaluate his worthiness in his own way. "Sit." He says sharply, making room in our small group.

"So, what is it you can do?" Ivan queries.

"I do give you my bond. I'm a well-honed fighter. Trained from a wee lad. My name is well known amongst my people. I'm here to offer my skills. Stocky as I am, I am a swift as an arrow. None pass by me." He informs us.

"Very well. We are here to finalise our moves. Your knowledge will be helpful no doubt." Confirms Ivan.

"Aye that I shall. You'll nay be disappointed with ma skill," Angus assures.

We mull over our objectives, our choices. After much consideration, Gwyneth draws her sword, and describes with it our attack plan on the ground.

"We will start here. Just north of Carlingford. Men will go ahead of us. Dig trenches in the night along the main entryway. As soon as men step onto the path, ours shall rise, discard their camouflage. Kill all but one. Allow the one that thought he got away to report back. He will be our coercion. The rest of us will wait down the valley, hidden in the woods. Maire, Angus and I shall lead the ambush. Ivan, you are to ride the first chariot, laden with weapons, decorated with my family's seats trophies. Driven by a lesser fighter. Directly behind us. The other chariots shall follow you. The rest of the horsemen will then flank the remaining chariots. We are to take the form of migrating birds. Archers are to remain hidden until required. The unsuspecting will be torn to shreds, unable to penetrate our flanks. Remember no prisoners. Once the defeated lie scattered, let their guts spill, blood flow. Take their heads for us to parade. Then store for any future terror. The warrior declared champion, shall have first pick at the loot."

Whilst heading back to join the entertainment, Angus takes a bag with pipes attached from his back.

"Permission to play my Piob Mhor, amidst your drummers war call?"

"Why not, I've heard they pierce, motivate." I smile to him. Back within the circle, warming by the fire, Angus assembles his instrument. Puts it to his mouth, draws a large breath opening his chest. He blows. Following the beat of the drums, the sound prophetic, immediately arouses the hearts in us all. We sway, taken in a trance, to another world. The druid steadfast, watches over us. As I freshly look to the stones in the dimming light. Flushed with delight. The fae who presented in the cave are playing amongst them. Their animals too. Joining in with the scene in the aether. The tiny white horse gallivants, galloping in and out of the circle, around the stones. His rider firmly seated, waves her arms in glee. The other small folk ride their rams, foxes, goats. They simulate battle amongst themselves. Whoop with delight. Other fae clamber around the rocks. Leaping, pirouetting. Aodh sits atop the highest stone, little elves preen and stroke him. He delights. The white horse runs to me. Stops abruptly before me. His dark rider salutes. He then bares his teeth, spins, takes off to re-join his army. We are blessed indeed.

KELLY 13

Awakening to the soft sound of Jim's breathing is pure pleasure. I study his half covered body. His face chiselled, handsome. His limbs toned, his muscular outline plain to see even whilst in slumber. A fine blanket of hair adorns his broad chest. How lucky am I? I roll onto my side, snuggle up, play with his man hair. Running my fingers through, twirling. I love it. Why some men shave everything off these days is beyond me. Can't beat a real man. He stirs. Turns to me with a huge smile on his face. Good, no regrets then. Gives me a peck on the cheek. "Would you like a drink?" I sleepily ask him.

"Arhh. Yes. However, you serve all day. I'll take charge, go downstairs. Bring my Kell breakfast in bed. What do you fancy?"

"Surprise me food wise, though I need a coffee, black. One sugar."

"Coming your way. He rises out of the bed, his six foot frame is hard not to admire. He goes to the corner chair. Picks up my blue fluffy dressing down. Puts it on.

"Oh my." I state, bursting into giggles. He gives me a twirl with it loose, then fastens it.

"You doze my dear. Your butler will be back soon." Jim goes downstairs. I can hear him clattering about, it amuses me.

He returns with a tray. Two hot coffees, two plates of scrambled eggs with sliced avocado. "Yummy. Thank you." He places my coffee on the bedside table. Hands me my food. "This is wonderfully done. You secret chef." Once eaten, Jim suggests we shower together. Oh lord, quite intimate my mind says. Blow it.

"Ok. I'll lather you up good. Will have to be a quickie though as I need to leave at eight for work." I respond. I get out of bed, still naked. Jim takes my hand, leads me to the bathroom. The room not huge, does have a powerful modern shower, with a waterfall shower set into the ceiling. Together with a hand shower, ideal for reaching under bits. I step in. Turn the water on. Jim turns his back to me, slowly lowers the dressing down to the floor. I admire his taut bum. Shame he couldn't use it to pound me last night. Just being with him, in this moment though, is enough.

The water warms, he joins me. Our lips kiss, softly, passionately. He grabs the shower gel, pours it into his hand. Suggests I turn around. He rubs the gel into my back, up over my shoulders, his powerful hands massage my tight muscles. I throw my hair back in delight. I feel more cool gel being applied lower. He sweeps over my whole back, over my buttocks, I arch in response. Jim runs a finger down my crack, up to the front, fingers me from behind. I wasn't expecting sexual activity after last night. I'm getting it. I smile to the glass partition. Glimpse the image of our passion. It excites me more. I turn round. "You now, you dirty boy." I tease Jim. He readily turns round. I copy his moves, relishing the firmness of his body. His breathing changes. The water washes away the foam. I take my mouth to his back, nibble him over and over. Take myself down. Hold onto his waist. Kiss his clenched cheeks. Bite tiny bites.

He switches to face me. His cock is up! "I think Kell has worked her magic." He grins. Without wishing to waste this opportunity. He roughly turns me around, pushes me against the marble tiles. I stick out my arse in deep anticipation. He is within me in seconds. I squeal thrilled. He places one hand against my shoulder, the other to the front of my hip. He starts his motion. Very slowly uses his placed hands to deepen his penetration. As his thrust quickens, I am drawn back to the music in my ears as I woke. His member follows the beating drums. For a moment I am lost. Then he kicks up his power, pounds me as no man has ever. Takes his hand from my shoulder, yanks my head back by my hair, moves round my face. We kiss, tongues flicking wildly with hot water flowing over us. Releases his grasp on my hips. Reaches for the hand shower, switches the water flow to it. Turns the dial to a jet. Places it hard against my clitoris. I howl. My whole body starts to shake. My legs give way. I lose the ability to hold myself up. Jim takes control, uses his bulk to support me. Squashes me into the tiles. My breasts heave against the now cold tiles. Every piece of me stimulated. My pleasure rises. "I'm coming. I'm coming." Jim yells. I feel his sperm travel up his shaft, deep into my dwelling. My body quivers. The pressure builds. He picks me up, supports my thighs on his. Every inch of him inside me. The top of his penis reaches my g spot. I explode in unison. My groin contracts over and over. The feelings rush over me entirely. I am in wonderland. He slowly draws out of me. Helps me to stand. Turns me to face him. He kisses my face, my neck. Looks me straight in the eye. "Kell, there is a part of you that scares me, I have to admit. I'm scared I'll never see you again."

"Oh Jim." I reply, placing my face into his wonderful wet chest.

The water now off. Jim grabs a towel. Pats me down like a little tender child. I am bewitched. Jim wraps me up, pulls a towel down from the rail. Rubs dry his hair and body. Secures it around his waist. Jim grabs my arms, pulls me to him once more. We embrace. He picks me up. Walks me back to my bed. Sits me gently down. I glance at my alarm clock.

"Heavens." I say aloud. "I'm going to be late." With no time to dry my hair, I tie it behind with a bobble. Quickly dress. Jim retrieves his clothes from the floor, puts them on.

"I know the café isn't far." He quips. "However I'll drive you there, may save a minute or two."

"Go on then, you're on." With that I race down the stairs. Quickly feed the cat. Am at the front door, ready within seconds. I ask Jim to drop me round the corner. Our village is small, gossip rife. I don't need that. Opening the back door. I'm aware my legs are still shaky. I can't quite believe the intensity of our love making. I'm ignited. Long may it continue! Jim has promised to spend the night with his family. He vowed to return tomorrow, late morning. Said we'd make a day of it. Take me to a special place. Asked if he could stay over again. Of course I agreed.

I hurriedly prepare the café's kitchen. Go to the front, turn the notice to open, unlock the bolts. Looking up, I'm taken aback. Ricky's face is pressed up against the glass. Pulling a ridiculous clown like grin. I open the door, he almost falls in. Throws himself at me. Squeezes me tight. "Why Aunt Kell, your legs are like jelly. Had a good time then." He cajoles me. I flush.

"How would you know that?" I reply, trying to appear innocent.

"I tell you Kell, there was this one girl, just this one. After our naughty sessions, it took her legs hours to calm down. You can't hide that one from me." Ricky taunts. "Tell me. Kell, come on."

"Oh, it's a guy I met last month. Its' early days really."

"Early days." He mocks. "Seems to be you've started with a rather big bang." He howls with laughter.

"Shh Ricky, the whole street might hear. Come inside." We quickly close the door behind us. "We can go in the back, I'll put on the kettle. "So, let's talk about you. You seem lighter."

"All that fear I'd held onto. What a sausage. Mother wasn't too shocked, although I did catch her weeping in her bedroom as she told my dad. I went to sleep petrified about how my father would react. I was summoned to his study the next morning. He had an old black and white photo on his desk. "You see this son, this is a picture of you great great-grandfather. Harry. Take a look." I took the photo from him. On it was a man in uniform, looking proud as punch, standing next to a Spitfire. "Fought for his country he did. He was shot down in June, nineteen forty, during the battle of Britain. We always had patriarchal blood in our bones. After he died, I'm afraid the women of the family took over. There was to be no more such talk of joining any military field. My father was banned, I was banned too. My dreams of flying shattered. Therefore Ricky. I am not ashamed of your career choice. I'm overwhelmed with pride." He stood up, embraced me. We both sobbed. Me with joy, Dad I suspect from his own unadventurous life, together with sense of new found freedom, that sharing my journey with him will resolve his disappointment."

"Oh, what a story Ricky, I feel moved myself. So have you made any plans yet?" I ask.

"Yes. I've decided to finish my education, it will be my first step in discipline. I've downloaded the army fit app. I've started to train at the gym, take long runs. I'm improving each week. When I feel fit enough, I will apply online. All going well, I'll then have to go to a two day assessment centre, in Aldershot. I've been told to dress smartly. I have no medical conditions, so I know I'll get in. Kell. I'm so excited I could burst. However I must keep grounded, focused."

"Ricky. I am so pleased. You seem to have matured so much in the last six weeks. You will do brilliantly well in the army. Congratulations."

"I might make a Lance Corporal yet Kell. I'll whip off now. Going to have a legs session today. I just wanted to salute you for your support. My bravery tested." Ricky plants a little kiss on my cheek.

"Bye private. Take care."

Ricky leaves. I am left satisfied, my work there done.

MAIRE 13

June fourth, fourteen thirty three. Twenty one years of
age. The eve of our battle. I follow the druid deep into the
undergrowth, Aodh accompanies us. Leaving my army to
roast the venison, settle their final preparations hidden in the
woods. Dusk is settling. A sure calmness resides with uneasy
apprehension, even fear. After twenty minutes of clearing
our way through, there is a lightness in the air. We stop by
a large oak tree. A large raven calls overhead. "Look to the
bark Maire." The druid orders me. I do. I'm wearing a blank
expression. "Look harder, delve deeper." I try. Right before
my eyes, the bark morphs into doorway. It is pushed from the
inside. Megan of the Morrigan steps out. Presenting herself
as a young, lithe maiden. She takes three vials from an inner
pocket, draws the corks. "We are to take this simultaneously.
She hands two to us. We follow her direction. Drink in one
swallow. My body starts to buzz, I'm panicked, allow trust to
encase me. My body shakes, I feel sick, bend over to vomit.
Straighten myself. "What is this?" I ask the druid.

"We need to be small to enter the fairy kingdom."

All the foliage looms around my now half sized frame.

"We will open a portal for you Maire. Are you ready?"
Surprised, I answer, I am. Megan removes the familiar

wands, again hands one to the druid. They both hold them up in front of themselves to the air of nothingness. I soon stop pondering, where upon a glimmering dome forms. Made of all the colours of the rainbow. Its beauty radiates. "Come with us." Meghan instructs. "Aodh is to protect the opening. The druid and Meghan just walk right though, disappear from my sight. I follow them in. Laid before us is a site to behold. A circular village of buildings, white, tiny, perfect. Fairies hover above the ground, playing. Their garments gossamer-thin. Animals roam freely. "We have been invited to their temple." Meghan informs me. Follow me." I am entranced. The fairies, now distracted, fly at us. Their tiny wings emit a quiet hum. They fly right up to our faces. Peer at us, stare at our clothes. Giggle amongst themselves amused. Follow us. On our way we pass what appears to be a working area. Gnomes are gathering baskets of stones. Piles of catapults lye beside. Along with minute glowing bows and arrows. Elves are busily polishing wooden carts. Flowers spring up all over, perfume the air, their hues transparent. They seem to whisper to each other. Clusters of bright red mushrooms abound. A great privilege encases me.

We approach the temple, the fairies leave us. Pure white marble steps lead to a golden archway. We are greeted by the black fae, riding her miniature horse. He seems enormous now. He bends one knee, outstretches his other leg. Bows before us. All menace gone. My eyes are drawn to a fire pit, which sits in the middle of the round temple. Fay of the Fae dismounts, tells us to sit by the fire. Her eyes are brilliant green, enchanting. We all sit cross legged on silk cushions. "Dear Maire." Faye starts. "At first dawn we shall assemble ourselves on the edge of the woods. We are to charge immediately before your tomorrow. I will lead with Tinker. Her horse snorts above her. His breath breaking the fire's flames. None on the battle field except you shall see us. Do

not be distracted by our assault. You are to remain focussed on the human task. For whilst our stones and arrows will weaken the etheric bodies of our foe, they shall not kill."
A life size hooded crow glides through the open doorway. Lands by Faye. Tinker, cross, flicks his neck to the bird. "He's harmless Tink." Tink backs off. The crow places his beady eyes before Fayes. They communicate telepathically. He then squawks, leaves us in a flurry, drops a tail feather. "You will have your fill tomorrow." Fay shouts after the bird. "Patience."

"I need to show you something of importance to you Maire." Faye says, getting up. I follow her towards the inner walls. Along the side sits a marble pillar, with a glass bowl atop. She takes her finger, licks it. Places it in the centre. Starts to stir. Look into the bowl. I obey. As her finger swirls outward towards the bowl's edge, the water takes on a life of its own. Colours start to form. The water seems to solidify. A picture emerges. In the bowl is a moving scene. A little girl, feeding, petting chickens. A woman stands to the edge of vision. It is the woman from Desmond Castle. Reality hits me. This is my child. My Fianna. "See, she is well comforted. She's a happy child. Fret for her not. You will be reunited in time. The woman tells her stories of you. Fianna listens with glee. At two and a half years old, she has the understanding." I place my hand to my heart. Use the other to blow her a kiss. The child looks up, straight at me. Smiles. I am thrown, amazed. How is this possible? Faye answers my thoughts. "All is possible in our realms." Meghan calls out to me. "Time is running out, the portal shall close soon. Come now. We must leave. I quickly thank Fay for her cooperation and care. Risen from the knowledge of Fianna's safety, I had been informed many times of her progress, this confirms it.

The three of us depart. Acknowledge the little people bustling around. The ferocious animals now lie around, huddled together, dopey, gathering their energy. We wave, express our gratitude. I laugh as we return to the opening. Aodh's beak is poking through, his eyes darting, taking in the wonder. As we walk through, we are instantly transformed back to our former selves. Megan has turned, the young damsel now back to the crone. She places her back against the oak tree. Raises her arms. Her gnarled appearance sinks into the gnarled bark. She is once again gone. I outstretch my arm. Aodh hops onto it.

Back at our bivouac, I see much has been done. My troops have energised. Tents are all erect. Weapons collected, laid on the chariots. The chariots themselves have been decorated as I ordered. The two chests from my father's hallway were brought to us. The skulls of enemies past, now menacingly adorn the sides. I am satisfied. The druid bids farewell, roams deep into the woods to perform his rites. Ivan approaches. Informs me the first men have advanced for their initial attack. I retire to my makeshift abode. Sleep fitfully.

MAIRE 14

The day of reckoning is here. In the art of war for us. Our appearance is vital. We need to strike fear in the enemy. We rose early. Gwyneth and I each ceremonially decorate each other. Our hair braided from the top to the sides, hers glorious blonde, mine brazenly red. The remaining locks swing free, interwoven with chains. We tie our hair high above our crowns, fit our adapted helmets on, pulling the pony tail through. We each wear necklaces of owl bones. Sacred to us for wisdom in battle. Ivan who has dropped his usual loose robes, is dressed like us and the other fighters. His large stomach protrudes. We brandish colours of our arms. Red shirts, the martyr's colour, concealed under our back and breast plates. Mail skirts protect our thighs. Foot soldiers wear armoured vests. The sign of a chevron across our chests for protection. Gauntlets cover our hands. We finish off with green, unfastened cloaks, which shall camouflage us in the woods, until we are ready to roar.

The horses too are adorned. Mine alone has scrolling tendrils, depicting ravens, down his reins. Bright green material cover their backs, to match our garb. Each wear a shaffron, crinet, flanchard and crupper, made from toughened leather and iron. Their forelocks cut short, to heighten their sight. Despite Angus's weight, he has insisted on the smallest charging horse, swears he can dismount and remount at the speed of light. Prefers to be seated at neck height to slice them open. Some of the horses are becoming agitated, sensing drama. The charioteers have laden their mediums. Swords, shields, pike axes, lances, javelins. Yet others contain spare falchion swords, polearms. Mallets. Along with my death traps. Extra strong nets to ensnare, the remainder of the household skulls, entwined along their edges.

The sun is rising. Its heat creeping along the woods behind us. Ready to blight the oncoming English. Six horseman gallop to us. They are the ambushers returning. They hold at the edge of the wood, duck under the branches, enter into the inner, where branches have been cleared. Go straight to Ivan as planned. He sounds his horn. Confirmation to the garrison of a fruitful start, to stand by. The watchers, placed some distance away, beat their drums. Fifty of us emerge, find our places, take-up our arms. The rest stay behind, await command. I am the head of our triangle, Angus and Gwyneth flank either side. The sound of horses' hooves gets closer. The English come into view. Upon seeing our numbers they swiftly curtail, for they are few. We hold our positions. The bowmen and crossbowmen hiding in the foliage too, ease their weapons. We await their infinite return.

Our drums resound. Over the horizon the English garrison spills. Swallow-tailed heraldic flags, flap above them. White, in the sky, with a red Saint George's Cross painted upon. So much pomp. A waste of a good limb. The men wear the livery of blue, gold. Their armour more updated than ours, still has gaps for our hooks, spikes, blades.

I scream my war cry. Dig my spurs into my horse, he leaps into full speed and we are charging towards our foe. A mist rises from the earth. The little folk before us, as promised. They fan out with great haste to encircle the English. I watch as the gnomes throw stones continuously. Faye and her band intricately begin their combat. Weave in and out, unseen, jabbing at legs, spooking the horses. Charging. Flying onto the English shoulders, slicing, stabbing at their astral throats with tiny shiny daggers, throwing the riders off balance. Tinker, ears back, teeth bared, rears and bucks, bright blue eyes ablaze. The foxes, badgers, gnaw where they can. The goats butt. We start our Celtic cries. We roar, scream. Intimidate and terrify our opponents with our ferocious calls. We leave behind our humanity, become primeval.

The two opposing parties clash in a frenzy. I take up my sword, swing, it slashes into my target, a soldier. His head half severed, lolls to one side, his gullet ripped open. "Hark!", I yell in bloodlust. A ball and chain rushes through the air towards my horse, I parry. It falls hungry to the ground. Angus strides out before me now. One, two, three struck with his spiked club in a matter of seconds. Prowess proven. I concentrate on my offensive, proud of Gwyneth's shared battle skills. I hurl myself into the violence. A huge man takes me on. He has a double sided axe. The brute leers. The axe sweeps down my shoulder, just missing my flesh. I nimbly use my point of percussion, catch out his eye. Which hangs like a bloody oyster on his ruddy, fleshy cheek. He lashes out, again misses, falls to the ground. Drowning in his own blood. Deep in the affray I now need to be weary, watchful like a hawk. I stand in my stirrups. A soldier wielding a spear, his eyes ablaze with hate, takes his chance. Thrusts it against my side. The blade is not sharp enough to pierce through my armour, the spear hangs loose. I retaliate, pull it out. Swipe my blade under his armpit, twist, he cries out. Holds tightly to his horse, blood flows down his side, with his right arm weakened, tendons and muscles detached, hang like broken violin strings leaving the bearer unfunctional, soon to perish. I move on.

Ivan comes to my side. He points to the hill. English infantry
are running towards the rabble. I twist round, see that ours
too are evacuating the woods, to draw their fire. "Ivan,
time for the sign to raise the bows." His driver passes Ivan
the pole, he raises it. The small red flag atop signals attack.
They are well drilled, will do their duty. "Man at arms."
Ivan shouts to me. I swiftly flick my body to the right. Just
in time to block a sharp blow. I bear my teeth to the bearer.
My sword slams into his helmet, he is stunned, I swiftly
lower the sword, plunge it into his right leg at the knee.
Blood courses, ligaments on show, His eyes glare into mine.
I remember Ivan's tuition. Use stealth tactics. I take the
crow hammer strapped to my back. Slam it into his groin,
before he has time to retaliate. His horse rears, he falls back.
My hammer crushes the eye of his horse. The horse falls
crushing him. "Next." I snarl through gritted teeth.

Infantries from both sides now intercept the cavalry.
The charioteers furnish fresh weapons. I take a long axe.
The sharpened gleaming blade cleaves right through the
foot shoulders, the axe thrusts right through their chain
mail. Two are dead instantly, with the old one, two. Their
bowels leaking through the mesh, squirming, pump out
their foulness. The fighting spreads, the skilled bowmen
start their assault. Arrows fly to their destinations like
swallows. Unlikely to kill, they puncture, enfeeble, disable.
The crossbows yet to be released. The archers told strictly
to fire only if necessary. We don't want to show our full
arsenal unless we need to. Ivan is having murderous fury
with his extended ball and chain. Gwyneth and Angus
now dismounted, are decimating the enemy with their steel
swords. Her hair stained with blood, flicks with no mercy.
With my horse tiring, I dismount, fling myself into the fray.
Stride to a chariot, take a mighty axe and my heraldic shield.
Join the chaos.

Then with my short sword, race into the thick mass of whirling bodies. I take a savage blow to my back, Gwyneth has parried the impact. I fall to my knees. Quickly recover. Heightened adrenalin flows. I crouch like a panther, lunge to my attacker, my sword up under his chin, into his neck and into his brains. He falters on the blade. I withdraw the blade. He stumbles, tumbles, collapses to his death. Angus goes volcanic, with swiftness unsurpassed he rages through the remaining attackers. Gwyneth and I survey the surreal drama before us. We slam our hands together with glee. Then win the battle.

We fight back to back, hurling our blades at any unwise enough to approach. Another, then another, then another. All without fear, inspired by hate. We cut them to pieces. Our years of experience providing annihilation on the field. I am drawn to the activity of the Fae. Animals are jumping on the dying. Tinker rears up, stamps his hooves repeatedly on a wounded soldier. Rams, ram. The Fae whoop with delight. Stabbing with their minute translucent daggers. Necks extended. Grinning heinously. Then I spy him. Johnny. For a moment my motherly instinct sets in. Swiftly followed by the knowledge that many a woman has killed her child's father. I sign to Gwyneth, protect my back. Wearily I approach my tall, regal opponent.

Boldly he stands five paces before me. The man I once loved, I who took his sperm. Hands on hips. Wielding his broad shield, his long sharp blade. His physical advantage looms. I give him a longing look, lure him into a false sense of pity. I shall match him, blow for blow. Surprise him. I begin. I step forward. My mind clear of the past. Lurch, on balls of feet, swing my sword, over and over, side to side, above, below. He parries each attempt. I have met my match. I get in closer. Determined to kill him. I speed up my manoeuvres. With each effective sharp swift shot, hatred oozes from my mouth like froth. He appears aghast. Continues to deflect. I drop my shield. Take both hands to the hilt on my sword. A vicious blow downs him, he flips back, stumbles. I stand over him, usher my insult. "Turnabout." This angers him. He retrieves his position before me. With my agility, my balance training, I'm in the ascendant. With great speed, I rain down many blows. I open his right arm to the bone. He tries to lunge at me once more. My blade accurately finds the soft tissue of his belly. It plunges in. Defeated, yet still at war with me. He crudely attempts to stab me. His wound takes greater hold. He leans forward, yawls, drops like a bull awaiting the kill. Johnny's eyes question mine, pleading. Mine do not answer. I take from my belt, my dagger of mercy. Thrust the point through his eye. Lay him down. Smile. Savour this moment I have longed for. Twist the dagger, blood spurts. His body jolts, goblets of brain erupt. I spit in his oozing eye socket. "My country never sleeps." The last words his ears hear. He lies expired, slain. Remorse does not touch.

I turn my back. Look to the carnage. His army beaten, lies on our soil. Blood of revenge does indeed seep to our land. We have dead and maimed. The enemy has more. The clear up commences. Angus will sever the heads. "Not that one." I yell. Leave that one on a spike in the middle of the corpses." I want to make sure Johnny's brothers know he has perished. Fallen to a female warlord. No doubt there will be reprisals. I hold my soaked sword to the sky. "Take your spoils." I shout to my flock. The crossbowmen, collect the bodies of our dead, load them onto the chariots. They will be prayed over soon, before being respectively thrown in bog land, to preserve their sacrifice. Men go to gather the scattered horses. Gwyneth and Ivan assemble the wounded. The Fae have vanished, their part completed. Wearily, wend our way to our

secret hideout. News will travel fast. More of our kinsmen
will join us.

Reaching our destination. We disrobe of blood stained garb.
The blood that stains our skin will sleep with us this night.
Merriment of victory begins. I do not rejoice, the beginning
battle won, not the war. Sitting in contemplation on a lonely
rock. Reflecting the days passing. Marvelling at our first
victory. Ponder what shall ensue. Killing Johnny did not
fell me as I'd worried, it enhanced me. It had to be done,
tis done. The sounds of the night still my thoughts. Aodh
silently glides through the night air, joins me. I rest my hand
on his back. Cast back to my inauguration day. The death
of my father, the birth of my daughter. The druid led the
procession, carrying a lantern. Raphael carried me to the
entrance. It was a blowing day. A moist mist surrounded us
at the north circle of dragon's teeth. Stood before my people.
Barefoot on a bed of beetles laid on the ground, depicting the
Celtic cross, the druid removed my dress. I stood naked. Bare
except for my amber necklace. Primitive, before the crowd.
The druid then draped a hooded cloak over me, made of
seal skins, offering transformative power. Control over land
and sea. I vowed to serve. Pledged to be faithful. The druid
performed the right of passage, ordered from on high. I knelt,
kissed this emerald isle. All hailed. I peruse. Have I fulfilled
my promise? Have I adapted myself well to my heritage? I
lick my surface wounds, unfelt at impact, in the climax of
creating a carcass mound. Yes, I am satisfied. Without doubt
a good auspicious start. I thank the gods.

Suddenly my body starts to jolt, through short sharp breaths,
large salty tears trace like snail trails through the blood on
my face. Why do I weep? A battlefield is not a field of joy.
Corpses like broken marionettes. These men fought, not for
glory, but for their mothers, wives, families relying on the

money they earned. I conjure images of flies swarming on congealed blood, maggots to emerge from ripped intestines, the hooded crows will peck with delight. A herd of wild boar rush past me, to emerge from the woods, to tear at dead lifeless flesh.

I weep to denounce myself for revelling in death. I feel the cuts of a thousand wounds. Screams ring in my ears. Clashing metal resounds. Last gasps of the dying shroud me. I retch, choke. Has my humanity gone? Hypocrites will wave flags and rejoice, the righteous, the pious will vilify, impugn, condemn – I spit on them. Then it came, reality or no that death will come upon them. I weep for me – I know that death will overtake me too. Let me die a hero.

I achingly trundle back to the camp, to offer congratulations. For ale to quench my thirst. On the battlefield the victors took their spoils. The English were stripped of their armour, their weapons. I find my troops sat round small fires, laid in a circle. Performing a ritual practised for centuries. Eating hearts and brains. Blood corses down their mouths, cheeks, necks. Hearts eaten to embrace the spirit of war, brains of the commanders to filch wisdom. I find Gwyneth squatting, holding a thin branch over a flame. Pieces of flesh dangle from it, fat drips, sizzles in the heat. We look to each other. I retire to my tent.

MAIRE 15

I awake. Do not stir. A musky smell pervades. My hands are held high and together above my head. A weight sits on my chest. Legs clamp either side of my ribs. Think. How would the guards allow this? My dagger rests under my pillow. I remain, eyes shut. Not wanting to alert the person above me to my knowledge. "Ha." A voice I recognise as Gwyneth. "Time for my reward." My heart calms. I raise my eyelids, whereupon I spy Gwyneth in all her naked glory sat above. Her vagina open, gaping, wet, calls eagerly to my promise made at the deal in the castle. I rise my gaze to her eyes. They are questioning mine. I nod. She moves her body up further. Rests her womanhood above my mouth, rubs it back and forth. Releases my wrists.

The short wiry pubic hairs tickle my chin and nose. Her odour heightens. She must have washed, the smell of horse sweat, the dried blood have both disappeared. This is my first time eye to eye with another woman's sex flesh. New to this, however I know what pleases me, so I start. To disappoint would be the greatest insult. Gingerly I open my mouth, slip out my tongue. Curl it to make a point. The curled end reaches her clitoris, encases it. I start to flick from the bottom to top. Gwyneth arches her back, her blonde hair falls over her shoulders. I absorb the contours of her body. It is leaner, tighter than mine. Her tattoos now in full view seem to take on a life of their own. The snakes on her arms writhe. Move up and down with her. The dragon upon her chest, comes to, bringing its own force of fire. I admire her masculine beauty, muscles honed as the best of men. She pushes the full weight of her upper body down on my face. My face encased in inner and outer labia. Their heat intensifies. I move my tongue into her, they swell, flush. She groans. Falls forward, my tongue is taken in deeper as she climaxes and throbs against it.

She straightens herself once more, moves away slightly. I take my hands, place them to her hips, up onto her pert, pink nipples. Her breasts which are highly held, tilt upwards. I encircle the dragon tattoo. My fingers trace its outline. She roars. Takes a hold of my right wrist, forces my fingers into a cup position. Grabs my arm. Violently slams my hand into her hungry orifice. "Now make a fist. Fuck me like a man." She demands, I do so. Holding onto her taught left buttock with my free hand to steady her. "Harder, harder." She insists. "Deeper bitch. Satisfy me as I have satisfied you. Give me all your power." Gwyneth commands. I push my arm deeper into her, pummel with all my might. Her ferocious passion rises, her legs begin to twitch, pin me tighter in her grip. We both gasp for air to fuel our bodies. Her from passion. I from work, grateful to have my mouth free for air.

Gwyneth starts to grunt. I am shocked by her guttural tone. She drops her body wantonly as far as she can onto my arm, my elbow now firmly wedged against my bed, with no reprise. My muscles weakened by battle, cry for release. Sweat trickles down my forehead, behind my ears, into my hair. Gwyneth rides my fist faster and faster. She lets out a cry. A sudden gush of water flows down my arm. It is not urine, I'm baffled. There is no odour to this clear liquid, perhaps inside her somewhere is the organ of a man.

Gwyneth puts her hands to my headboard. Shoves her wet throbbing pussy back to my mouth. I am bewildered and not amused.

Gwyneth gets off me, dresses. She leaves without a word. I go to wash her off me.

KELLY 14

"Jim, would you mind if I went to church this morning?"
I question. I've woken quite perplexed. There's a feeling of
violation I cannot shake off."

"What is it my special one? Is it me? Have I pushed too much,
dropping in unannounced last night?" he enquires.

"No Jim. No. I'm feeling odd, like I've been trampled by a
herd of cows."

"Well, I can assure you that's not happened here." He
chuckles, pulling me in closer. Let me help you feel better."

"Jim, I'm sorry. I really need to go to church. Take
communion. Be cleansed of whatever this is. It's odd, and
certainly nothing to do with you. I'll rustle us a quick bite to
eat. Then get ready to go to Mass."

"Would you like me to come with you?" He gently asks.

"It's ok dear. I wish to go alone. To find some peace. I'll
probably go for a walk after. To reenergise. If you'd like to
meet for early doors later, that would be lovely."

"Kelly, I'm sorry, I've a plane to catch this evening if you
remember. Work calls." He says.

"Oh, yes sorry I forgot. My head's just fuzzy. I do apologise. I know I need God."

"You're a funny little thing." He cajoles, stroking my cheek.

"Please don't see me as mad," I plead as he leaves. I have kept my strange dreams to myself. Telling him too much may make him turn and run.

"You are not mad Kelly, just different, delightfully so." I have a few days on a big case which shall take up much of my time this week. I'll call you on Friday evening, or earlier if it settles sooner. I don't mean to be aloof. It's just a big one. One which the outcome certainly matters to me for my career, and more importantly for the child concerned."

"I understand. You do honourable work indeed. I can wait." I reply. Secretly dreading that I've made a boo-boo. I quickly tidy the kitchen. Grab my bag and coat. Head to Seapatrick Church.

Whilst walking, my mind takes over. Am I being punished for sleeping with a man who I hardly know? Yet deep down we seem intrinsically connected. Why did I wake up feeling odd? Jim so far has shown me nothing but kindness. Have I perhaps had yet another strange dream which has imprinted in my waking mind? How can I feel so shit, when I've just had the most perfect few days? I cannot understand my woe. What has made me feel so contaminated, as if my very guts have been torn from me? My soul has been encroached? I have heard vaguely how a man's sperm can integrate with more than a woman's body. But how? And why would Jim's sperm disempower me? No. It has to be something else. Something I have yet to...perhaps shall never fathom.

I am not let down by today's sermon. The Canon starts. "Today I have chosen to read from Ephesians 6: 10-18. The Whole Armour of God. "Finally be strong in the Lord and in the strength of his might. Put on the whole armour of God, that you may be able to stand against the schemes of the devil. For we do not wrestle against flesh and blood, but against the rules, against the authorities, against the cosmic powers over this present darkness, against the spiritual forces of evil in heavenly places. Therefore take up the armour of God, that you may be able to withstand in the evil day, and having done all, to stand firm. Stand therefore, having fastened the belt of truth, and having put on the breast plate of righteousness, and, as shoes for your feet, having put the readiness given by the gospel of peace. In all your circumstances take up the shield of faith, with which you can extinguish all the flaming darts of the evil one, and take the helmet of salvation, and the sword of the spirit, which is the word of God, praying at all times in the spirit, with all prayer and supplication. To that end, keep alert with all perseverance, making supplication for all the saints." The congregation remain hushed. "The peace of God, which passes all understanding, will guard your hearts and your minds in Christ Jesus. Philippians 4: 6-7." Again, he pauses, we remain quiet. "In the same way, the spirit helps us in our weakness. We do not know what we ought to pray for, but the Spirit himself intercedes for us through wordless groans, and he who searches our hearts knows the mind of the Spirit, because the Spirit intercedes for God's people in accordance with the will of God. Romans 8: 26-27." Canon Stevenson invites us to kneel.

"Dear Lord, father of us all, Holy Mary, mother of God, may you bring your sanctuary to those weary in heart. The saddened, the lost. Give us your grace to fulfil our needs. Today we pray for ourselves, each and every one of us. For, what is prayer if it does not start with the self? Be selfless God's children, yet start at home. For what strength can you offer if you are yourselves weakened? I say to you, rise up, seize the day, in confidence that Our Lord and Lady are by your side. The Holy Spirit resides in each of us. We need merely to ask for supplication for it to be received. God has created many kingdoms, whereupon we shall all reside. Trust in the Holy Spirit to rid you of your demons. It is he, in his kindness and wisdom that can cast aside your troubles. If you feel yourselves touched or damned by misfortune. Turn to Our Lord, for he alone knows the truth. He, when asked will while away what haunts. Clear the remnants of the past. Hold you tenderly in his gracious arms. Lift you from despair. Cast aside the things that under misguidance have entered your mind. Know that you are cherished beyond your knowing. Ask God now to lift your spirit, to take it unto himself, so that you may dance in the cleansing waters of love. I invite you all now, to take a few moments for your private prayers."

I pray to Our Lord and Lady. "I do humbly ask that you rid me of the dread from which I woke. Restore my soul to peace, to love." Already I'm aware of the heaviness lifting. "God the Father, Son and Holy Spirit, return me to my serenity. Remove the garb that befell me through the night. Guide me in my meanderings, in my trust, on my path. Enlighten me. Keep me strong and purposeful. Give me this day your daily bread, and deliver me from evil. Amen. Oh, and help Jim with his case." I can't help myself, so used I am to praying for others. I sign the cross.

The Minister sets the incense to the burning coals of the thurible. Its essence is wafted, swung across the altar to purify the eucharist. Once this ceremony is complete, we dutifully line up to take Holy Communion. I await my turn with reverence, anxious to partake. It comes. The Canon administers to me "The body of Christ." Kneeling I open my mouth, savour our Saviour. "The blood of Christ." I drink from the chalice of life. My body involuntarily shudders. I intrinsically know my pallor has lifted. My gloom taken away by the power of God. Halleluiah. I cross my chest three times in reverence and thanks. Return to my pew, bow my head and praise the Lord with all my heart. Gaze up at my favourite stained glass window. The last supper. This act of Christ in his final hours brings such hope to us all. Our selfless, forethinking Jesus.

MAIRE 16

Having washed the liquid from my face and neck, I change my nightdress, put on some sandals. Wonder out in the quiet night. A new moon hangs gracefully in a clear cerulean blue sky. My mind starts to whirl. What of the men slain, unmothered, unprotected, crying. Dying alone, with no ease. Perished, dead, mortality has mortified. With no mourners in our bones. Souls unheard, not respected in their fate. They lie in a field mortuary well beyond their time. Annihilated in a moment of non-satisfaction. The dead walk alone. Death walks alone. Oblivion, obsolete, not encompassed. Their kingdom shall not come, their hearts eaten, broken. Christ be warned, there is an army of hollow souls tapping at your door.

Merriment has taken its toll. Men drunk with victory lie passed out in various positions, dotted along the bracken, the moss. Some are still, others twitch like sleeping dogs, reliving in their dreams the last hours of yesterday's horror. I take myself further from the camp. Seeking solitude. Become slightly bewildered, when a movement across in the trees catches my attention. I creep closer, then stop, hide behind a large oak tree, to spy on what I behold. There two people are engaging with each other, against a tree with two trunks split like twins. Two naked bodies, their filthy backs to me, are leaning into the trunks. The one behind is tall, fair. Fit.

Am I a monster to watch this spectacle? No. Curious! The one that he is fucking is smaller, squat, unkempt locks of dark hair rocks on their shoulders, as the two trunks support their body from the forward thrusts of the fair haired one. His penis as it draws out to thrust some more, is like nothing I've witnessed before. It is huge. Groans emit. The fair haired man rests his left forearm atop his prizes arm. His right hand is hidden from me. Yet plain to see is manoeuvring in a wanking action to the front of his maiden. As if his fist is banging against the woman's clitoris. I'm not sure I'd be grateful for this action. It would not serve me.

Groans become grunts. I am taken aback, having presumed one of the cooks was getting a good seeing too. Both tones are male. Pleasure now eludes their throats. The actions quicken. Two sighs of absolute pleasure release simultaneously. The one in front turns his head to kiss the fair haired chest. Angus's face, illuminated by the slight moon reveals itself. I take care not to emit surprise. They turn to each other, caress. Stroke. Two dampened, hard penises glisten, touch. Exchange of the last drops of sperm takes place, as each takes a finger to the dew, and passes to the others lips. Scrotums rub together gleefully in appreciation of the gift in time. I turn my back to my tree, drop silently to the ground. Hug up my knees. I am brought to thought. Why was Gwyneth merciless, mirthless? Thankless? Her eyes looked to me as blades. I'd been repulsed by her act, concluded same sex interaction was uncivilized. Now, upon witnessing the tenderness in the dark, I question her intentions, her release.

Is there something I am choosing not to acknowledge? Am I in peril? Or have I grown cynical, untrusting, from loneliness that abounds my task, yet protects. I am a diamond admired, yet uncut. Nothing will break me. I will henceforth borrow Aodh's eyes to search for treachery. Order the Druid to select feet and hand bones from the dead from both sides, to use in sorcery. I shall be weary, more alert. Better informed.

MAIRE 17

I am down at Whiterocks beach. Fianna is playing happily before me, turning cartwheels and squealing with delight. I am content. Fianna is five years of age. Her beauty surpasses mine. She will grow into a strong independent woman like myself, I have no doubt of that. I have started to instil the qualities passed down to me. The last year has been blood free. I look to the calmed sea, which emanates our collective thoughts. For two years we fought ferociously. Drilled battalions of gallowglass came down from Antrim. The MacDonnells of the glen, connected to Angus, joined forces. Brought with them their great and mighty bodies, who'd rather die than yield. Marauding kernes set our lands alight with their flesh destroying tactics. Together we pushed the Pale into paler significance. The British have dug fortified ditches to protect what remains of their territory. Those two years saw an influx of flies.

Fianna has my competitive nature. She will not give up until she perfects all she does. Already she rides Raphael unaccompanied, he seems to sense her greenness, obeys gracefully to her commands. He is set free to munch among the white rocks. Aodh effortlessly circles above, cooing to himself. I treasure this scene, this serenity. Long may it last! I've left my home to spend two weeks with my daughter this summer. Guests of the MacDonnells. The sands are enchanting. I take my daughters hand. Kiss her sweet cheek. Sweep my fingers through her ruffled hair. Run towards the water's edge. She giggles, her thin legs follow mine. We paddle, play jumping the waves. Throwing caution to the wind, I undress. Fianna squeals. Pulls her frock over her shoulders. I throw our clothes to a safe distance. Pick her up. Wrap my arm under her bottom, snuggle into her neck. Mother and daughter take to the sea. It's cooling. Blissful. My feet sense the sand breaking under my steps. I meander in further, until the water is at waist height. I spin, Fianna lets go of me, leans back. Her long dark hair skits along the waves. I am in love. Looking back to the cove, I see Aodh has settled himself on Raphael's withers, they too have an unbreakable bond. We head back to the sands, lay out our garments. Lay down on our backs. Stare to the blue sparkling sky with content. Hours pass. We return to our dwelling, all on my horses back. Wrapped in bliss.

A delicious spread of food was laid out for us upon our return. Fianna gobbled as much as her stomach could stand. She peacefully went to sleep, murmuring of the fairy stories I'd passed on. I am sat outside awaiting the druid, who is to take me in the night to a magical place. I have an inkling of where this is, but have not revealed my thoughts. The druid likes to surprise me. As the sun dips out of view, I spot him walking towards me. His dark hooded cloak billows in the wind, as his feet carry him closer over the horizon. The weather has changed. Rain threatens. I pull my soft green cloak around me. He greets me. We set off.

The moon full in the night sky guides us on our path. It takes a few hours to reach our destination. From the top of a cliff we hastily descend. The scent of the ocean grows stronger. Waves clash against yet unseen rocks. Clouds loom. Release their rain. The moon amongst them lights up the stream of rain drops in front of us. Creating shards of light about us. With each trepid step we take, the sheer power of our destination intensifies. We speak not a word, not wishing to disturb the dominion emanating around us.

The site that beholds me mesmerises, as we turn our final bend. Hexagonal pillars of all lengths loom, in their secluded bay. Mist sits over smaller ones besides the sea. The clouds shift, the moon lights. I shudder. The druid smiles. He leads me to the water's edge. We take off our shoes. Energy shoots up my soles. He warns me to guard whilst walking over the slippery circular rocks. A few feet in, he instructs me to sit upon a designated seat. He stands steadfast to my right. "You can be a soul destroyer or soul bringer Maire. The choice is yours. We are given our tools, teeth, nails, thoughts. Our actions are ours to decide." "There is madness in me, I cannot deny, promises too." I reply. "That is why I have brought you here. You are no fool. The gods wish to thank you for your purpose fulfilled. Be silent now and close your eyes. Let your very substance drop into the seat. Immerse yourself into the rocks, become part of them. Let their mastery enfold you."

I let myself glide down into the cold damp rock, trickles of sea foam cleanse my feet. The sound of pebbles being wafted along the sea floor enchant my ears. I feel my body drift down. My bones become the stone. I fall into the deepness of this splendid place, my body seems to disappear unto itself. I merge with the entire scene. Becoming smaller and smaller. When nothingness takes over, I am suddenly huge, magnificent. A kaleidoscope of brilliant colours start to flood over me. They seem to come from the above. The form of an angel appears, tall as the sky. The colours radiate from her, to me. Filling me with a love of nature, transcending human love. Indescribable. As I am held in the arms of this angel, an immense gratitude flows between us. I am aware too of the druid basking in her glory. Time stands still. Humility abounds. I fall asleep. Soon the druid wakes me. The area still throbs, the angel is gone. I look to him. He speaks. "This is one of the few remaining areas in our world, where an earth angel is still attached. Men's demonic, selfish thoughts have driven most of them away. Their purity threatened their existence, they had to return to their realms, before they shrivelled."

"Such sad tidings," I sign.

"We must head back now before the rise of the sun, the rise of your daughter. Tell no one of your experience, for sharing it will dissipate its force, the power unleashed tonight was for you alone." He takes my hand. We retrace our steps, return to the cliff. Follow the trodden path of the animals back to the MacDonnells abode. Along the way the druid stops, faces me.

"Maire, I have to share, there is a personal peril on its way. I know not what. However, remember this. Worry only distorts. You, as a magnolia tree, can take the rain, winds, frost. Yet every year it shows its glory. Remember this my child. I shrug. Everything has a place, a reason, a time.

MAIRE 18

It's that time of year again, when I take myself off into the oak forest to gather mushrooms, which will be hung to dry in our barn. I come alone. To this place, the mighty oak is our symbol and strength and survival. It is my time of reflection. I am wearing my mother's amber necklace. A simple brown long dress. My green cloak. Leather ankle boots protect my feet from the undergrowth. My hair tied behind me in a single plait. Acorns are starting to fall under the canopy. Squirrels collect them one by one, take off to their secret places to bury them. I have left Raphael down by the stream. He is so greedy he'd eat anything. I need to keep him away from the acorns as they are bad for horses to consume. I gently hum to myself, in my own world. Placing the mushrooms and fungi into my sack. I hear rustling, small twigs snap. Alerted, I stand up to check out my surroundings. As I do, a beautiful badger startles and runs. Unusual, is this auspicious? "Relax Maire." I tell myself. The forest is teeming with life. A mother deer and fawn jump, scamper from danger.

The forest floor is damp, autumnal leaves of various shades carpet the undergrowth. A gently blowing wind brings with it scents. I delight. The winds blows leaves in a joyful dance. One reveals a hunter's trap. I dread these things. Poor animals, they are often left caught, badly injured, left

to die in agony, while the drunken hunter forgets where
he laid the damn thing. As is my custom, I go to set it off.
Bend slightly over it, place in its jaws an old broken branch.
Snap. It shuts, unfed. The noise echoes in the peaceful
surroundings. Temporarily shutting down my excellent
hearing. With total horror, I realise I've been set up in a trap
myself, as a heavy fishing net falls from above, capturing me.
And five masked men set upon the task of gathering their
bait. They manhandle me. I fight with all my might. Then
realise it is futile; better to preserve my strength for what I
am to face. With my whole body tightly bound, I am carried
to an opening where seven horses are tied. Roughly they
manhandle me, three men throw me on my stomach across
one of the waiting horses back, like a sack. "Got you bitch."
One snarls. First mistake I think to myself. A voice I never
forget. When I'm free, he will be sought.

We set off. One horse remains behind. I think of Raphael,
hope his ears picked up the drama. Hope he gallops straight
home. We travel out of the trees. I'm aware we are heading
south. Some hours pass. We climb into a mountainous area,
the route unfamiliar to me. The terrain changes. From my
viewpoint, which is mostly looking down, the horse carries
me over sparse land. Hawthorn bushes and heathers, close
to the end of their natural cycle motivate me. It is not my
time to die. We reach a mountain peak and stop. One man
drags me down to the ground, I land with a thud. They
turn me round. "Look what we've planned out for you
princess." Quotes the man who spoke before. I see nothing,
say nothing. I am hauled on my back across the rough
scattered stones. My head is battered, bashed. My back too.
To my utter dismay my cherished heirloom leaves my neck.
"There my lovely." The man mocks, showing me an open
grave, containing a roughly hewn coffin. Now I panic, to

their delight. The men laugh. "Heave ho." They chant as I am picked up and dumped inside.

"Untie me." I plead.

"Piss off." One answers

"You deserve this. You foul woman." With that the lid is closed. "Don't panic. Don't panic." I say to myself. Listening the drumming of soil falling from their shovels, the sounds of doom.

The rattling of small stones mingled with dirt dim as the grave fills. The men whoop, jump on top of me to tighten the earths grip. I detect a horse approaching at full speed. Pull up to an immediate stop. The rider dismounts. "Is it done?" The rider questions. To my utter dismay, the voice belongs to Gwyneth. I am shaken to my core, feel utterly condemned to death, my fate cruelly sealed. The horse left behind must have been for her. For her alone knew of my yearly forest jaunt. I force myself to breath slowly and cautiously. Knowing full well once the air is consumed, I shall perish. I hear the party dissipate. Tones of course laughter rip out, as the villains congratulate each other. Then silence, naught but black silence, and the gentle heaving of my chest. I bend my knees up to the top of the coffin. Use my feet to gather momentum. Push against the rough wood with all my might. The wood cracks, gives a little. Soil and grit begin to filter through. The meekest shard of light appears, the earth above me trickles in slowly. I cannot move any further being bound, however I am able to push myself back hard against the headrest. I remain still, suspended in time, in hope. I remember the tomb voyage, how I hated it, until I calmed myself. So I force myself to sleep for protection against insanity.

I awake, unaware how long I have been incarcerated. Yet aware of my shortening life span, as the air thins. My heart palpitates. My body is stiff, sore. I ache inside too as I feel my organs slowing. I give my knees one more blast at the cracked wood. To no avail. The earth above has filled the tiny, precious gap. Darkness enfolds, holds me in its grip. I shudder. The cold has chilled me now. I shake uncontrollably. In my final moments, madness takes over. I imagine hooves thundering over the land. Pass out.

I come to, lying on wet ground. Hands turn me, unfasten me. Hands I know well. Ivan is on his knees. A terrified look on his face, mixed in with relief. Aodh stands above my head, his wings stretched out. His beak stretched to the sky, open, complaining profusely. A dozen of my father's trusted men, are around us, covered in wet soil. Horses' heads hang low, smothered in white frothing sweat, held by two men. Their flanks bellowing, their nostrils flared, sucking in air. Ivan gently strokes my face. Sits me upright. I am dizzy. Little stars swim about me. "Take a moment. Do not fret. Remain still. Nothing can get to you. Now allow me to replace this."

He takes from his large coat inner pocket my necklace, places it tenderly back where it belongs. I try to get up.

"Too soon Maire." Ivan states. For once I listen. He sits besides me. Aodh calms, comes to my side too. I rub my eyes, they are sore.

"Here", Ivan passes me his water flask. I splash the water into my eyes to clear fragments of soil. "That's it my warrior." Ivan speaks to me as my father would have.

I come back to myself. My senses returned. Realize something is missing. Alerted, I cry out. "Raphael, where is

Raphael?" "Calm yourself Maire, he is fine, he has a few cuts. I will explain. Your faithful horse came to the hold. His reins had snapped, he must have gotten them tangled and fallen. But come he did. Whinnying, tossing his head in distress. The men at the gate spotted him. We were immediately alerted that something was amiss. He is being cared for. Do not worry. His cuts are slight. He's a strong one. We gathered these men with great haste. Aodh went ahead. Raphael had enough left in him to guide us to the spot where you were ambushed. Raphael found a torn piece of your cloak amongst the foliage. He was then taken back to rest, as we started out search. We were not far away when it started to rain. Alas, this is the reason for our delaying in reaching you. The tracks were washed away. Being in the mountains, it was impossible to know where they took you. Aodh searched for two hours. He then found us, dropped your necklace from his claws. He used his head, his body, wings to give us direction. We followed him up this mountainside. We got to you just in time Maire, as the rain had densened the soil above you. My child. We thank the heavens for your safe retrieval. Let's get you home. I am in no state to go into my ordeal. I'm helped onto a horses back. We slowly descend.

Upon my arrival home. All are gathered solemnly in the main yard. I speak one sentence. "Worry not. Together we are indestructible." Heads lift and smile. I go straight to my horse. He is lying down in his stable. He lifts his head. Glee emanates from his gaze, he starts to rise. "No my love. Stay down." I coo to him. Aodh lands on his open stable door. I then kneel by his side, let my body fall over his. Sob and sob with gratefulness for my divine creatures. I settle after some minutes, notice Ivan is stood in the doorway. His eyes question. "Gwyneth." I shout out. His face reddens. He storms out. I sleep on my horse, he sleeps with me.

KELLY 15

I'm just about to shut up shop. It's Thursday the eighth of February. We've had a pretty miserable week weather-wise. Which is no surprise for Northern Ireland. Locking the back door, turning the key, I get a little tap on my back. I lift my head to see Jackie's round, happy face smiling. "Hey, Kelly, How's tricks? Thought I'd bob down to say a quick hello whilst I was in Banbridge, lovely little town isn't it. Do you fancy a quick one?"

"Well, why not." I reply. It will certainly take my mind off Jim.

"I'll take you to Harry's bar. It's close and comfy."

We arrive, seat ourselves at the end of a large table. Settle in. It's quiet. The barman takes our order. We both go for a large glass of merlot. He brings them over, we say "Cheers." Clink our glasses.

"So Kelly, how have you been, since your last visit?"

"Well, guess what, after five years of being single, I seem to be entwined." Jackie raises her eyebrows, her eyes sparkle.

"That is good news. How do you feel about it?"

"Jim is kind, sweet. I've not heard from him since Sunday which troubles me."

"Is this how he normally behaves?" Is her next question.

"Umm. Well, he did take a while to get in touch after we first met. And, to tell you the truth, he does have a job which occupies his mind. He warned me of the case he's working on, said it was important, so I guess I'm perhaps being over anxious. I do like him. It's odd the bond we seem to have after such little contact. But it's there alright. I'm just worried of being too hopeful. Making a mockery of myself." "Don't be silly Kelly, look at you, you are delicious, a good catch. I sense your great kindness and self-sacrifice. It is certainly time you had some fun. What does he do?" I inform her of Jim's job. Jackie helps me settle my mind. "Barristers do have mountains of paperwork bundles to scour through. They need to be sharp. Perhaps he couldn't distract himself with your soothing voice. Sometimes, it is good to make first contact. I bet if you phone him tonight he will pick up, if even only for a few minutes."

"Ok, I'll give it a go, the silence is killing me."

"Do that, oh and to spice it up a little you could try phone sex," Jackie laughs. "What's that?" I ask with a puzzled expression. We spend the next half hour giggling like school girls. Whiling over the content of the supposed call.

"I've got a good feeling over this one Kell, good luck." Jackie says. As she leaves she gives her bum a little waggle.

At home, I greet my cat. Start to fluster. Jackie suggested I send him a saucy photo. That's easy enough to say, but what of? I rack my brains. Think Kelly, think! My blue dressing down? Nah stupid! I know. The new underwear that I'd ordered from La Senza. Umm cheeky little number. Rather like a vintage lace French basque with attached suspender belt. That might get his juices flowing. It's worth a go. I carefully place the black basque against a backdrop of pink tissue paper, together with the packet of black seam stockings. Take the photo. Get ready to send the text. Gulp. Push send. Yikes. I start to shake a little. Grow up woman, what could go wrong? Plenty. To my utter joy, within five minutes I get one back.

He sends me a picture of his wig and gown, thrown haplessly on his bed. Together with the words, "Give me ten minutes." I start to heat up. Cinders looks at me like I'm crazy. I rush upstairs to prepare myself.

The phone rings. I put it on loud speaker. "Good evening my honourable gentleman, do you wish to dishonour me?"

"Why yes fine lady, I wish to turn you into my slut." Jim rasps to me.

"Be my guest. Tell me what you wish me to do." I tease.

"Are you wearing your basque?" Jim enquires.

"Why yes, I am, my stockings too. Would you like me to keep them on?"

"Everything on. Everything. Go to your wardrobe, take out your highest shoes. Put them on." He commands. "Now do as I say." I lay back on my soft sheets. "Push out your breasts from under the basque Kell. Fondle them as I would. Imagine I am atop you. You are running your fingers through the wig on my head. My gown covers us both in this mysterious moment. I am naked bar for that. You are mine, only mine, surrendering there for me to pleasure. Now wet your fingers, take them to your nipples. As you do, I am sucking on your pink flesh. Your nipples arouse into my mouth. I hear your pleasure, I hear your arousal. Your breath is reaching down to my forehead. Now. Move your fingers down, down, part your knickers and open up your labia."

"Yes Jim, yes. What are you going to do to me?"

"I'm going to gobble you up my dear. Wet your fingers again, so your clitoris can sense the moistness of my tongue. I am upon you now. My tongue dances on your clitoris, licking in a fashion unfelt before. Move your fingers up and down, where my tongue is seeking its desire. I am erect. Move your knickers far enough aside for my throbbing cock to enter you."

I groan out in pleasure. "Good girl. Prepare yourself for my thunderous entrance. Slam your fingers hard into your pleasure pond." I gasp. I can hear Jim too, as his excitement grows. His fever rises. "You are not allowed to come until I tell you. If you do I shall punish you, do you understand?"

"Yes, Jim, yes. I'm ready, I seek your approval, just tell me when to climax." "Not yet my little whore. Wait for your master to judge that."

"Of course, of course." I can barely respond, my body is trembling. "Now woman now." He falls silent, I hear in the background him lashing his penis. "I'm coming, I'm coming." Jim informs. We groan together in joint fulfilment. The only conversation now our heavy breathing in unison. Finally we both settle. Jim disconnects the call. I am temporarily shocked, until a text comes through. I will be with you at 7.30 tomorrow night. Be ready for me, I expect everything utterly. I squeal with glee. Yes. Yes. Yes.

MAIRE 19

My father came to me in the ether last night. I was lying in bed, in the early hours, unable to sleep. When suddenly a feeling came over me. From the space above my head, my father's hand appeared. I recognised it immediately. I was so emotional. Shortly he said to me, "I'll see you when you get here." Confirming our belief that the dead live. He then went on to tell me that he is absolutely adamant that Gwyneth be sought, taken, killed. He told me to gather my council, together with the wisest of his men. We are to use wit, cunning. Then once we have her to be very open about her internment, death.

"Lucifer shall knock at her door." His last words as he departed.

We are gathered now in the main dining room, which is decorated with tapestries depicting battle scenes. A few new ones hang in place, commissioned by myself to provide an everlasting memory of our combat. I look to one now. Gwyneth sits proudly on her horse, axe held high. I shall slash it to pieces. Her image erased for ever. Another shall be made portraying the death of the traitor. A warning to others of her fate. I have yet to decide how to plan it, draw it out. We sit along a large oblong wooden table, on the benches at the sides. Two large white candles placed at the centre flicker away. Ivan is pacing the room, pure fury flows from his face, which is still as red as it was yesterday. I sit at the head, the druid sits opposite me. With a large sack before him.

The druid speaks. "Ivan, sit down, I need your energy to combine with ours. My powers require the number of thirteen sat. Ivan looks cross. Pacing is his way of thinking. He obliges. The druid stands, raises his arms fully outstretched. Tips back his head. Chants in his mystical language. He then grabs the bag, holds it high. Utters more words. Replaces it on the table. Releases the string. Tipples the contents out in a forward motion. Bones collected at our first battle spill out. The way they lie, is of great importance. One of the candles is knocked to its side. Hot wax cools to leave a pattern. The druid spends some time analysing the formation before he speaks. "Knowledge of Maire's survival is to be kept secret, within the boundaries of our walls. Maire you are to be bound here until the time is right." I nod. "Gwyneth is by the sea, above the port of Dublin. She is mingling with the British. Her jealousy of you, Maire, fed her wish for your demise. We are to wait for their Christmas celebrations to commence. Much merriment will make light our work amongst the drunken idiots."

"Maire is to remain here. She is too easily recognised. We have one and a half moons to properly plan our attack. The rest of us in this room will set off a few days prior. Then we need to split into two groups of six. Half will remain beyond the boundary, the others to go in at nightfall on foot. Ivan, too will be easily spied, for this reason you are to remain back. The gaiety of the British will protect you from exposure. Kill no one, do not arouse suspicion. Remember our target is Gwyneth alone. The time we have shall be used to plan our course, our entry, our capture, our escape. We have the blessing of the gods to do this. We need their patience to prevent us from going any earlier. We are all ablast with wrath, bitterness. Once Gwyneth is securely brought here, it is your decision alone to scheme her extermination Maire. Enjoy the task. The bones are to remain here untouched for three days. Make sure a fresh candle burns throughout. This will seal the magic. I shall myself collect the bones at the end of their gestation."

I find the next few weeks frustrating. Being unable to take my horse out into the wild. I envy Aodh's freedom. Yet it has sure given me enough time to conceive Gwyneth's end. I am pleased with my thoughts. I have set my carpenter to work. Michaelmas is almost upon us. I almost drool, fantasying my revenge. The men have set off. I am hungry to carry out my work. It is at sunrise that they return. A cart is driven as arranged. I look forward to inspecting its cargo. As the men ride into the homestead. Six lead. The horse and cart is in the middle. The rest follow on. Ivan and the druid come in last. The druid expressionless, Ivan maliciously grinning. I stand and watch as they come to a stop in front of my home. The kinsmen are called. I want witnesses galore. Gwyneth, tied to the cart, is bound as I was. Writhing like a raging dog. Her hair matted from fruitless attempts to free herself. Her body a mass of struggle, grazes, bruises, cuts and wounds are clearly seen. This excites me.

"Bring her out. Stand her before me."

She's a feisty one indeed. It takes four of our men to do so. She immediately hurls a gobbet of spit towards me, misses. I go up to her. Grab her chin, raise her face. Make sure she sees my furious gaze. She spits again. It hits my chest. I punch her with all my might. The men secure her upright position. Blood trickles from her nose. She bares her teeth. I apprise her to her predicament. She refuses pain. I click my fingers in the air, signal to my carpenter to bring her doom. The crowd makes way for him and his apprentice. They carry a large wooden cross. "Let out her arms, make loose her legs." I bellow. The cross is held behind her. More men help now as she is secured to her final destination. She still remains silent. Once secured, I order the men to take her to the outside of the fort gate. There I have myself dug a hole for the cross. There, her life will yield, slowly, torturously.

Just as Gwyneth is about to be risen, she starts lashing around, ranting like a mad woman. "You bitch, you fucking bitch. How dare you. He was mine, you took him. Johnny was mine, my love. My life. You interceded, stopped our match. I've plotted my revenge for years. Pretended to be your ally. Watched as you played with that bastard of yours. She's next, mark my word. Johnny's brothers will see an end to your bloodline. The very thought of his blood suffusing in her veins sickens them. I ate his penis back at the camp that night. Claimed it back into my body. His manhood is grown in me now." I scream. "Put her down." Retrieve from my side my finest dagger. "Take this you mouthy slut." I shout out as I cut out her wicked tongue. Blood spews. Gwyneth chokes. Tries to talk, fails. "Ha." I bark. "Cock is it you want, cock? Men un-tie her legs. Hold them down. Take your pleasure. For Gwyneth may have her last wish. Fuck her, anyone who wishes to. Fuck her until she passes out. Knock out her teeth, then fill her throat, fill it with your semen. You have my permission to take which ever delight pleases you, even her arse. Then shut her mouth with cloth, hoist her up. Let the blood trickle down her thighs. Leave her there. She is not to die yet." I pound my chest with pride. Raise my fist. "Hail Mac. Hail Sept O'Ciaragain."

With that I take my leave. Go saddle my horse. Gallop out into the open, triumphant.

184

MAIRE 20

I return early afternoon. Gwyneth still hangs unconscious. Her body ravished, covered in blood and semen. Battered, her head drapes to one side. Pleased, I seek the druid to assist me in my further plan. The grand finale. I trust he will. I find him in the back courtyard playing with his prayer beads. I explain my proposal. He looks shocked. Nevertheless, for whatever reason, he agrees to help me. "We must go down to the brook to talk this over, to gather power, to choose the right one. I also need to call on the help of the Morrigan. I will need you to hold my space whilst I travel in the astral world. Walking to the brook, we gather twigs, dried wood, old moss to make a fire.

We choose to seat ourselves on a small sand bank where the brook swells. A small rickety bridge is to our left. We lay out the fodder for our fire. Light it. Scheme, plot. Choose. A light wind blows. Then the druid falls silent, crosses his legs. Holds out the palm of his hands upon his knees. His eyes roll up into his head. He does not close his eyelids. I guard him as promised. If his enchantment takes him too deep, I am to call him back. He hums, quietly at first, then louder. He reaches a crescendo. I am just about to retrieve him, as he is falling back. When there is an almighty crack in the air. Raven feathers start to fall over the bridge. The Morrigan appears, first as three ravens, then merging to become the large one. Finally she shows herself as the crone. Older and more withered than I've seen her before. He drops his head forwards, his eyes roll back to face her.

"Do you know what you are asking?" she questions, her face distorted. I stand up. "Indeed I do." I firmly answer her.

"One last time Maire, are you sure? There could be consequences."

"I do not care. Nor am I troubled. If I can do this. Then I am powerful enough to protect myself too."

"Very well. Your wish is granted. At the time chosen, call out to the prince of lust. Use your eyes as well as your omnipotent voice. Roar out his name with great power. Close yourself down this night. Withdraw unto yourself. You must sleep in virginal white. Lay salt around the edges of your bedroom. Do not cross the line until dawn." She shouts out to me.

"I shall obey. I give thee my heartiest thanks." I reply.

"Oh, I know you do, and so you should." She opens her mouth, lets out a horrifying squawk. Is sucked into a vacuum which appears in the air around her and vanishes. A single feather rests at my feet.

"Take it," the druid tells me. "Put it under your pillow this night." I bend over to pick it up, look at the beautiful hues hiding in the blackness. Put it to my heart between my breasts.

Arriving back at home, I don't even look to Gwyneth. Saving my hatred for later, I call to my servants. I instruct them to build a fire to surround the base of the cross. To make it waist height, thick, dense. They look thrilled. "Gather round at sundown today for the spectacle." They agree. Around six pm. We are all stood around the cross. The sun shimmers over the horizon. A small fire has been lit to the side. Four men stand around with a torch each, awaiting my command to set her ablaze. One of you fetch an axe. Amputate her right hand, well above the wrist. I want to dry it out, keep it. Hang it in the main room as a token of this day alongside the new tapestry I shall design. A young lad, keen to show his lack of fear obliges. It drops off in one swoop. Gwyneth, semi-conscious, half-alive, lets out a howling scream. The boy collects it, shows it to the jeering people. Blood pumps out of the severed artery. "I want you all here. But you are to turn away, do not look to her. Eyes scorned can curse. Do not allow her that otherworldly pleasure. Do not allow her to place mischievous thoughts in your mind. Give her no comfort." I run my finger over my bottom lip. Snarl. "Now." I shout out. The four men dutifully carry out their task. Ensure the fire takes. Join the rest with their backs to her. I position myself in the middle, facing. Staring her out as the flames start to rise. "Asmodeus. Asmodeus. Prince of revenge. Prince of lust. I call upon you. Asmodeus." I cry out as loud as I can. The ground beneath the fire starts to shake. The flames rise at enormous pace. The three heads of the demon start to break through the earth. A bull. A human. A ram. Three tongues flick in sordid delight. Two black spiked wings too start to break through. They bellow through the earth, make way for his body to be released. One last push, then the King of the Jinn reveals all of himself. His hardened dark, dried out, grey skinned body. Naked he ascends from hell. His serpent tail lashes around. He roars. Turns to the fire. Roars into its flame. His second roar rips through Gwyneth's belly, hundreds of worms drop out. Sizzle in the heat.

"Take her soul." I command. My lips risen in pure hatred.
Make good use of her. Digest her, ravish her. Take her to the
second level of hell. Hold her there for five hundred years.
The malevolent force before me, flies up to me. I do not flinch.
He lets out a devilish sound, smiles. Turns back to his treat.
Gwyneth has long stopped screaming. Her body blackening
has succumbed. The demon uses his talons. Lands on her
shoulders, takes up flight. I see her wicked, slimy grey soul
being pulled up from her feet, over her charred body, out of
her crown. Gwyneth's face contorts. The leader of seventy
two legions takes her up high into the darkening sky. Then
hurtles straight down, head first back into the earth with a
clap of thunder, dragging down with him a hapless lost soul.

I clap my hands. "You may turn." I whoop. My people gasp
at the sight before them. Never before have they seen such a
thing. The dead body that has melted into the wooden cross,
appears inhuman. Like a gnarled demoness has perished, not
a person. I leave the scene. My job done, with no regard for
my victim.

MAIRE 21

The coldest of days. I am galloping, I mull over the fields of my desire. We shall tear treachery down. How fucking dare Johnny's brothers call to kill my child. I shout out into the prevailing winds, as snow tickles my face, my ditty. "Hey ho, tip top, watch where you go. Fingers pointing. Murder anointing. Smiles killing. Something is chilling." Safe in the knowledge that I have the support of Tom Fitzgerald, known as Thomas of Drogheda. This is where we are heading Ivan and I. He has lured the first brother James to his plight. The Earl took some persuading. His honour of my father was what turned him. He owes him a huge debt, I am claiming it. We slow the horses. Our destination is close, we do not want to bring heaving horses to the tavern, that sits to the south of the river Boyne. We follow the river now, getting closer. The edges of the river have frozen. I'm so on fire, the freezing air does not distract me. Our journey perfectly timed, darkness falls.

Ivan takes the horses. He tethers them to the fencing, goes in, to make sure Thomas is fulfilling his role. He will add to the spilling of ale. I make to the water's edge. Take from my belt the sharpened dagger. I kneel, put on my gloves, cut out a large slab of ice. My rhyme fills my head, as my hands carve out a perfect ten inch square, thin it to fit nicely in my grasp, chisel one edge to make it lethal. It is done. I lay it in the snow by my side to keep it frozen, deadly. I crouch under a well-placed holly bush. My body starts to shake, to shiver and shake, is it the intense cold, or adrenalin? I force myself to remain calm. It will happen, it will happen. I take my cloak, pull it tighter to me. Pull up the hood, to conceal my unmistakable hair.

I hear voices, loud, shouting, I recognise neither, yet I know who they are. Thomas supports a rather drunken Louis to the river bank. Both relieve themselves in the water. Louis, is swaying and lewdly demonstrating how much higher a British man can piss. Ivan creeps up behind me. Always there to protect. "Do it Maire. Do it for your daughter." I pick up my self-made weapon. Kiss it. Silently manoeuvre myself into position. Thomas turns. This is his way of letting me know which man is which in the darkness. I poise directly behind my victim. Place my left arm to his shoulder swiftly as I unleash my fury. In seconds his throat is opened to the bone. His hands fly to stem the blood spouting out, covering the snow in my glory. His trousers wrapped around his ankles, he tries to move, but flops back to the bloody snow. I place a foot on his chest, press his emptying body hard to the reddened snow. He catches a glimpse of me. Ties to talk, he can't. He twitches and merely groans. Globules of blubber bounce out from his wound. "For your niece Louis. You lot chose to come to our land, you do not get to choose who we lie with. You do not get to kill our chosen bloodlines. I do this in the name of Ireland. "Now Ivan." I remove my foot. Ivan drags the bleeding pig to the water by his arms. Hurls him with his great might out into the foaming torrent of water.

Thomas quakes in shock at the ferocity of my feral act. "Forsake the British Earl, we are mightier. I do this for Ireland." I bellow, then gather myself. "I am grateful to you

for upholding your honour this night. Your debt is paid."
All three of us nod our goodbyes. We go to get the horses.
Mount, move on from Drogheda to our place of rest to mull
over our next plot.

MAIRE 22

It's been a few months now since I wiped out the White brothers. News still filters from the Pale I am told, which pleases, of how the father vigilantly searched in vain for his missing sons. Oblivious to the fact that John's heart still beats in another. Those with the knowledge from there have all long since rotted. Spring is in action. Buds are shooting, sap rising. New life emerging. Whilst others tend to their hoeing beyond the walls, I'm helping Fianna plant our seeds for growth in her small vegetable plot. Telling her how vital it is to sow our own seeds in life. I have lovingly braided her long dark hair, entwined with soft crocus flowers, which illumine her stunning blue eyes. She looks a beauty. Aodh joins us, he swoops in. Lands where we are bent over tending the soil. He waddles over to the shallow bowl of seeds, bobs his head in. "Oy, no." I yell to him. He lifts his head, full of seeds, gives me one of his looks. Takes the seeds to a small trench Fianna has prepared. Drops in the seeds. Stands tall, his eyes face mine. "Clever boy," I say, "I'm sorry, should have known." Fianna giggles. I watch as the two of them meticulously, lovingly plant and cover over the seeds, Aodh is a little unbalanced whilst drawing the soil over the seeds with his talons. I am tickled.

I decide to teach her my learnings. "Fianna." "Yes mother." "My dear, you know I am a gentle person, as are you. But it is important to not let yourself be treated like a fool. Some people just need annihilating. Just as we trim plants, as you grow you will experience wounds, but convert them into victory. There are times we need to surplant our human given dignity. On occasion you will have to use cunning, be cold. Cull when necessary, swiftly, but only the guilty. Always stand on your feet, let no man thwart your intentions. Do not trust anyone who won't look you in the eye, even if their words convince." She looks to me inquisitively, yet I know my words have been understood. After my episode with Gwyneth, I have decided to instil wisdom into my cherished daughter. She may be only three, yet she's an O'Ciaragain without doubt. I commend her on her efforts. "Now child, time for us to go back to the house, clean those fingernails, put you in some fine gowns fit for a queen." Our spring equinox celebrations shall begin soon. Aodh takes leave.

This is the first time Fianna will join us. Having myself had a sheltered childhood. I have cultivated her into a precious bloom, to help her fully embrace her strength, purpose, at this tender age. No knowledge can be enough. She will not be taught to embroider. She will be taught the way of man. The way of beasts. The way of kindness and integrity. I have asked the Druid to give her a special blessing tonight. Because of the recent happenings, we shall celebrate with only our own people. The joiners have constructed an awning outside the front of the house. We go upstairs leaving the women to adorn the long tables and benches. A bonfire sits in the centre of the courtyard, waiting for dusk.

Fianna and I join the guests who are well underway with their feasting. All chatter stops, all stand. All clap. I look down to my child. Fianna's eyes light up. Her face beams. I have dressed her and myself in the finest matching garments of muted and emerald greens. Ivan leaves his place, approaches. Bows, guides us to our seats. I signal for all to sit. "Pass me the wine." I shout out in humour. The raucous festivities resume.

With the food consumed, wild boar, braised swan, barons of beef. The tables cleared, the musicians gather their drums. This is my favourite time of the celebration. The beating on the skins raises my spirits to the gods. Ivan winks to me and takes Fianna away. "Don't worry, she'll be fine." He tells me. I sanction him taking her. Place my attention back to the young who have lit the fire, and proceeded to dance round it. The flames take well. After a short while I am taken aback by a sight. From the stables, Fianna reappears, seated bareback on Raphael's back. The druid leads him on one side, Ivan the other. I stare in wonderment. What a splendid idea these men have conjured. What better way to bless the child than atop a pure white stallion. Raphael shows fear to the flames, Ivan calms him. They halt within a safe distance, away from the wind-blown smoke. I step towards them. The dancers widen their circle, giving us space, encasing us for the blessing. The druid removes from his bag a neat little crown made from holly. Fianna drops her head briefly for him to place it. The deep green holly leaves blend in perfectly with her shining hair and the blue flowers. This is my proudest moment. A lump rises in my throat.

The druid moves towards the fire. Places his hand in his pocket, draws out handfuls of brown powder. Throws it into the fire, as he circles it. The powder, known to me, is ground tinder fungus. The fire crackles and sparks fly out. The dancers rise their heat. Fianna lets out a squeal of delight. The druid asks the drummer to stop. The dancers to sit down, hold hands, close their eyes. He goes to my daughter, takes her from the horses back. Sits crossed legged

in front of the fire. Places Fianna in his lap. He unties a
small pouch from his belt. Removes three thin white dried
mushrooms. Instructs her to eat one, then to try to sleep. He
then ingests two of the same. He tells us to remain quiet.
Ivan is instructed to stand behind him. I to sit by his side.
I am grateful for a calm evening to enhance this sacred
rite. Raphael remains alone, still, the light from the flames
shinning in his eyes.

Time passes. The fire enchants me, draws me in. I remember
the day I gave Fianna into the care of goddess Brighid's.
She is the patron of healing, poetry, a solar deity known to
inspire, encourage. Another of her names The Fiery Arrow. I
feel she has taken a grip of us, flung us into the heart of the
fire before us. Swaddled us with her magical powers. I hear
Fianna stir. A look of pleasure and bewilderment falls on
her face. The druid strokes her cheek. Passes her to me. We
embrace wholeheartedly. The druid speaks, "You may all
take your leave now." My people start to rise, disperse. "Ivan,
take the girl with you to settle the horse. Maire, we need a
private talk." I wait until all is tranquil.

"What is it?" I ask him. Maire, the goddess came to me,
to us all in fact. Her green passionate eyes met mine. She
announced to me I am to take Fianna." I gasp. "Not yet
Maire. When the child is seven, I am instructed to take her
with me to my abode by the holy well in Belcoo, close to
where you were born." I ponder on the meaning of his words
for a moment. "For what reason," I ask him, frightened of
the answer. "She is to be taught the way of my people. To be
cultured, leaned, travelled. She has your power, she is also
to be given mine, through my flesh and spirit. I shall raise
her as a Bandurai." My hands fly to my mouth, I am all too
aware that the training takes near on twenty years. "But, I."
"No buts Maire. We have to trust the goddess's word. Do not

worry yourself, I shall bring her to you as often as is possible. You may visit when I give my permission. I lower my eyes, bow in humble submission to Brighid's wishes. I turn, leave the druid to stare into the stars. Go towards the stables. I wonder if I made a mistake, asking for the blessing this night. Tonight my child shall lie with me.

KELLY 16

It's the last weekend in April. I can't believe I am actually doing this. The only time I've shut my café before was for Arthur and Miriam's wedding. And now. Opps. Sorry customers, adventure calls. I'm at Belfast airport, awaiting a flight, to join my beau. All paid for by his nibs. Having stuffed my face at the café earlier, to avoid wasted food, which I hate. I decide not to buy any food to take on the plane. Besides, I don't want to be too bloated for my special two days. Two whole days. A mini holiday, a break with my man. I still have to beat myself with how well this relationship is blossoming. I've got used to his long breaks, and fully understand his commitment to the children. That's him. Kind, considerate and extremely sharp. The tannoy announces my flight. "Easy Jet, flight number EZY 485 to Edinburgh, this flight is now boarding, please make your way to the gate." That's it, like a sheep I follow the footsteps ahead of me to my destination. Jimmy will meet me at the airport. He has a new case at the high court, starting next Wednesday, so our little trip fits in perfectly.

He greets me in the arrival hall, squeezes me tight. Takes my case. Leads me to his driver. "Come on Jim, tell me what we are doing, I'm here now. Why the big secret?" "Arhh well dear, you will find out bit by bit. I promise you, you will not be disappointed." My mind flips. I've packed what he suggested, pretty frock, casual and walking clothes. A warm coat in case of high winds. What does this mean? A long sleek Mercedes awaits. The driver jumps out, sees to my case. Opens the back doors for us. I'm not used to this, I muse. Driving through the city, I notice how busy it is and am somewhat surprised to how many people are milling around. "We are here," the driver announces, as he pulls up at a large building. My eyes are drawn to the building across the street, the city's cathedral stands large, omnipotent. "Come on," says Jim, "time to get to our room. We enter the building, "Old Town Chambers," is scrawled above the entrance. Jim goes to the reception desk, returns with a huge smile on his face. "Follow me Kell, the fun begins."

We approach our room, Jim unlocks the door. What lies before me makes me gasp. "Oh wow. Wow." I exclaim. I have never in my life seen such a room. The arched ceiling and walls are made up of old stone, a huge bed hugs one wall. A copper bath sits proudly in a corner. Hugh shuttered windows draw me to their view. I take Jim's hand move towards the glass. "Oh my God, look at our view, how on earth did you find this place?" Jim smirks, only the best for you, this is the oldest room available in Edinburgh. It dates back to the fifteenth century. The walls surrounding us are all original. They call it the Town House. I look down now to the cobbled streets, in excitement I hadn't noticed them before. We also have an up-close view of the cathedral. "This is amazing Jim." I turn to hug him.

"Let's see what's through there, he leads me through a small arched doorway, a stunning shower room is revealed. We walk back to the bedroom, behind the bath lie a few stone steps. Jim climbs, I follow. At the top a sumptuous lounge greets us, together with a dining area, and modern kitchenette. There is a second double bedroom too. "Just in case I snore," jokes Jim. "That's not all Kell, follow me." Unbelievably there is a second bathroom, wooden floors support a huge freestanding bath. Coves dug into the walls each hold medieval candelabras. The candles, pre-lit, enhance the wonder of this strange old building. "This has to be the most romantic place on the planet," I exclaim, tears well. "Don't be silly Kell, you deserve this treat. And of course, I too shall enjoy it." He winks. One can sense the history of this place, yet I do not find it creepy, stifling, but somehow comforting, familiar. "Come, let's go and explore," I suggest, "we can un-pack later, this old town is just drawing me to explore." "Whatever you wish." And out we go.

Outside the building, Jim pulls out a small guide book, this does not surprise me. He is meticulous. "Let's walk up the Royal Mile," he suggests, I agree. A fresh cobbled pavement carries our feet along. We head to the castle sat upon what's known as castle rock. We amble along, taking in the towering tenements, the little side streets, the stairwells that sit along the path. We climb up to the castle, cross the raised stone footbridge, buy our tickets, and start to take in the magnificence of the place. It is awe-inspiring. Great rooms loom before us. Huge fireplaces, suits of armour, wooden panelled walls. Jim consults his guide book. "Let's go out to the battlement area." He doesn't wait for an answer, boys will be boys. We find it. Cannons line the walls where they are cut out to fit them. We find a spot to stop, take a breath and imbibe the wonderful atmosphere.

I take the guide book from him, flick through, to find myself strangely drawn to visit the prison of war museum. "Must we Kell?" Jim questions. "Yes, I don't know why, I'm just interested." "Ok." We follow the map, enter a room that has displayed a replica of the cells. Jim shudders, I find it intriguing. I can see that Jim is uncomfortable, so we quickly move on, to meander around the other attractions. "Time to head back." States Jim. We walk back up the Royal Mile, stop at a quant café for a coffee and chocolate muffin. Instead of returning to the apartment, Jim tells me to close my eyes. He leads me onwards by the hand, "wait and see, wait and see." Jim gives me the same answer to my questions. "Now, look, open your eyes. We are in the mouth of St. Giles cathedral. A lot of the seats are taken, Jim leads us to two empty seats. "What are we doing here, I've already been to mass today?" "Aha, I thought I'd get your there. I did some googling, there is a musical performance due to start shortly." Oh, how thoughtful. Thank you." We both take in the evenings performances. Leave with elevated spirits.

Back in the apartment, Jim is running us a bath in the upstairs bathroom, he has also lit some incense sticks he brought with him. Bubbles amass atop the steaming water, just what we need after a full day. We slowly bathe each other, it's so lovely to feel so treasured. I am grateful to have washed my hair this morning, it can take ages to get it straight. We both emerge, Jim gets a warm towel off the rail, wraps it round him, retrieves another, proceeds to gently dry me. Memories of my childhood flood back. I feel so blessed to be in the company of this man. "Let's prepare ourselves for dinner, I've booked a fine restaurant. And no, don't ask."

We turn back up the royal mile, Jim holds onto me dearly, shortly we stop. "This is it." We are facing a restaurant, the name "Angels with Bagpipes," above the entrance invites us in. "What a beautiful name," I exclaim. The maitre d, shows us up the stairs to a table on the first floor. It is beautifully laid out to a high standard, statues of angels abound. Jim, being the gentleman he is offers me the seat with the best view of the room. We sit down, I thank him. In no time a bottle of champagne arrives. "Did you pre-order this?" I ask.

"Of course." He replies in a deep sultry tone. I am beginning to long for him now, we had no time to cuddle earlier. I'll be patient. We clink our glasses, say "cheers, to us." Jim directs me to choose from the menu, having checked their signature dishes. We eat, chatter, exchange looks of love. Hold hands. Just as I think the meal is over, three Scots march in, dressed in swirling kilts, sporrans, full highland gear with bagpipes. "Especially for you," Jim coos. They stand back, Celtic tradition flourishes, then commence to play old highland tunes. I am overwhelmed with emotion, I have long wished to hear the bagpipes for real. What have I done to be treated with such thought? They finish. We thank them profusely. "Let's head back now Kell." "Ok," I reply. We slowly get up, place our napkins back on the table. Head out into the cool night air.

Dawdling up down the street. I can feel the sexual chemistry rising. I am so lucky, this man seems to cherish everything about me. He laughingly opens the door, scoops me into his arms Carries me through. Carefully puts me down. We silently make our way up to the lounge. Jim goes to the sound system. Clicks play. The voices of Boys to Men echo out. Jim snuggles into me, we sway to the words. "…I'll make love to you, like you want me to." The moment could not be more perfect. I close my eyes, allow Jim to guide my movement as our bodies interlink in motion. Every song thereafter is a love song, I'm in heaven! Jim guides me back down into the master bedroom, the ambience is electric. He stands me before the bed, we slowly undress and caress each other. We lie down. My kind, generous man, proceeds to make love to me with a tenderness, like never before, as the music from upstairs distils. We spend the whole night is a time capsule of true appreciation.

MAIRE 23

I cannot stop the druid taking Fianna in four years, yet there is something I can. I sent word, requesting an invitation to join the chief of the O'Neills, Eoghan mac Neill. To celebrate Beltane with his clan this year. I received prompt news, that I may indeed attend and bring three guests. Perfect. The location, the castle of Henry Aimbreidh O'Neill, in the barony of Strabane Lower. I shall take Ivan. I hence sent a messenger to locate my intended, ask him to meet me there. He has confirmed his attendance, and shall bring along a friend. All is in place.

April 30th, 1434, Ivan and I are in the foothills of the Sperrin Mountains. We journeyed over two days, sleeping out at night under the stars. Raphael has carried me, Ivan chose to walk. He hates burdening a beast, if he can carry himself. The scenery on route has been inspiring. The hills offer up a mix of intoxicating pines, dancing heathers, and waterways that twinkle with gold. Music starts to pour over from the distance, confirming we're almost there.

The castle looms atop a man-made mound. Two large half-circular shaped towers dominate the countryside to the north. We approach the southern entrance to the courtyard. I hand Raphael over to a stable boy. "Feed him well," I request with a smile. Ivan and I head to the tower at the south. We are directed up a spiral staircase to meet our host. The great hall is teeming with life. I spy Eoghan immediately. He too me, he rushes to greet. "Maire, my, my, what a reputation you have, perhaps I am a fool to invite you here." He laughs. I give him a kiss on his ruddy cheek. "Is that the kiss of death oh mighty warrior?" Eoghan jests. "You are a descendant of the Kings of Tir Eogain. Do you really think I would even try to overthrow you?" "I would put nothing past you my dearest, and however, I am fully aware that we are bonded."

We simultaneously raise our right hands, clash them together like two massive boulders colliding. "United in victory, time shall honour our souls. Transgressions shall become voluntary cries for remissions. Now, please make merry, your other guests have not yet arrived. You will have noticed the feast is prepared on the field to the east. We've quite a display for you, you shall not be disappointed." I thank him, briefly introduce him to Ivan. Grab myself a cup of ale, start to explore our surroundings. Ivan decides go outside, sit in the sun, rest his heavy bones.

I meander up a mural stair, which takes me up to a parapet. Here I can fully see the layout for the evening, beyond the curtain wall. Women and children hurry around, bringing dishes from the courtyard kitchen, place them in the middle of many set tables. Tankerds of beer, wine. Spring flowers are scattered amongst them. A large fire, hungry to be lit sits away back. It is our tradition to light all the hearths in our homes from the fire of Beltane. Beyond, the men sweat erecting ornate tents for the guests to retire to. I take a few moments, plan in my head how I am going to achieve my objective. Then go back outside, to the other entrance. Each tower has a set of stairs, I go up the one to the left. I come across a small room, having just one window. The other side I find identical. I go back down, I am interested in the stairs that go down. They are not lit, I gingerly make my way. Underneath, I find a vaulted basement. The stone archways protect stored foods and beverages. I retrace my steps into the fresh air. Go to find Ivan.

"Any news, have they arrived?" "No sign yet." I sigh. Patience is not my forte. We sit together in the courtyard, legs dangling over a flat wall, staring into the landscape, each with our own thoughts, taking in the building excitement buzzing from the young ones. Ivan knows nothing of my plans, for he would surely disagree. I lower my head, saddened, where are they? A wry smile passes my lips. I am jolted by a jab in my back, turn hastily, alarmed. Only to be relieved. "Maire, didn't think I'd let you down, did you?" Angus's face is lit up. "Allow me to introduce Ronan." I acknowledge a tall skinny blonde boy. "It's been a while. How are you and Fianna? And thanks for asking me here this day." "It wouldn't be the same without you, trust me." I raise my brows. He looks confused. All shall be revealed.

Bells ring, we are summoned to join the feast. I make sure I am seated next to Angus. Wait for him to drown some beers, relax. Put my arm around his shoulder, bend my head to whisper in his ear. "How would you like to be a father?" Shocked by my question Angus stutters his reply. "Maire, you know, I know you do. I can't be a father, would not be right. "Yes, but, if you could, think about it, would you, I mean would you father a child?" "It's never crossed my mind." "Well, let it cross you now. Come let us go for a walk." Angus's face looks worried. However he follows me away from the feast. I stop at a tall broad oak tree. Sit. Pat the ground besides me to indicate he should do the same.

"Maire, what is it? I do not understand the importance of your questioning." "Take a deep breath Angus. What I am about to suggest, I am aware will shock." Angus heavily exhales, with a baffled expression, which soon turns to awareness. "Maire, I'd do anything for you, really I would, but, am I right to believe you wish me to father a child for you?" "Yes. Angus." He swiftly arises. "Maire, without being rude, it is not possible. You may be beautiful, wise; even witty. However you are a woman!" he exclaims in exasperation. "Surely you of all, can find an appropriate mate." "I don't want a mate, I want to entwine our blood, our stock, our fierceness. I want a child to be strong, cunning, agile; indestructible. I want an heir, one who will take over my sept. If we combine, we would bring forth a child of unprecedented valour." Angus frowns, scratches his head. "Relax Angus, you have until midnight tonight to decide." With that I leave Angus to muse.

Midnight approaches. I spot Angus heading off with his lover Ronan. I can't let this happen. Not yet. I want his balls full for my purpose. I skit across the shadowy land, cut them off ahead. Reveal myself. "Angus, a word please." His companion looks puzzled. "Very well," he hesitantly utters. "Await my return Ronan, I shall not be long." He's wrong there. I have yet to use my full power of persuasion. We head back towards the castle. I lead Angus to the back towers, go to the one that has a near full moon shining at its window. He follows me to look out. "Look here Maire, what you are asking is not normal." "Normal, there is nothing normal about you and I! Do you not see how beneficial this would be to us? We are both born of excellent stock. We could not fail to bring into this world one that would be a champion. Our lands need our blood to mingle, reproduce, we would be honouring our ancestors and appeasing the gods."

I sense Angus yielding. I continue. "Should you wish this to remain between us, I will understand. However, I believe that we will be doing our people a great service. Producing one who can still keep the hated English at bay with fortitude. Prevail Angus, you can pretend I am male." "No," comes his stark answer, "if we are to do this then I will only do it with respect for you and our offspring." I am taken aback.

"Maire, I love you as a sister, as a dutiful brother, I will carry out your request. However, I wish for this to be hallowed. I need to do this my way." "Very well," I place my hand in his in thanks. He moves in front of me. Gently lifts my dress. His eyes do not leave mine. I can tell this is his first time with a woman. He is shaking a little, apprehensive of the task required. I place my left leg to the window sill, to assist him in his efforts. Before long he is inside me. He very carefully manoeuvres himself back and forth. I stare out to the moon. Calling out quietly to the goddess Cerridwen, the white crafty one, who rules the realms of fertility, nature, enchantment; knowledge. Angus remains silent. His breath increases, yet he does not increase his motion, remaining soft. A serenity fills the room. I spot on the land in the moonlight, a herd of deer. This is a good omen, it tells me that Herne too is here. Lord of the wild, the horned god of fertility. Male and female deities have joined to enhance our encounter. I can feel Angus's penis ejaculate inside me. I make myself orgasm at the exact same time, to help his liquid rise. I know inside me lies the sperm that shall fertilise, the day of true conception will take place in two days, on the very night the moon is at its greatest. I give thanks to the gods. Blessed be.

The encounter makes me question, how many British women lay back without sense, just a sense of duty? Crushed over and over again, all in the name of a good match. Whilst their parents say "quite a good arrangement, don't you think?" Handing them a life of conduit woe.

KELLY 17

I wake early. Jimmy is snoring. However, not wishing to
disturb him, I gently roll him onto his side, he snuffles. I
snuggle into his broad warm back. I smile. Nuzzle. Give
thanks to Our Lord and Lady for bringing me such a
gift. Fall back into light sleep. I stir to the smell of warm
croissants, fresh coffee. Just as I rise myself against the
headrest, Jim appears with a breakfast tray. "For my lady," he
jokes, placing the tray in the middle of the bed and hopping
back in. "Fancy a little stroll today my dear?"" Why not."
"There's a glorious walk along the water of Leith, we can
grab a taxi there. What do you think?" "Jim, I love rivers.
That would be lovely. Thank you." "No need to thank me,
I'll enjoy it just as much, especially with you by my side." We
take our time, no need to rush. The day awaits.

We leave the apartment at eleven, grab a taxi. Jim asks him
to take us to Dean Village. A short drive, Jim consults his
booklet and we are there. He guides us to the start of the
walk. I am enamoured, we travel downhill, following a
walled path. The river ripples, bubbles bounce off the banks
of ferns and wild flowers. Small houses lean over cobbled
stones. After a while, we cross a metal bridge to the other
side. Lines of washing flutter in the peaceful wind. We
breathe in the fresh scents that surround the entire walk as
we snake along with the water. "Now, shortly we shall come

across a well, called St Bernard's. It contains a natural spring. The dome was designed by a painter, known as Alexander Nasymth in 1789. There, ahead." I put my arm through his. Enjoying every moment of our time together. There is a Greek statue inside. "That my darling is Hygeia, goddess of health. It is believed that if you drink from the spring, you shall have never ending health, though I wouldn't recommend it, as the locals say it tastes awful." "Oh Jim, that is so interesting, what a mine of methodical information you are." I tease. "You are not at work now." I laugh at him, grabbing the booklet from his pocket. I throw it in a nearby bin. "Let's just be now. See where our footsteps take us."

We make for the main road, turn into Ann Street. Fall across a place called Healthy Burgers. A queue is formed outside. My tummy grumbles. I look to Jim. "Well if the locals are prepared to wait, it must be good." He states. We join the line. I love eavesdropping, people are talking about a Beltane Festival. I turn to Jim. "What's this festival people are talking about?" I innocently ask. "Not a clue." Comes his reply with a straight face. "Oh ok." After a short time we are allocated a place on the end of a long table. The restaurant is packed. I am thankful they do veggie burgers, we order, eat. Natter. Pay the bill. One of the staff orders us a taxi back.

The journey takes us twice as long, I'm curious. "Jim, why the heavy traffic." "No clue petal. Don't worry we'll get there." Outside the apartment the streets are alive. The atmosphere buzzing. "Come on Kell, let's go in, we need a siesta, after last night's frolicking. And we may have a late one tonight. What do you think? Shall we pretend we are teenagers again, and stay out late?" "Anything Jim. Anything we do makes me super happy."

We nuzzle into each other, drift off. Jim's alarm goes off at 6.30pm. "Right Kelly, let's shower. We do so. "Put on layers tonight, it may get chilly. We shall dine alfresco tonight." I catch Jim shuffling some tickets into his jacket pocket. "What are those for?" I query. "Oh, er, I thought I'd take you to the city's Playhouse before we eat. They have a splendid performance tonight." "Whoop, who's the lucky girl. Thanks Jimmy." We set off. It's still warm, so I wrap my jumper around my waist, tying the arms at the front. "Blimey what a crowd Jimmy, and why are they so revved up?" "Not a clue petal. Let's get going, the performance is due to start shortly. We walk up the streets, the crowds teeming in the same general direction. "Here this way." Jim remarks, whilst pointing to a sign showing the way to the playhouse.

Then we take an unexpected right turn. "Why are we off course?" "You'll see, patience Kelly." I am confused. We join the others, walking up towards a hill top, signed, Calton Hill. We wait in line to pass an entrance. Jim pulls out the tickets. "This my dear is your very special surprise. He hands one to me. I read the words, "Beltane Fire Festival. April 30th 2018. What is this?" "Aha, remember those dreams you've mentioned to me?" I nod. "This my dear is a celebration the ancient Celts used to perform each night before the 1st of May. I thought it would be fun to bring you here." Then it dawns on me. Jim has probably lined up his court case for this week, so he could do this. I throw my arms around his neck. "You are my knight in shining armour alright. What a wonderful, thoughtful thing." Although deep down, I am rather hesitant, worried he thinks I'm mad. "Well you're a good liar!" "I have to be, I'm a barrister after all."

We walk up the hill towards the National Monument. Luckily we are in time to get a good view of what's to come from behind the metal barriers. Jim proceeds to tutor me

in on all the other monuments up here; who built them
and why. Although it's fascinating, I am more interested
in witnessing the goings on, feeling the anticipation. On
our way up, youngster dressed in all sorts of outfits played
pranks on us and others. At first this shook me, then I
saw the humour. Drums roll. Smoke starts to billow from
behind the pillars. A man with a Tannoy announces the
start "Honour nature and fire of earth." He shouts out.
The May Queen steps forwards with The Green Man. The
crowd go crazy. I join in the whooping. Jim smiles, pleased,
squeezes my hand. Jim explains to me the queen represents
growth and purity, whilst the green man denotes life on
earth. He has certainly done his homework. We follow part
of the procession, as the story of their courtship is played
out. They walk through an arch set on fire just before
their arrival. White maidens follow, one protector walks
in front of the queen the other behind, dressed in blue and
wafting branches. Various groups of outrageously dressed
individuals perform along the way. Some depict innocence,
whilst others mischief. "Let's head back to the city," Jim
suggests, "there's plenty going on there, we can come back
later for the main show. I fancy some street food." "Street
food it is."

Throngs of people line the streets, police try to keep the
peace. There is such a cacophony, from high pitched
screaming, jeering, drums, base trumpets. One street
performance is followed by another. The whole thing is so
theatrical, I presume the dancers are trained. A semi naked
group of young people painted red show off their acrobatic
skills on a centre stage, along with their allure. The whole
night is mesmerising. Then we head back up. Jim being
anxious to get a good viewpoint for the remaining acts. Boy
is time flying its 10.30pm already.

We head to the main bonfire site. The Queen arrives again with the Green Man. The green man enacts a ritual of death and rebirth, accompanied by loud trumpeting. The queen amid roars from the crowd descends the stage, goes to light the bonfire. Groups of performers dance, hoot, holler, in a trance like fashion, increasing the amazing ambience. We wait until the fire starts to die down. Jim leads me to a place known as the Bower. Reds and whites entertain with their Celtic traditional dance routines. Then we take our leave, before the festival closes, to avoid getting caught up in the human traffic.

Returning to our apartment, I feel a little saddened; this is our last night. However, we are certainly ignited from all energy raised by the naked horseplay and passions of the show. Jim throws me on the bed, rips off my clothes as fast as he can. Drops his trousers, steps out. Unable to contain himself, he leaps on top of me still half dressed, steamily and with great prowess he ravishes me. Finally, panting, he falls back onto the sheets, I cover him with the soft duvet. Our breathing quietens, with all the excitement of the day, we both soon fall asleep.

I wake up late to Jim gently stroking my back. "Morning my star." I want to say "I love you," but I hold myself back. "We can have a late breakfast in a café, then I'll ask the driver to run us to the airport, where I shall bid you personally farewell." "Thank you for all your kindness Jim, I really appreciate the effort you've gone to, I couldn't have asked for anything more. You really are a dream." Dream, shit, I remember, in the early hours, I woke up, not knowing what had just happened. I swear I was transported to another time. All I can recall is looking out of a stone framed window, a burnt out fire in a field, lit up by a full moon. The moon calling me in. A family of deer. I was standing, a rugged man, short. His hair, black, curly, slightly matted was having sex with me. Oh what next? I decide not to let Jim know. For sure this time, he'd think I was nuts.

KELLY 18

Oh boy. What a trip. I need to come back down to earth. I'll make a camomile tea, settle myself for an early start. Back to life. I turn the key in my front door. Flick on the lights. Cinders rushes to me, I bend down to pick her up, until a ferocious banging at the back door startles me. Scared, my heart starts to pound. I peek round the door leading to the kitchen, there, half masked by the back doorframe is Ian. I tentatively open it. Not sure what to expect. Ian's face is red, his eyes swollen. He barges in, thrusts a crumpled letter into my hand. "Read this." He commands. Slumps himself over the work top, quivering. "Are you alright," I enquire in a small voice. "Just read the letter Kelly." He demands again.

I open up the folded paper, start to read. Start to shake.

"Dear Ian,

This on reading will hurt you!

Am I that unworthy; that crap? Am I nought but a sparrows shit? You mock me, your friends laugh at me. You ignore my love for you! I cannot get the image out of my head, it rules my every breath. I want to believe it is not real, yet it is. Why the fuck did you have to do this? I cannot escape my pain. I fear for my sanity. My hatred to myself grows, menacing me, torturing me. Satan's tongue lavishes at my wounds. Oblivion shall meet me at the gates of hell. You may enter into this space with me, for it belongs to you. I'm telling myself to shut up, piss off. To crawl under moss, to be eaten by foragers. Shame on you, you disturb yourself. You do not care. Beware of badness, it seeps from the very earth. I've become a god-forgotten person. I suck. You have hurt me beyond believe. Am I that despicable? I shall die broken at the thought of you, the photo which flashed up on your I-pad, whilst you told me you were in a meeting, shall follow me to my end. Could you not say "no" to lust, entwined with harlots? Why did you not settle for love, kindness? I succumb to my forced fate. For I am now nothing. Oh pooh, oh pooh, why did you have to do this? Look after the children, I have left them a memory box for each of them to open when you feel the time is right. For you have full responsibility for their souls now. Cherish them, do not deceive them as you have I. My time has come. I feel like I don't deserve to live, that somewhere deep inside I must be a horrid person."

Your ex-wife.

Teagan."

I am stunned. "Where is she Ian?" I solemnly enquire. "Ian sobs uncontrollably. He straightens himself, tries to latch on to me. I back him away, keep my boundary. His mighty strength has left him. "Please Kell, you're the only one I can talk to. "Ian. What's happened? Tell me she is ok!" Ian's words come out bit by bit. "She did it Kelly, she took her life." He drops to the floor. I put my hand to the centre of his back. "Come on, get up. Take a seat" I guide him to the kitchen table. Go to my medicine cabinet. Take out the whisky, pour him a large one. Place it in front of him. "Take this. It will help to calm you." Ian drinks the whole lot in one go. I replace it with another. Pour one for myself. Ian places his head in his hands, tears drip onto the table surface.

"I'm a fool, a fool; a bloody fool. Why did I do this, why?" He breaks down again. I give him time to gather himself. Lift his chin, look into his bloodshot eyes. "Ian, what on earth did you do?" "I, I, oh god, I can't tell you. The shame, the shame. He closes his eyes, curls up like an infant. "Take the whisky Ian." He plays with the glass, lifts it. Sips as a child suckling on a teat. "I dishonoured her Kell, my beautiful Teagan, her, the children. The entire family. I'm too ashamed to share the details with you. I shall carry this burden myself. Pray I can make amends to Connor and Sophie. I don't know what to do." He judders. "I will tell you part of it, you must promise to keep it to yourself, I feel that if I don't I too shall fall apart." "Ok Ian. In your own time." "I went to London last Thursday on business. And me, the dick head, got in contact with Jess. Her and her friend Mia, offered me a, you know, a threesome." He hangs his head, takes away eye contact. "I took one stupid photo. Just one. Why, I will ask myself to the day I die. I left my I-pad behind by mistake, it is linked to my phone. You can imagine the rest." He pauses. Resumes.

"Teagan asked her mother to look after the children so she could take the weekend off, visit a friend. Her mother thought it strange that she'd taken such a large suitcase. After she didn't answer her phone, and failed to return on Sunday night we became worried. On Monday we called the police. They found her car parked on the strand at Blackrocks, this letter inside. They found tied to the sundial, the, the place where I proposed to her, the dried bouquet she'd kept from our wedding day, the ribbon with our names and the date still attached. They found two large bottles of absinthe on the ground, together with her wedding shoes. They found, oh god, they found her body, washed up, battered by the rocks.

She was wearing her wedding dress Kell, her wedding dress. Kell, what have I done?" He reaches out with his hands to hold onto mine. "Her mother has taken the children to stay at hers for a while. Kell, I'm so alone." As much as I feel for the man, I feel anger too. I'd feel disrespectful to Teagan if I comforted him more. I shall hold my tongue, not give the man my thoughts, as he is suffering enough. One day, maybe. One day.

"Ian, your secret is safe, though things do tend to have a way of coming out. I'm going to take you home now. Where you belong." I drive him back to his house, he tells me the worst thing was listening to Terry Jacks, "seasons in the sun," which Teagan had left to play in her car. I watch as he enters his empty home, hunched over. Wait for the door to close. Head for home. I take myself straight to bed, too in shock to cry, I simply stare at the ceiling until I fall asleep.

MAIRE 24

We are sat on a deserted sandbank of Loch Neagh, by the village of Maghery. Ivan accompanied us down, then set off to barter for some iron. Our reaping baskets are full from our earlier catches. Fianna has caught many young yellow eels, with each one her chest puffed with pride. I myself, being able to wade deeper have caught two huge brown trout. The day is drawing to a pleasant end. I point to Cooney Island, where the two rivers meet. Charm Fianna in with the folk lore of this charming place, whilst wild geese called away for winter honk above.

"Did you know fairies pass here at night?" Her eyes widen. "The boatmen often catch the soft tunes floating in the air. They glide from island to island, it's said they ride on moonbeams." "Mother, really." "Yes dearest one. People say the men folk are all dressed in green, with funny little red caps. The girl fairies dress in silver gossamer. It is said that one man was wholly protected by them." "Why mother?" "Well, he used to leave a little poteen in a flask for them to sup on. They rewarded him with great prosperity. They would lead the gaugers into the bogs. So they could not take the fish." "Tell me more." "There is more; it happens indeed, on a full moon and especially around the time of Samhain, once the light dims. On a calm clear moon lit night, like it is now. And only to those who are pure in heart and have the fairy vision gift. That just under the waters you can see their kingdom." "Really mother, tell me more," she tugs at my dress. "They hold festivals too, just like us beneath the surface of the lake. If you look hard enough you will be able to see columns and walls of their beautiful kingdom, with glimmering sparkling lights. It is said all sorts of folk live here, Silkies, and even Merrows too." Happily I sense Fianna's enthusiasm growing.

"Mother, can we stay, please," she tugs again "I so want to see them, I know I can." "I know you can do dearest, this is why I've brought you here, to gather our nourishment, leave our poteen in thanks. And to see if they will allow us to peak into their wonderful world. Ivan will be back soon, I've asked him to return before dark, so that he can guard us. Women may be strong, yet we still need someone to watch our backs. Whilst we wait for him, stare deep into the waters, and make a wish."

Whilst Fianna is occupied, I think back over the last few months. Pretty soon the bats come out, darting and dashing over the river, catching the last of the summer flies and midges. Since the druid's revelation, I've spent every moment I can with my daughter. Earlier this day we went searching for snails. Each choosing one to race against the other. Sadly Fianna's snail trailed behind mine to the finishing line. Although this is a lesson for her indeed, that not all can be won. I've taught her how to wean the calves. Our stunning herd of cows produced well this year. It is nearly the time for them to come down from the mountains, to an area of reserved grass for the winter. Cows are cherished by us, they boost our livelihoods with gifts of milk, meat and hides. I've also engaged Fianna watching the crops grow and how to protect them from scavengers. Ivan got her a sweet black cat, eyes bright green, Fianna was given the task of encouraging her to catch the mice that like to dominate in the corn barn. We went to the woods a few weeks ago, where the unspeakable happened, of course this time we were well shielded. Fianna hooted with joy watching the pigs snuffle around for acorns, which fatten them up nicely. I also put her in charge of collecting the eggs from our hens. She delights when her basket overflows.

I place my hand to my swollen stomach. Now is the time to share the good news. "Fianna, may I have your attention a moment." She lifts her eyes from the water. "Fianna, you are to have a sibling." "What does that mean?" "I am to have another baby." "Oh, gosh, how wonderful mother, will it look like me?" "Maybe a little; you never know." I remember the druid foretelling of me having a son. I wonder if he is correct. I've had reservations of late. I know I need to trust him, yet the mother in me already overflows with loss for the child by my side. I must stay focussed. Take the upmost influence in Fianna before she is schooled by him. I'd called her Fianna as the name relates to groups of warriors. I always thought she'd emulate me. Now intimations are she is to be a warrior of ancient magic. I sigh. "Here child, place your hand on my stomach, say hello to the little one." Eagerly she slaps her hand to my belly. "Easy child, you don't want him to be scared of his big sister already do you?" "Fianna laughs. "Maybe. Can we look for the fairy folk again?" "Of course." I hear Ivan's heavy steps approaching. Good timing. "We are going to see the fairies beneath the waters in a while." Fianna gleefully informs Ivan. "Oh really." Comes his reply. He has never quite believed in the tales of old.

"May I be excused?" He politely requests. I dip my chin to confirm my agreement. He finds a spot in the long browning grasses. Lays down his massive frame, crosses his arms behind his head to make a pillow with his hands. I know he will only doze, his sharp ears shall catch any untoward sounds. I take my daughters hand, join her in her search.

With the leaving of the sun, the bright moon lights up the sky. Its reflection is illuminating before us. A magic feeling abounds. From afar, the waters start to ripple, as if a giant eel is approaching. I can feel Fianna bubbling with anticipation. It is not a fish that surfaces, but a beautiful young maiden emerging. Water cascades enticingly from her face as she rises. She looks us deep in the eyes. She then jumps up, flips, reveals her tail, proceeds to swim in full vision, we stand up to see further where she is headed. She raises her body out of the water again like a dolphin, leaps and dives head first deep into the lake.

As soon as she disappears bright sparks flash under the water line, a whole city begins to illuminate before us. Ecclesiastical towers and spires form, breaking through the lake pointing high above the water. The city lights up. The sparks flame and dance around the buildings. Then transform into the little folk known to me; that Fianna has been hoping to see. "Mother, Mother." She jumps around. "Stay still child, we do not wish to disturb them. This is their time, we can watch, quietly, respectfully from where we are. She settles, her face full of wonder. I pick her up, place her to my hip. Entranced we observe the fairy folk, bewitched by the lyrical sounds of their plaintive singing. I am blessed, happy in the knowledge that Fianna has had her most enchanting experience so far with me. This is one that she shall never forget, nor I.

KELLY 19

The last few months have seen Jim embroiled in some pretty heavy cases, time together has had to be sporadic; we did however manage to escape on a sailing holiday. Heather, bless her, now that Ricky is at training jumped at the opportunity to run the café in my absence, seems she's been at sixes and sevens since his departure. She loves to talk, gossip, warble, so thoroughly enjoyed it. And, blow me has offered to help out any time I need it. The timing couldn't have been better. I'm grateful to hand her the reins without too much ado.

My first experience of a boating holiday did not disappoint. We spent a week sailing each day to a new destination, in mainland Greece, and onto a few of its quieter islands. The place that we enjoyed the most was Mongonissi. Our skipper, Nick meandered through a small outlet, to a mooring where twenty or so other boats of various sizes were already anchored up. A line of sunbeds awaited us. There were two left together, we quickly grabbed them and whiled away the afternoon. Nick made us a reservation at the island's only restaurant, "Trust me," he said, "This place gets busy."

No sooner had we started to snooze when a neighbouring boat started to play annoying music extremely loudly. The Italian man on board was yelling and carrying on, desperate to get attention, whilst he squirted champagne over a squealing bikini clad girl, who looked half his age. This scene took me back to Teagan's funeral. A tragic, sad day. Expectedly Teagan's mother ushered the children in behind the coffin, straight into a front pew. Ian walked alone at the front, head bowed. Took a seat to the other side. Whilst his parents and relatives sat around him, none offered him solace. No doubt he felt the eyes of the congregation boring into him. Stupid man. What did he expect? News spread of his affair, and following up liaison. In his anxiety he'd wiped the offending item off his I-pad, yet not realised Teagan has sent herself a copy. As proof no doubt, for any impending divorce, which her mother, Michelle discovered whilst tying up loose ends. Jim and I stared rudely at the obnoxious man on the yacht, he dimmed his music, whilst his crew faffed around, result. We enjoyed the rest of the evening, watching the sun go down over the tree splattered coastline in peace. Whilst the crickets struck up their songs.

The night unfolded, I was so pleased Nick has not told us what to expect. It was the most memorable one of the holiday. We just finished eating an amazing array of fresh Mediterranean food; when music took over. A group of young boys and girls gave us a wonderful show of traditional Greek dancing, with costumes to match. Wow, the energy of those guys. When they had finished, a young man gallantly asked for my hand and led me to join in, as did others with fellow diners. Pretty soon I was out of breath, though I did my best. After that the whole restaurant was invited to join in a line dance, boy those young men could kick their legs up high.

Just when we thought the night was closing. The owner, who had served us earlier appeared on the central floor. The music restarted, the original dancers formed a semi-circle behind him and proceeded to clap. The funniest thing, this Greek man, middle aged, rotund, astounded us with his moves, just as agile as the youngsters. Only this time he started to remove his clothes one by one, tossing them into the crowd, we all roared. Before he took off his trousers, he went in his pockets and proceeded to hand out ten euro notes to his customers. The whole thing was a spoof, he collected his cash back at the end. "For the show," he yelled, "not to keep." We all saw the humour. We'd been travelling for four nights now. Jim and I cuddled in one cabin, yet each slept in our own, as they were tiny and darned hot. I went to bed that night praying that I would not wake up feeling sick to the bobbing of our boat. The sickness tablets helped, but only after lunch times.

Now, months later I am perched in the doctor's waiting room, waiting, waiting. Aptly called. Finally I am called, it is a locum doctor whom I've not met before. "Take a seat." She waits until I am settled. "Now, what can I do for you?" I'm unsure what to say really, I'm not ill as such, just suffering from constipation, bloating and heart burn; along with irregular bouts of bleeding. I share this with the woman sat before me. "Oh and, I started my menopause early, so I don't understand why my periods have kind of started up again, does this mean my hormone levels have gone up again?" "Yes, I can see you started that early, it's on the notes." God I hate the patronising tones. She proceeds to ask me a whole load of irrelevant questions. "Do you eat a healthy diet?" "Yes." "Do you smoke?" "No." "Do you drink?" "Occasionally. Why?" She raises her eyebrows. "I'm just trying to ascertain what is causing you these niggling problems! Would it be alright if I put you on the table, feel around your liver?" My liver, why, does she think I'm a raving lunatic, or an alcoholic?

On the table, my shoes removed. I dutifully lie down. She puts on some rubber gloves. "Right I'm just going to prod you gently on your right side, see if there's any underlying pain." She starts to kneed my stomach. "How does that feel." She asks. "Just hard I guess, must be the bloating I've been experiencing. She prods some more, moves her hands over my entire stomach area, starts to kneed from the top towards the bottom. "Ok, get yourself up, and come to sit back down. She looks concerned. It worries me. "Kelly, there's nothing wrong with you as such. In fact, I believe you are pregnant." My eyes flash wide. "Pregnant, I can't be, what are you on about?" "Miss Duffy, you are most definitely pregnant, about five months by my calculation." "What." I jump out of my seat. My mind a blast. Doctor, I know I'm slightly over-weight, but surely you must be mistaken." "It is not that uncommon for someone in your situation to fall pregnant, and you won't be the first not to spot the signs." I start to flap. "Oh god, this is not planned, not one bit. Are you sure, really sure?" "I'm as sure as I can be, I'll make an appointment for you to attend the nearest anti-natal clinic, to book you a scan. Perhaps that will put your mind at rest. The receptionist will call you later with the time and date." My mind at rest, is she kidding? I don't know what else to say, so I thank her. Leave, too stunned to even think.

MR WHITE

I am announced. Entering the grand room atop of
Carrickfergus Castle by the pompous door boy. "M Lord,
I present to you Mr James White, Deputy Constable of
Carlingford." "Welcome dear man," replies my friend, the
eighth Earl of Ulster, also known as Richard, Duke of York.

Having written to him some months ago, it has taken an age
for this meeting to take place. I asked for his generous help
in finding my sons. He agreed, sent me a letter insisting I join
him here. Informing me he believes he has found a solution
to my situation. I am curious. "Sit a while." Richard clicks
his fingers, a youth appears with a goblet of wine, two brass
cups, pours us both a drink and disappears from sight. The
room is magnificent, huge arched windows allow sunlight to
pour through, domed arches loom above. The walls adorned
by flags on poles, bring colour.

"Now then James, I can see this situation has been troubling
you for some time. There is literally no word at all on their
whereabouts. I have however devised a rather unethical plan,
one which may just remedy your malady." Richard shouts
to the valet, "fetch her now." The boy bows, shuts the large
doors, leaves to fulfil his mission. We both raise our cups
in mutual respect. "What does your lordship consider has
happened?" "I fear the worst, however, this shall shortly be

clarified. Many young men have disappeared over the last few years, you are not alone."

The doors fly open, two burly men walk through, either side of a nun. "Bring her to me." Richard instructs. A small quant woman, dressed in a basic habit approaches, quaking a little, clinging a small bible, with a set of rosemary beads hanging from her free arm. "James, this is Sister Agnes." I am puzzled. Richard picks up on my expression. "Stick with me old boy." "Sister Agnes, closer please, now kneel. "I shall only kneel to our Lord." Comes her timid reply. "Kneel," he thunders out, she obeys.

"Child of God are you?" Richard questions. "I am sir," Agnes answers. "Not what I've heard," he pokes his face towards her. She looks troubled, clutches her bible so tightly her fingers turn white. He turns to me. "This is the daughter of a prominent British gentleman, at least she was. He paid a large dowry for her to be sent to a convent, having since disowned her." He again juts his head towards the cowering woman. "This is true, is it not?" She does not respond. Lowers her head in shame. I question Richard, "Sir, how is this feeble creature to help us?" "Wait," he responds, lowering his tone.

"Sister Agnes, it is true indeed, that when you were ten years of age, you horrified your mother, when she discovered you at the bottom of the garden, rubbing your genitals and speaking in tongues?" The nun flushes. "That was thirteen years ago, it was but a mere experiment." "Some experiment for a child. Tell me, do you still dabble in sin, and to what purpose was the action?" She places the bible and beads to her forehead. "I will not speak of it." Comes her reply, with fear emanating from her. "I am married to our Lord, Jesus Christ is my protector now. You had no right to bring me here." The thing which terrifies her seems to be giving her strength. "You have one more chance to willingly help with our crusade, take it." "I shall not," she shouts out loudly. "Men, pick her up, take her down, a few nights in the dungeons may quell her spirit. Bring forth the one we are interested in." "No, no," Sister Agnes screams in protests, over and over, as she is taken away. "Two days should do it, break her, in the meantime, a room has been prepared. You are to be my guest."

Two days have passed, Richard has asked me to meet him at the priest house after luncheon. I tap on the old wooden door, a priest answers, ushers me in. Richard is knelt in the first of two small pews. "Join me, sit by my side, we are to be blessed before our undertaking." I kneel besides him. The priest lights candles atop the meagre altar. Uses a candle to smoulder a frankincense burner, the odour from which soon fills the small chapel. I'm still unsure where this is leading, each time I have questioned, I'm told to "wait, wait." I believe Richard is enjoying the game. The priest utters words in Latin, flicks holy water over our crowns. "It is complete, your souls are sealed. You may now carry out your task without concern." The priest stands before the altar. Crosses himself, falls into prayer. "Now, with our bellies full, our souls shielded, we can commence. He guides me out of the chapel, back towards the castle.

The walk down to the dungeon proves most unpleasant. The stench of excrement and urine hits my nostrils immediately. A feeling of sickly dread invades with each step down. Wailing, grunts and moans fill the air. We pass open barred cells to each side. Pitiful women caked in weeping sores plead with their eyes. Angry men boar with theirs. Two men are at guard. We come to an iron door, Richard indicates for it to be opened. Inside is Agnes, chained with both hands separately above her head, which has lolled to one side. "Wake up." Richard kicks her shins. She lifts her head, menacingly raises her eyes. Swaying her lower body from side to side in a seductive manner, she speaks. "You've done this," she hisses. "You've released the beast. Her expression changes again to the serene one we beheld in the grand room. "Please, you must help me, this cannot be allowed. I cannot control it without the guidance of Sister Superior. "She will help you not, you are to fulfil your duty as a citizen of Britain. You have to endure your penance. Play your part in striking up against the savages."

Her head falls forward in resignation, the swaying resumes. A dark and evil voice calls out deep from her chest. "What is it you want?" Richard takes a step back from the exuding evil. "You are to use your powers to locate this man James' sons!" He states. "Why should I help you, to what benefit?" "You are not in a position to gamble." He firmly tells her. "Oh yes I am, I've had my powers diminished by years of subjugation. The only way to raise them is for this body to get sustenance food, flesh inside me." She bears her teeth, curls her lip, gives a twisted snarl. Richard looks repulsed, calls in one of the guards. "You, fuck her now." The guard is startled. His gaze flies from side to side. "She's no nun," Richard exclaims, "Now, do as I say."

Agnes has already started to enjoy the scene, her body writhes with anticipated satisfaction. She turns her neck from side to side, not taking her eyes of her victim. Guttural sounds flow from her throat. She opens her legs wide. The guard approaches, drops his trousers, reveals his manhood, lifts her habit. Swiftly enters her, she throws back her head, then brings it forward, as the guard pleasures himself. "Bite me, bite my cursed breasts." She instructs the man. He obliges. Enjoying himself. "What is your desire?" She laughs, "My friend here, James White, wishes to know the whereabouts of his sons." "Give me their names." She commands. I speak with hope, "Christopher, Louis, Patrick." "Fuck me harder," comes her reply. Her eyes roll into the back of her head, leaving only the whites to be seen. Agnes seems to disappear for a moment into another satanic world. "Dead, dead, all dead." She cackles.

"At whose hands?" I bark, shaking with fury. "The woman, the red woman from Armagh. A bestial warrior indeed. She defeated you, she did." "I demand revenge." I bellow to the beast within. "Get this bugger to bugger me then." The guard pulls out of her lost virginity, she turns side-wards, sticks out her cheeks. The guard fumbles around for a moment gets his dick in her arched arse. She slaps her palms to the cold damp walls. Places her forehead between. "Fuck me harder you fool. Get inside me up to my guts, till the blood runs black. If you want answers, I want it all, now." The guard picks up his rhythm, now savagely thrusts himself in a frenzy at the bride of god. She grunts, grits her teeth, snarls like an attacking wolf, sneering, chomping. Her body convulses. "Take away her chariot, and take away her wings." Saliva drips from her lips. "To lessen her power, you need to take away what keeps her pure." The guard withdraws. Her body slouches exhausted, her innocence returns.

MAIRE 25

Beginning of May, 1436. Angus and I are walking out towards the woods, Raphael carries me. Aodh circles above. I hold my dear child Mac in a sling to my chest. He's gurgling happily away. His mop of bright red hair bounces in ringlets. It is grown quite long for a child of his months, and frames his rounded face. He has the depth of his father's bones, his eyes piecing blue, shout out "O'Ciaragain." He wishes to feed, I pull aside my top, allow him to suckle in, stroke his rosy cheek. Whilst Angus takes hold of the reins. We while away in the bright sunshine. Aodh coos above in rhythm with Mac. Angus has indeed been a great father, he visits frequently. Has such passion for his son. I tease him over the initial reluctance to his being.

The Druid has been staying the last few days. He is teaching Fianna to draw our ancient sacred symbols. Today they, with Ivan have gone to the river to collect small stones. The druid is to help her create her own set of runes. Runes represent the trees, knowledge, life, guidance and healing. To make her own, will empower them, and they shall advise her through her journey.

Mac, satisfied, nods off against my breast. I unlock him gently from my raised, wet nipple. A piercing sound from above startles me. Angus and I look to the sky. Aodh has been pierced by an arrow, his wings refuse to flap. He drops like a stone, crashes to the ground behind us, my heart stops. Three dowdily dressed women, whom we had barely noticed, rush towards us. I presume to help. I'm wrong. Within seconds each brandish a large knife. One thrusts hers towards Raphael's belly, I kick her away. Another lunges, this time again to my horse, Angus stabs her with his small dagger just above the heart. At the same time, another attempt is made on Raphael, Angus blocks the move, tries to deflect the blow, a knife slices his neck. Adrenalin kicks in. I boot my nervous horse hard, he leaps straight into a gallop. I take up the reins, my child secure, head home as fast as I can. The horse's mane whips at my face, my prince has saved my king. I remain focused. My head screams. "Stupid, stupid, stupid."

I pelt through the front gates, unleash the child from my chest, throw him to the first person I see. Scream from the top of my lungs, "Men, now, five on horseback, gather arms." "What?" One asks. "Just do it, no time to explain." Within three minutes my band is formed. We rush out into the fields, towards the place of treachery. "Pass me a sword," I yell to the man closest, he rides asides me, does so. "Faster, faster." I shout out. "There." We pull the horses to an abrupt stop before Angus, he is still breathing just. I jump off a heaving Raphael, drop to my knees, lift up Angus's head. "Men, one was injured, find her, bring her to me. Give no pity, but keep her alive." Angus weakly raises a hand, points in the direction of the trees. "Ma, Ma," he tries to call my name. "Shh Angus, I will speak. This act will not go unrewarded, the gods will honour your soul. I shall honour your son. He shall be known as a fierce revered fighter as yourself. Do not worry about us. I am strong, my appetite now more ferocious will revenge. You rest. Let the earth take you." He manages a slight smile, his eyes show gratefulness and peace. They glaze over, I close the lids, dip to kiss his reddened cheek.

I walk in great sadness towards my beloved bird. I know if the arrow didn't kill him, the fall will have. He lies in long, fresh grass, blood surrounds his clean wound and pools from his beak. I fall to the ground. Pick up his already stiffening, still warm body. Tears course down my face. "My sweet one, my saviour, what have they done? What have I allowed to happen? I gently remove the arrow. My pained heart places him to my chest, I wrap in the same sling, which only a short time ago suspended my son to my breast. I place the arrow beside him, for I already know what purpose it has. I walk solemnly back to my horse, and Angus's corpse. The men arrive, dragging along the injured woman. They stand her before me. She is shaking. "I'm so sorry, I had no choice. My bairns are starving. The British keep us hungry. Forgive me."

I must be thinking irrationally, I go with my gut. "Woman, you have only one way to save yourself from certain death, for if we leave you out here unattended, you shall surely die." "Anything." She desperately replies. Again my thoughts question my action, yet I know the predicament that many of my country men have had to endure since the British arrived, I shall use her to my advantage, give her one chance. "You tell me now, right now who ordered this." The woman spits it out. "It was The Duke of Ulster mam, he and a Mr White." I fume. "Those bastards will have to die, do they not learn." I screech. "Men, place Angus over Raphael's back." They do so with great respect. I lead my horse back home, stroking the dead bird, sweetly sing to him. The woman walks besides me head down. The men remount and follow.

Upon returning, I give orders for the woman to be taken, her wound to be cleaned. Her movements to be watched at all times. Go into the house, retrieve coins from the hall chest. Go back outside. Call four young men. "Here, take these coins, ride north. Take Angus's body. Accompany him across the seas to his land. For we must uphold his traditions, it's where he'd want to be laid to rest. I help them pull him down, wrap his body in finest cloth. The young men return with two horses attached to a cart. We lay Angus in the back. I touch him one last time. "Farewell my true friend. I will see you on the other side when I join you." My people silently watch him leave. Some follow, throwing flowers and soft fruits in with him.

I turn my attention now to Aodh. Time has flashed by, I await with dread the return of the Druid and Ivan, and particularly Fianna, who will be distraught as am I. Still cradled, I take him to the stables. Raphael is standing still, looking exhausted and low. I approach. He snuggles his muzzle into my neck, then carefully down to Aodh stiff and still in death, he blows at him as if he is trying to waken him up. Realisation hits, a tear rolls from his eyes. His companion is no more. I head back to the house, to sit and wait for the others.

An hour passes, I have decided that Aodh shall be buried this night, just as the sun sets. For tomorrow is another day, one for decisive action. They return, I say nothing, for I do not need to. Fianna rushes to me, the Druid and Ivan look grim. I tell them of the woeful afternoon. Their faces drop. Ivan's raises in anger, the druid goes within, Fianna weeps huge tears over his feathers. The Druid speaks. "Fianna is to come with me, we shall prepare the stones she collected from the river bed now, so that they are ready for a sunrise ritual. This will be her first initiation into our arts." I agree. Ivan and I go to my people. "Prepare for burial this night, I want all the horses, and the strongest bulls present with us. The joiners are to prepare a coffin of the finest wood. Have his grave dug by the vegetable plot, in the area of full sunlight, and where the moon shines also at its strongest through the trees.

The sun becomes sleepy, falls silently, slowly down the sky. We place Aodh in his opened coffin, which sits on a high plinth. Fianna brings her gift. "Look mother, my cat caught him especially." In her hands is a freshly killed mouse. She places it by his beak. I take from my pocket one of the amber beads from my cherished necklace, place it in a claw. The druid steps forwards, removes dried sticks and flowers. Places one at a time in the tiny coffin. "A rose bud for love, lavender for peace, holly for resurrection, birch for rebirth, elder for transformation and yew for protection." Ivan closes the casket. I pick it up, walk to the back of the house, the horses together with Raphael follow untethered, as do the bulls. Our people mingle with them. There is indeed peace this night, all are one in our sorrow. The cat meows its death chorus. Grief fills the air. I raise the coffin to the stars. Lower it, kiss the top. Ivan picks up Fianna to do the same. Each and every person gathered then follow suit. The animals do not move in reverence. The druid silently takes the coffin, lowers it into the prepared hole. Throws in the first handful of dirt, Fianna and I do the same together. Then Ivan, who is unusually showing pain. My people proceed to walk up one by one, each showing their appreciation for such a magnificent bird. Raphael lowers his head, steps forward with one foot, bows, the other horses copy him. The bulls bellow. For indeed human and beast intertwined, serve along together in our world.

I take Raphael back to his stable. Bring in the mounting block, stride him. Let my upper body fall forwards onto his neck, lay my head sideways on the crest of his mane. Reach down my left hand to stroke his strong white shoulder. Within moments I start to feel the familiar tingle, coming up from his heart into mine which sits directly above. The tingle becomes a stream, of the most delightful love between us. Raphael has healed me this way before after times of great sorrow. My heart lifts. Soars in pure love.

MAIRE 26

Rising before day break, I peer from my window, spy Fianna walking close with the druid, Ivan respectfully paced behind. Fianna is clutching a small hessian sack, as if it's filled with gold. No doubt her runes, which I know I will never be allowed to see, as this would break their magic. Where they are going also is not my concern. I shall patiently await their return, and my instructions.

I ready my men for action. For action in fury we shall take. The druid and my sweet child shall conjure the plan. I sit dressed prepared on a bench by the north wall, taking in the sunshine, wondering what it shall be. Knowing that it shall be perfection, the druid taps into the all seeing-eye. Fianna skips through the entrance, rushes up to me. Jingles her bag of stones, sits, smiles. The druid joins us. Ivan hurries to the stables. "Maire, your child is blessed indeed, she has the sight. The Fiery Arrow chose her subject well." Fianna jumps around with glee. "Mr White shall take leave from Carrickfergus in two days, to return to Carlingford. He will be travelling with four other men. He shall have to travel through the lands of O'Neill of Clandeboye. He will stick to the coast. There you shall capture them. It will not be so easy without Aodh's guidance. However, Fianna saw his spirit. So listen with all you heart to the winds, the skies. Look to the clouds for guidance, their shapes shall point for you.

When you return with your captives, Fianna and I will have prepared a real treat, a meal of revenge."

Ivan and I leave with our small garrison, no need to borrow fighters from our neighbours, natural warriors abound in our lands, if so required. We head towards the place where the sea comes in tightest, where it will be easier to lay a trap. Once laid, I head back into hiding with Ivan, for I am easily recognised. I look up, three clouds swell from the north, carrying rain. I watch and wait, in the knowledge that when the rain scurries my men shall attack. The British are not as hardy as us. They shall take shelter, shelter in the newly laid cover. A horn blasts, our signal to approach the foray. Fighting has commenced, my men have stood their ground, two British slashed, dying. The three remaining see us approaching and surrender. I swirl Raphael around in a tight circle, over and over, my sword held high. My shrill cries pierce the quiet. "Bound them." I yell out. I recognise my main target, by his aged face, which resembles his begotten sons. I spit at him. Take their horses, tie them together, the men shall walk.

After two days we return home. During which my men have whipped and provoked the enemy, wearing them down, smearing them in their own excrement. Glad, and victorious with the weary prisoners. Triumphantly walk into my homestead. The people gather and cheer. The prisoners are tied to a post erected in the main courtyard. I wash, change. I take with me also the deadly arrow. I find Fianna carefully rocking her brother's cradle in the nursery. I smile. "We've done something marvellous for you mother, Aodh spoke. We listened. You will be very happy." "I am pleased my dearest, pray tell me." "No, the druid wants to amaze you. You'll see." She giggles, returns to helping her brother into sleep.

Down in the main hall, I and Fianna greet Ivan. We step out, my people have the three traitors roped together; being dragged out of the gates. Fianna and I ride my horse, Ivan follows. Insults are hurled at them, I remain quiet. We make our way to the hill top beyond the meadows. What greets my eyes takes my breath away. A huge crowd of local clans is gathered, a small fire lit, hand held torches light the night. By the side stands a huge wicker man, only it is not a man, it is the shape of a bird its wings outstretched, my Aodh. A ladder leads from between his legs, into his belly. Surrounding the blessed sight in white chalk, is the Celtic sign of Triskelion, the three legged. The crowd makes way for us to pass. Jeering at our captives. This is intoxicating, I could not have devised a better scenario. An extra Beltane fire. The Druid stands before. The traitors are led, flailing limbs, hopeless pleading screams of cowardice, up the ladder, into the belly and tied down. The druid starts to speak.

"British, fear their gods, we revere ours. They employ thieves. Believe that in killing our treasured animals they will rip out our hearts, kill our spirit, to form an allegiance with their fake god, in the hope of making Maire flounder into imminent destruction. They are wrong. The Triskelion speaks of this, "no matter what you do to us, or how many times you assault us, we will always stand and move forward." We know the difference between passion and vengeance. We commend you into the bellows of our bowels, dead already, like fallen leaves, unable to avoid their destiny. Do you not learn?"

The torch bearers gather round the base of the wicker structure. I dismount with Fianna. "Allow us." I shout above them. Take from my saddle the arrow, I am handed a bow. Light it from a torch. Bend a little, invite Fianna to hold the bow with me, aim the arrow deep into the effigy. The torches are stuck into Aodh's legs, the sweet fire takes. The clansmen stand and watch as the flames rise, listen as the screams start. For they shall not suffocate in the flames, no their skin shall sizzle as pigs on a spit. Their fat shall drip to enhance the heat. The crowd hollers and hoots. Fianna, the druid, Ivan and I, watch every blissful moment of their torment. First it warms, second it stings, third it scolds, fourth it turns into the nightmare you began. Fifth, skin melts, drops away, every nerve cries out in protest. Sixth you're burnt beyond recognition. Then one last tiny noise. I watch their bodies fold, fold; fold. My spine held onto badness, every bone, now released. Vengeance is sweet. Love unsurpassed wins.

A whooshing whirling sound, starts in the lightened sky above the burning mess. It intensifies. Hundreds of buzzards circle above, in the middle is my Aodh. I gasp. Fianna squeals. Raphael whinnies. He gracefully leaves the flock, swoops down, I stretch out my arm. He lands. Stares deeply into my eyes. I sense him telling me that we are bonded in happiness. Angus has successfully traversed over the Mule of Kintyre. He too is being honoured this night. He thanks me for finding him, bringing him into this world. He is happy to have been a part of the grand onslaught of the British. I am to call on him whenever it is desired. Then he lowers his head, opens his beak. Places in my hand the amber bead that rests in his coffin. Then bids me adieu, ascends to join the circle above, which disappears before our eyes. I fall to the ground in wonder.

"That is not all." The druid breaks the silence. Two men are bringing the woman we brought here five days ago. Her eyes full of terror, she wriggles against the men. "Kneel her before the burning mass," the Druid commands. Ivan stands behind him with weapons in his grip.

The druid makes her drink Ergot, for I know what this is, he takes a rope from Ivan. "For Toutatis, god of the tribe." He shouts, proceeding to strangle her whilst the men hold her still. "For Taranis, god of thunder." He caves in her head in with a large stone. "For Esus, god of vegetation." He stabs her in her heart. Upon her death, he turns to face us. "For her people, those tricked, robbed, mutilated in the name of the King of Britain. She is their sacrifice, so that they may find strength in warding off their evil. Help the Irish to evolve and fight for their liberty, not succumb. I need four volunteers to carry her to the nearby bog. Her spirit shall be sealed for thousands of years, to continue to support the weakened willed." The theatre over, we disperse laughing, reciting the scene, back to our homes.

MAIRE 27

Bugger, the Earl of Ulster has been called back to his lands, to serve the King. Bugger, I'd devised his loss of life. I will not let this man get escape his insolence. I have little choice but to return to the dark arts. The druid wishes me to do this alone. He needs to keep his energy pure to teach Fianna. He has warned me of the power of words, to make my spell more effective. To create bane. The carpenters have made up a small coffin, just large enough to fit in my two palms. I've made a small doll from wool that fits neatly inside. The lid left ajar until I perform my ritual. I've waited for the next full moon. Tonight it is at its closest to the earth, tonight it is. I've been given enough time to prepare this meticulously. I am set.

I am close enough to home to be able to make a run should I detect movement in the moons beams. Raphael waits by my side. I've brought him with me to witness the power of a maddened Celt. I go to his saddle, release the small spade to dig a grave. Replace it, retrieve my saddle bag. I crouch down, Raphael lowers his head to watch. I lay the small coffin by the graveside. Use my pouch of salt to enclose a magic circle around us. Pick up the article, hold it in my hands. Remove the lid. Take out the flask, pour the goats blood onto the heart area of the doll. The wool absorbs it immediately, lines like veins spread out, until it is drenched.

Satisfied I close the lid. Scratch on the top with my dagger his initials, together with the sigil, chaosphere. Wrap the coffin seven times in black yarn, away from me, each time reciting my curse.

"May my boiling blood disturb you, enforce upon you a long unfruitful life. May you be surrounded by death! Rot. Your allies will your foe be. Feud upon feud will blight your days. Your personal ambition quashed. That which you desire the most shall never be grasped, until it is just out of reach. Then a great misfortune shall befall you. A paper crown shall adorn your severed head." I tie the yarn to form a tight knot. "So mote it be."

I bury the coffin with sinister pleasure, kick dirt over the top. I place a tight circle with the salt clockwise to seal the deed. To keep the power working. Go to Raphael, kiss him on his muzzle, "there see, no-one threatens you and gets away with it. I mount, Raphael rears up in majesty. In silent joy we canter home in the light of the moon.

MAIRE 28

Seven years have passed since Fianna's birth. There were a few skirmishes, forays in the year that followed when Angus and Aodh took their leave. The last year has seen the British power wane, their armies needed elsewhere. Always trying to conquer land that doesn't belong to them, in pursuit of more wealth. Thieves. This time they despatched their garrisons to France. Trying to lay claim to the French throne. The Duke of York their leader, good he will not perish yet, however his life is tied up in battle, angst. Imbolc is shortly upon us. The Druid has prepared a journey of discovery for Fianna, myself and Ivan shall accompany.

On foot to Croc Na Teamhrach. The Druid had us stop by a holy well. Beautifully set amongst large rambling rocks. The water flowed out from one of them into small streams. He removed Fianna's hood from her warm red cloak, lay her on her back, her long, luscious hair fell into and flowed with the water. He gently supported her. Three times he cupped his hand, poured fresh water onto her forehead to initiate her into the sacred dwelling place of the gods. Known as an entrance into the otherworld. "This is a place of great prospect child, which I pass to you."

We head up to a chambered cairn. Ivan goes to gather old dry wood. The air is alive, my feet tingle with the enormous amount of energy coming from our mother. We drop down to the entrance, enter. To the left a huge decorated stone. The Druid stops, follows the carved patterns with his finger, he invites Fianna to do the same, and intones magic words. The dark winter's night is starting to draw. We go into the centre of the cairn, I lay out mats made from rushes for us to sleep on. Ivan joins us. A fire is lit close to the entrance, sealing us in. We eat the bread, cheese and a leg of mutton, a gift from a guest house host.

We bed down early. The Druid advises us not to be alarmed by any noises in the night; it is the earth herself speaking to us. I doubt anything would disturb Ivan. I am wrong. Oddly we all slept soundly. Then, just before dawn a cataclysm. A loud clashing, the stone walls regurgitating their anger. Thunder rolls over the mound. Forked lightening barges in through a curtain of thrashing rain. A giant's face looms from the flaming spears, filling the entire space. His face trembles with rage. "How many of the Irish have succumbed to British rule. They have denied our heirs their rightful lands. Thieves, vagabonds! Do they not see, the harm they are doing? This Isle is full of mystery. The little people have been banished from the pale. The Fairy kings are outraged at having to vacate the very port that represents the island's birthing place. A time will dawn when this great port falls back to Irish hands, but alas the damage is done. Too many with selfish thoughts have distorted the precious plot. Fianna will exhort the fairy people with prayers; incantations, to enhance their new kingdoms. It is her destiny to restore peace, balance. To enable them to carry on their great works in nature." He smiles, draws out of the ether a perfect white wand made from birch. He hands it to Fianna, she does not flinch, nor show fear; only childlike honour. The giant disappears, the storm abates in an instance. A dazzling beam of sunlight shines straight through the opening, lighting up the back wall. We are in awe. The Druid is not surprised.

He walks over to the burnt out fire, calls Fianna. "Look here child. In the ashes, do you see the cross? This is a sign that Brigid was amongst in the night. Always look for omens in the remains. They will guide you, clarify your thoughts and direction. Come, we must leave now whilst the sun still shines through upon us.

Together we walk out, the sunlight intensifies, almost blinds us. From inside the brightness the youthful Morigan appears. She asks Fianna and the Druid to step forward. Takes out the two wands from her cloak. Passes one to the Druid. They hold them up together, the tips touching. Morigan asks Fianna to place hers in the middle. She obliges. Immediately there is a flash of white light from the three tips, which surrounds us entirely. The light diminishes. Before us are Faye on Tinker and her fellows beside. They are cheering for Fianna. They jostle for attention. Faye laughs. "Follow us."

They lead us onto one of two mounds close by. A slight splattering of snow covers the top. In the middle stands a single upright stone. The Morigan speaks. "This was brought to us by the gods, known as Tuatha De Danann, the Stone of Destiny. Touch your wand to it Fianna." She does. The stone emits a great roar. The fairies jump and whoop. "This confirms that you are the chosen one. For Ireland may need Kings, she also needs a keeper of our realms. You have been trusted with the task of human guardianship, to maintain respect. The Druid will teach you well the ways of his craft. Our relationship has started. I will always come when you need me, just call my name three times. But be warned, I don't always appear this way." She laughs.

Enormous wings sprout on her back, they spread over the little people. She flaps them rigorously, on the third sweep all vanish. Leaving the four of us enveloped in wonder. We gather our things, commence our long walk back up north. The Druid and Fianna are to go their own way after tomorrow. I spend every last second by her side. Stroking her hair, admiring her valour, her maturity. The Druid has told me to visit in May. So in May I shall indeed make my way back to my place of birth, Fermanagh, with my son Little Mac. He is safe at home, guarding his father's treasure; the small dagger. Ivan and I are already, unfortunately training my son in the art of war.

MAIRE 29

Having waved, snuggled and kissed the life out of my daughter some two hours ago, I have maintained my poise. Until now. My legs will carry me no longer. I collapse to my knees in the fresh falling snow. An almighty cry stirs from deep inside. Demanding release. The sounds that emit my voice are unrecognisable, a deepening symphony of unearthly howls, condemn with rising discourse. My mind goes wild, reminisces. Wound upon wound. The indignation brought on by the British oppressors. Lives distorted, dispersed. The horribleness endured. Countless men and women jolted into barbarity to protect. The death, the sacrifice. Parentless bairns. My lips part and pull to exaggeration. I take deep long breaths, then let out my horror, with widened owl like eyes. Whilst the demon of a thousand memories expels from my soul. Ivan in his wisdom leaves me alone, whilst I break my bondage of raging battles.

A haunting voice rides out from the shadows on the hills before us, to the valley where I kneel. A stunning figure appears, dressed in a white flowing gown. Her white hair floats around her, her skin pale. She glides through the air towards us. Her left arm, devoid of flesh is merely bone. She halts, suspended before us, singing a sorrowful lonely sound. The Wailing Banshee. I tremble, why is the warner of impending death here? She stretches out her bony hand to my heart, it enters my body. Our eyes lock, interchange. "Fear not child. I am not here to take you yet. I am here to collect what you've tethered to yourself for far too long. I am here to unleash the vexation deeply imbedded in your mighty heart." I feel an immense tugging, black mist pours out of me to her. The mist starts to cover her white dress, forms a shroud. She becomes as old as old can be. Her pale blue eyes turn red, pools of blood flood to her cheeks, spill to stain her gown. She lets out a harrowing screech, flies up through the snow flakes and vanishes.

I fall to the ground, exhausted, curl up like a new born. Feel the relief of the lifted burdens. My father's favourite phrase comes to my thoughts. "Onwards and upwards, Maire, onwards and upwards." I start to rise, Ivan's large warm hand helps me up. "Well done." He puts his arm around my back. We continue our homebound journey in peace. "Hail to Mac."

KELLY 20

The height of summer, a glorious hot day. We are in the garden of the house Jimmy brought for us. He insisted I kept my terrace house, to rent, to give me some independence. "Nothing worse than a man who totally takes away a woman's freedom!" His words. "Frankie, oh I'll get you, you little monkey." My darling son, three and a half now, is having me on again. Always the prankster. He's charging round the garden, trying to pelt poor Cinders with the chocolate cupcakes we made earlier. He's marked her once already, she, displeased, has hidden under a bush to clean herself. "Come here, come on, that's enough now." He turns his attention to me. "Going to get you now Mummy." "Don't you dare," I laugh at him. One thing I must remember is never to dare Frankie to do anything. He is absolutely fearless. He lands one right on my stomach. It plops, splatters.

Frankie jumps, hoots, twirls in the tartan kilt he refuses to take off. Since a reminiscing visit to Edinburgh a year last May, where Jimmy proposed to me, that's all I can get him to wear; even at our cosy wedding. Come rain or shine, he's oblivious to the temperature. So we ordered him various ones in different colours and weights. It's a shame there are no Scottish schools here, god knows how I'm going to coerce him to wear trousers come September. Oh well, another bridge. And the fact he won't have his hair cut short. Well, the schools going to have to accept the hair at least, fine golden ringlets bounce around as he dances. The last time I tried to shorten it, he turned into a monster. Screaming at the top of his lungs, rushed out into the road, nearly getting himself killed. I gave up. He looks really cute in truth. I'm glad he knows his own mind.

I've had no further dreams since his birth. Yet, each night, when I lay him down, for as long as I remember, he pools into my eyes. It's like he's trying to communicate something serious. Now that his vocabulary has improved, he's starting to talk in his sleep. The names he calls out are the ones from the dreams. This has really began to worry me. I decided to get back in touch with Jackie, to see if she can shed any light onto the matter. I am either going doolally, or something really bizarre is happening. Heather is coming round after she's closed the café. She has been a wonder indeed. We share the days at work, and with my little one. All's panned out there perfectly. She's a gem.

She arrives at five, runs in; lifts my monkey into her arms. He clings on, showers her is kisses. She lifts him into the air. "Dance with me, dance with me." He pleads. "Wait until your mother has left dear, then we can dance all you like." Frankie delights. We named him Frank after Jimmy's grandfather, with the second name Angus to honour where he was conceived. He insists we call him Frankie, he prefers it. In fact the clever so and so, totally ignores anyone who uses his given name. He certainly can be stubborn, yet in a delightfully amusing way. "Right I'm off now," I shout to him. "And behave!" "Yes mummy, I always do." I wish. Though I wouldn't change a thing. He has the face of an angel, and great doe chocolate brown eyes, that melt, so he mostly gets let off from his mischief. God help any woman that falls in love with him. I chuckle to myself.

250

Jackie has me sat in a comfy armchair, with a foot rest to match. I've tried to fill her in with the goings on, though there's so much, and not enough time. Jackie has convinced me to try hypnotherapy. "At last." She states. Then proceeds to explain the procedure for inducement. The formalities over, she begins.

"Stare at a point on the ceiling. As you do you will find your eyes getting heavier and heavier, until a point comes when they just close on their own. That's it." She then talks me through exercises of tensing and relaxing each muscle, from my toes up to my head. "Now I want you to imagine a gold spiral staircase. Start walking up each stair, counting backwards in your head, from twenty until you get to the last step. Once there, you will find yourself in a beautiful castle that has many rooms. This holds your Akashic records. Look around and find one with the name Maire on the door. When you have found it just raise a finger for me. Good. Open the door, and enter, you will see on a table an old leather bound book. Go to it. On the front of the book in italic writing will again be the name Maire O'Ciaragain. Open the book to the first page, and tell me what is written there."

I do as she asks in my imagination. The book feels somewhat familiar. It is thick, old; stained. "The story of Maire." I tell Jackie. "Good, now start to flick through until you see a scene from one of your dreams. With trepidation, I turn the pages. From the first page a large white horse jumps and forms before me, his main three foot long. He looks to me, I know him. "What do you see Kelly?" "There's a pure white horse standing before me. He's nuzzling the book, I think he wants me to turn another page." "Well do so." Jackie's voice is so calming, it helps me to stay focused, relaxed. I turn the third page. There's a druid with a beautiful young girl. I turn again, this time I see a kindly old man. Another page, a giant of a man. With each flick another character is shown. Until all the figures from my dream have been revealed to me. Then the book evaporates. I'm aware that I am not alone. The room is full of the people from the pictures, all smiling broadly.

"Tell me what's going on Kelly." "The room is full of the characters from my dreams, but I don't understand, where is Maire?" "Look to your feet." I do. Shocked I find myself wearing dark brown ankle boots, I draw my eyes upwards. I'm swathed in battle armour. There's a shining sword in my right hand. It is decorated with three ravens on the hilt. I sense a great strength rising in me. The horse nudges me, breathes his warm breath on my face. As he does my armour vanishes. I'm dressed in an opulent green gown. My hair, down to my waist, is a stunning red. I lift up my hands, they have tiny freckles. My skin is like milk. Oh my God, my pulse quickens. "What is it Kelly?" Jackie gently asks. "It's me; Maire is in me; how can this be?" "Just stay with it, is the horse still there?" "Yes." "Excellent, he is your guardian, he will keep you safe. Now, ask your guests, one by one, to step forward to introduce themselves."

The Druid steps forward first with the young girl. "Maire, we are so proud of you, all of us. This is your daughter Fianna, who grew up to do marvellous work. She tugs at my dress, a little black cat emerges from behind her cloak. I bend down, kiss her forehead. Ivan is next. He swoops me up with no effort, swirls me around, laughing. Johnny steps up. "Maire, I've always loved you. Sadly the times weren't right for us." I feel a little dizzy, he smiles. "Karma has brought us finally back together, I am your husband. The work to make amends for all the children's parents that we maimed, killed at the dictatorship of the king." "Gwyneth comes forward. She then morphs into Teagan, I can't believe what I am seeing. "Maire,

Kelly. I always had this feeling inside that I was not good enough, punctured, a failure. I never knew where it came from until I passed. I apologize for the pain I caused you. And thank you for all your support. What happened couldn't have been helped."

Next the kindly man greets me, he is carrying a young boy in his arms, I recognise them both immediately; it is my father and son. I look into the child's eyes. I am bewitched. They stare into me the same way Frankie's do. So this is what he's been trying to tell me. That Little Mac has come back into my life this time as my son again. His father, Angus comes to my side. "I he's my boy alright, a little fighter, a little awkward sometimes, but always carries valour." It's making sense to me now. The people in my dreams are the people I share my current life with. I take time to really peer into their souls. My father in this life, is Arthur. Ivan has become Ricky, no doubt he's joined forces to help those on the battle field, to alleviate guilt. "They were hard times Maire. We did what we had to do. We are all back, to make amends, to settle our karma." Ivan informs me.

The couple who helped me birth Fianna speak to me too. "We are the Earl of Desmond and his wife, now Brian and Heather. I laugh. "I'm impressed with the workings of the angels. Who'd have guessed? All this means so much. There is a tapping at the window. Tap, tap; tap. I turn to see a huge buzzard demanding entry. "Aodh," I scream, rush to open the window. He gallantly swoops in, circles above my head; settles himself on Raphael's back. The horse whinnies with satisfaction. A revelation, my whole past from the 15th century is before me.

The Druid speaks. "There is a natural spiritual law. There are those that have served their purpose, myself and Fianna are not required to return to earth, our lessons learnt, our souls journey complete. We honour you Maire for your steadfast tenacity, valour and rectitude. "I don't need to be honoured." I reply, "I'm clearly here to honour my people." It makes sense to me now, I didn't have to return, I chose to, to pay back those that helped me. Love surrounds, in a simple way; yes.

Lightning Source UK Ltd.
Milton Keynes UK
UKHW041340170920
369997UK00012B/7